Praise for Lambda Liter
It Should Be a Crime

"Taite is a real-life attorney so the prose jumps off the page with authority and authenticity...[*It Should be a Crime*] is just Taite's second novel...but it's as if she has bookshelves full of bestsellers under her belt. In fact, she manages to make the courtroom more exciting than Judge Judy bursting into flames while delivering a verdict."—*Gay List Daily*

"Law professor Morgan Bradley and her student Parker Casey are potential love interests, but throw in a high-profile murder trial, and you've got an entertaining book that can be read in one sitting. Taite also practices criminal law and she weaves her insider knowledge of the criminal justice system into the love story seamlessly and with excellent timing. I look forward to reading more from Taite."
—*Curve Magazine*

"Taite, a criminal defense attorney herself, has given her readers a behind the scenes look at what goes on during the days before a trial. Her descriptions of lawyer/client talks, investigations, police procedures, etc. are fascinating. Taite keeps the action moving, her characters clear, and never allows her story to get bogged down in paperwork. *It Should be a Crime* has a fast-moving plot and some extraordinarily hot sex."—*Just About Write*

By the Author

truelesbianlove.com

It Should Be a Crime

Do Not Disturb

Visit us at www.boldstrokesbooks.com

DO NOT DISTURB

by

Carsen Taite

2010

DO NOT DISTURB

ISBN 10: 1-60282-153-4
ISBN 13: 978-1-60282-153-8

This Trade Paperback Original Is Published By
Bold Strokes Books, Inc.
P.O. Box 249
Valley Falls, NY 12185

First Edition: June 2010

CREDITS
EDITORS: CINDY CRESAP AND STACIA SEAMAN
PRODUCTION DESIGN: STACIA SEAMAN
COVER DESIGN BY SHERI (GRAPHICARTIST2020@HOTMAIL.COM)

Acknowledgments

I spent close to a decade living in the Land of Enchantment, and I enjoyed visiting all my old haunts in the pages of this story. While I'm very familiar with northern New Mexico, I've never been a rock star or hotelier, and I'm grateful to the cool folks who helped me navigate those worlds. A big thanks to my good friend Sam Tucker, for all the fried food lunches spent discussing the ins and outs of the imaginary Steel Hotel line. A shout out as well to JD Glass for answering all my hypothetical guitar questions and sending me to the dictionary to look up "luthier." Special thanks to Jeanine Hoffman, Sue Stolz, Levine Sommers, Mary, and Barbara, who kindly shared their knowledge of that dreaded beast, cancer. Any factual errors on these subjects are mine and mine alone.

Sandy—your brutally honest first read made this a better book. You are indeed a good friend.

Cindy Cresap—thanks again for making the editing process seamless. You are always spot on when it comes to figuring out what's not quite right. I'm a better writer because of you.

Stacia—your attention to detail always makes me look more skillful than I am. Thank you.

Sheri—thanks for another blazing hot cover.

Rad—thanks for the great ride. I'm loving living my dream with Bold Strokes.

To all the other authors and behind-the-scenes folks at BSB—you are the greatest. I can't imagine a more nurturing family.

Lainey—without your encouragement, I don't know if I would have had the courage to write the first few words. Thanks for everything you do to make my dreams possible.

To my readers—thanks for the constant stream of encouragement, praise, and shouts for more. I save every note and every e-mail and read them whenever I need a boost.

Dedication

Lainey—we're always in the land of enchantment
when we're together. I love you.

CHAPTER ONE

W e're paying that publicist big money to get you on the front page, and she damn well better do it!" Rick shook the latest issue of *People* in the air.

Greer sighed and grabbed the magazine from her manager's hand. "Rick, dear, have you looked at the cover? A full-on feature of the Brangelina twins." Greer pointed at the photo of Brad Pitt and Angelina Jolie cradling their famous offspring for the camera. "I'm pretty sure they would trump a government-sponsored announcement about life on Mars." She shoved the magazine in the trash. "Besides, my only accomplishment this week was having my fifth album go double platinum. Nothing front-page about success."

Greer knew she sounded like a petulant child, but she didn't care. Her reputation hadn't seen the same upward trajectory as her rise on the charts. Even if she sold more records than the Beatles, she was sure her everyday mishaps would make bigger headlines. A simple comment to a waiter that her steak was overdone appeared in large print as: GREER DAVIS STARTS FOOD FIGHT. Photos of Greer with adoring female fans in various states of undress merited the keen observation: SHE'S SEX CRAZED!

So far this trip had gone better than usual, which translated into an absence of ripping headlines. Greer had arrived in Chicago yesterday morning for a well-choreographed press junket to promote her new album. Rick had planned every detail of the trip down to the minute, and the schedule didn't allow for anything off course. Greer was worn out after spending the day talking about her album and her upcoming tour. She repeated the same details over and over in the dozen interviews Rick had lined up for the day. She hated the public relations side of stardom, but Rick insisted she remain in the public eye at all times.

Rick Seavers was all business, and his business was all Greer Davis. His sleek style, from his custom suits made in London to his slick coif, was carefully crafted to project an air of confidence, and he used it to make sure his star client stayed on top. He was constantly thinking of new ways to get her mentioned by the press. Now was no different.

"Let's fix it," he said. "I've arranged for a VIP party tonight in your suite at the hotel. Macy Rivers is in town and I've invited her to attend. The two of you can pose for the cameras. Show you're Macy's gal-pal. Her sweet rep is bound to rub off. Oh, and I'm firing the damn publicist for not thinking of this herself."

Greer had long ago given up keeping track of who Rick hired and fired on her behalf. He had been the driving force behind her success for the past ten years. She didn't question his decisions. His idea to put her in front of the cameras with Macy was spot on. Macy Rivers was the darling of the press. She experienced the same level of success in the country music arena as Greer did on the top forty charts, but she didn't have as many bruises to show for it. Macy was pageant pretty with wholesome good looks and a smile worthy of toothpaste commercials. When Greer stood next to her, she felt like an outsider in high school. She knew she was attractive, but her spiky blond hair and edgy good looks didn't represent traditional beauty. Macy could do no wrong, unlike Greer, who found herself on the defensive every time she spoke to the press. Despite their differences, Greer liked Macy and the two had become friends over the years, an anathema to all who knew them. She figured Macy found the image of the prom queen hanging out with the bad girl had a certain allure. Hell, maybe tonight she'd see if she could get Macy liquored up. It might do her good to let loose.

❖

"Smile, girls."

Greer had told Rick to take the night off, but he couldn't resist directing the show, even if it was only from the sidelines. Greer supposed she should be grateful he took such a hands-on interest in her career, but sometimes she felt like she had a full-time babysitter. She paid Rick good money to take care of the details of her professional life, but the line between her professional and private life was blurred beyond recognition. Hell, she couldn't even throw a party without it being a publicity stunt. She felt a sudden desire to be bad.

"I should kiss you right here in front of all these flashing cameras."

Macy didn't even flinch. She spoke through a big smile. "You're all talk, Davis. I am so not your type."

"What? Straight and wholesome?" Greer answered. "You're absolutely right, but you sure make me look good."

"Happy to help, Davis. Happy to help."

Finally Rick eased the two away from the cameras, but not before they were blinded by dozens of flashing bulbs. "Why don't you girls head on upstairs? I'll let a couple of these photographers in to cover the party, but they'll stay out of your hair. Pictures only. Go, have fun."

Thank God. If I have to talk to one more of these vultures, I'll scream. She planned to let loose tonight. She deserved it after the last two days of constant scrutiny. She grabbed Macy's hand and led her to the penthouse elevator.

The party was in full swing before they ever reached the suite. Greer always stayed at the Tinsley when she was in Chicago, and her parties were a hot ticket event for any other celebrities who were visiting the Windy City. Her penthouse would be full of famous people in various states of inebriation. They all counted on the wait staff, who were skilled in keeping the guests' glasses full and their own mouths shut about the antics they would see during the evening. The token table of hors d'oeuvres would barely be touched. Greer's guests were more interested in partaking of what they could either drink from a glass or snort up their noses. The pretty food was there for decoration. By the end of the evening the food would look as wilted as the guests.

Greer grabbed two glasses of champagne from the tray of a passing waiter and handed one to Macy.

"Here. How about you let your hair down a little tonight?"

Macy tossed back the contents of the glass and handed it back to Greer. "How 'bout I let my hair down a lot?" She nodded at the empty glass. "Champagne was okay to start, but I'd like to try something a little more potent. Can you help me out?"

"Scotch, bourbon, vodka?" Greer asked.

"I was thinking of something, uh, not so liquid."

Greer smiled. "Good girl wants to let out her inner bad girl for the night?"

"Can you blame me?" Macy frowned. "I spend my days singing PG lyrics, plugging wholesome products, and hanging out with people who think a few too many drinks will land me a spot in hell. I deserve to cut loose a little, don't you think?"

"I do." Greer grabbed her hand. "Follow me." She took Macy's hand and elbowed her way through the crowd. The suite had two bedrooms, two living areas, and a dining room. Greer led Macy to the guest bedroom, where she knew someone would have what Macy wanted. The room was dimly lit, not to hide anything, but because the occupants didn't want bright lights to ruin their high. Greer shut the door behind them to keep out the light. The room was a vice cop's dream. Piles of snowy white coke were heaped on mirrored surfaces all around the room and guests were helping themselves. "Is this what you had in mind?" Greer asked.

"Exactly." Macy started toward the nearest table, but Greer held her back.

"Whoa there. Have you used this stuff before?"

"No."

Greer felt a pang of regret. She didn't mind getting Macy drunk, but she wasn't sure she wanted to be the one to introduce her to putting things up her nose. "Are you sure you want to try this?"

"I've never been more sure about anything in my life."

Greer heard the rebellious confidence in Macy's voice and

decided it wasn't her job to police anyone else's morals. "All right then, but wait here." Greer strode over to the nearest table and palmed a stainless steel bullet loaded with the powdery substance. She figured she could at least limit Macy's first experience to small bumps of high. Returning, she said to Macy, "Come with me," and led her out of the room.

Macy braced against the door frame. "Wait a minute. Why are we leaving?"

Greer leaned in close and whispered in her ear. "Little Mary Sunshine, do you want everyone in the world to see you snorting coke?" She waited until the idea registered with Macy. Then she held up her hand, closed tightly around the bullet. "I have what you want. Come to my room and try it there." Macy nodded and followed Greer to the master bedroom across the way. Greer placed her hand on the doorknob, but felt herself pulled back as she started to open the door. She looked over her shoulder and was surprised by the kiss Macy planted on her cheek. She raised her eyebrows.

"Thanks for being so sweet," Macy said. "I have a feeling this is going to be a night to remember."

Greer blushed and drew Macy into the suite.

Chapter Two

Ainsley Faraday hated being cornered first thing in the morning.

"Fluffy does not like the cedar bed you had delivered to her room. It is itchy. She prefers down. And not the synthetic rubbish people try to pass off as real, but mature goose down. It's the warmest. Our room is intolerably cold and Fluffy hates to be cold."

"Certainly, Mr. Withers. I apologize for any inconvenience to either you or Fluffy." Ainsley managed to summon a bright smile for the Maltipoo and his doting owner. She held the smile until Sebastian Withers and his sole heir prissed their way out of the lobby. Once she was sure they were out of earshot, she stalked to the concierge desk, her laser stare daring the two well-suited attendants to run for cover.

"Who the hell has been dealing with Sebastian Withers?"

One of the young men shuffled his feet while the other made darted glances seeking escape. Ainsley could smell their fear. She cultivated her reputation as the high supreme bitch of the Hotel Steel because she deemed it to be the most effective way to achieve results. One of these lackeys would provide her with results now or lose his job. "Answer me now or you're both fired."

Feet shuffler raised his head just high enough to assess the seriousness of his situation. With a slight nod at his coworker, he rattled off what he probably thought was a sufficient explanation.

"Ms. Faraday, he is impossible. You know we only have cedar beds on hand. I provided him with a brand-new one. It had never been used. I delivered it personally within seconds of his call. I've been waiting hand and foot on the hairball he calls a dog from the moment he checked in, but nothing I do is enough—"

Ainsley raised her hand and barked, "Stop!" He froze.

"I've heard enough." She looked at the coworker and began one of the quizzes she knew they had grown to despise. "We have no down beds, but a guest requests one. What do you do?"

Concierge number two shook in his shoes, obviously trying to discern what the mistake had been. Ainsley imagined he thought guests who could afford rates in excess of $500 a night for a standard room were generally eccentric freaks who had been put on earth to terrify those who could only afford to stay in a Motel 6, if they could afford to vacation at all. She could almost hear the frantic beat of his anxious heart. He was probably thinking it was one thing to have to answer to the erratic, unreasonable demands of people with money to burn, but it was quite another to have to be treated like garbage by his boss, who acted as if these guests were perfectly sane. He winced as if concentrating hard on the question before stammering his reply. "I'll try to find a down bed."

"No! You do not 'try' to do anything. You do it, and you do it fast. Your job is to make the guests happy. Fix Mr. Withers's problem or get out. Now."

Ainsley didn't wait for a response, but stalked off to her office. Once there, she fell into a chair and laughed. She knew the two young men thought Mr. Withers was crazy. They were right, but as the operations manager of the hotel, she had to set an example to her employees, which meant catering to the whims of her capricious guests. She couldn't for a minute let her employees see her true feelings. If she had her way, she would show Mr. Withers and his canine companion the door. As it was, she maintained a front, faking genuine concern for the needs of her guests, and no one was the wiser. Ainsley kicked off her shoes and pulled her feet up under her. It was going to be a long day. She was tired, but she knew despite her fatigue, she still looked polished and pressed. She prided herself on her ability to project an unflappable image, which started with impeccable appearance. Custom suits, designer shoes, flawless makeup, and a tight French braid painted a portrait of control. Only in the sanctuary of her office, with the door locked, would she ever let her hair down and curl up in comfort.

Her reverie was broken by the ringing of the telephone. She could tell by the ring that whoever it was had the number for her direct line. She glanced at the caller ID and noted the source of the call was the hotel's corporate office in New York. *Damn, did one of those brats out front already complain about my show of power?* She was used to fending off complaints by employees. Her ability to achieve results guaranteed her superiors would always side with her, but she would still have to explain away her displays of force. She sighed and picked up the phone.

"Faraday here."

"Ainsley," a big male voice boomed. "How the hell are you?"

"I'm good, Frank. Very good." She braced herself. "What can I do for you?"

"Cancel whatever dinner plans you have for tomorrow and send a car to the airport. I'll be landing at O'Hare at eight and I'd love to see you."

Ainsley caught her breath. Frank Evans didn't fly around the country. He summoned his minions to his plush offices on Park Avenue if he needed to talk to them in person. She wasn't fooled by his "I'd love to see you" comment. Ainsley knew she was his favorite location manager, but being favorite had never extended beyond professional accolades. She had no personal relationship with Frank. Dinner would be strictly business. Though she was dying of curiosity about the sudden visit, she knew better than to ask questions.

"I'll pick you up myself. Dinner at the hotel or somewhere else?"

"Let's check out the competition. Charlie Trotter's. Send a car and I'll meet you there for their nine o'clock seating." Frank clicked off the line.

Ainsley stared at the phone in her hand. Everything about Frank was a test, including his dinner suggestion. Charlie Trotter's was competition for no one. She was supposed to get dinner reservations a day in advance at a restaurant traditionally booked months ahead. On a Friday night, no less. Luckily, she had better connections and more savvy than the two rookies working the concierge desk. She made a few quick phone calls, wondering all the while what had prompted Frank's sudden visit to the Windy City.

❖

Greer silently cursed the hotel staff for not leaving the curtains drawn. She had stayed in the penthouse so often she didn't need to be reminded of the fabulous view of Lake Michigan. The blazing sunlight pouring through the window was a piercing reminder of how difficult it was to recover from her infamous parties. She knew it didn't matter how hard it became to keep up her playgirl lifestyle, she wouldn't let up. She barely knew half the people who attended her soirees, but at least they provided some sort of company in her otherwise solitary existence. Since she had taken the music business by storm at the age of twenty-one, she found herself surrounded by hordes of people—fans, staff, and paparazzi. The bigger the crowd, the lonelier she felt. Her rapid climb to success meant the crowds were huge, but with no friends in sight. She had learned the best she could hope for was an occasional close acquaintance, someone she could connect with once every six months or so when schedules and geography permitted their paths to cross. Macy was one of those people, but last night, after she'd tasted her first high, she became someone Greer no longer knew. Macy transformed from sweet girl next door to bigger-than-life prom queen, holding court for all her adoring subjects. Greer shrugged. She could hardly blame Macy for taking advantage of the freedom she found in the lines of coke. She was on top of the world the last time Greer had seen her and she'd probably left with one of the obsessed fans who'd wrangled their way into the party. Lord knows everyone there had been fascinated with the prom queen's animated personality.

Greer closed her eyes to block out the bright new day and climbed out of bed. Her only scheduled appearance for the day was an appearance on *Oprah*, which left her plenty of time to recover from the wild night. *Bathroom first, then coffee.* Not yet ready to face the day, she scrunched her eyes shut as she made her way to the oversized bathroom, cursing when she stumbled and fell into a heap on the floor.

"Fuck!" Greer's eyes flashed open. She was lying on the carpeted floor and she was now doubly pissed at the hotel staff since it was their fault she'd been walking with her eyes closed. Grunting, Greer rolled over and started to push herself, up but she stopped short. She wasn't the only one lying on the floor.

Macy didn't look like a prom queen anymore. A prom queen doesn't lie, half dressed, on the floor of a hotel suite with dried saliva caked on her chin. Her wide-open eyes showed hints of fear she obviously couldn't feel anymore, and her mouth was slack.

Greer's hand flew to her mouth. She clamped it shut, resisting the simultaneous urges to scream and vomit. Even as she reached out to shake Macy's shoulder, she felt the rest of her body recoil with fear. She shook Macy's still form, at first softly, then with increasing pressure. After a few moments, she let her fingers slip away from the futile task. She knew she should lean forward, check to see if Macy was breathing, but she balked at the thought of placing herself in such close proximity to what she knew was disaster. Her thoughts raced, finally skidding into a memory of something she had seen on television. Her eyes darted around the room, finally landing on Macy's purse lying nearby. She fished through the contents and pulled out a compact. She flipped it open and held the mirrored half near Macy's mouth, careful not to touch her lips. Greer waited for what seemed like an eternity for fog to show her signs of life, but the mirror remained clear and bright. Greer's hand began to shake with sharp, jerking motions, and the compact dropped to the floor. Greer's stomach rolled and her thoughts raced. *This can't be happening. What is she doing here, in my room? Is she dead? This can't be happening.*

She had no idea how much time has passed, but she knew she had to do something, and she had to do it now. Macy was either dead or dying, smack in the middle of Greer's suite, the likely victim of a drug overdose. Greer swallowed the lumps of fear rising up to choke her and stumbled over to the nightstand. She picked up the phone and hesitated only a moment before dialing Rick's room.

Greer was sitting on the balcony, but she could still hear the exchange taking place in her bedroom. She felt as if they must be talking about some other Ms. Davis. Surely she wasn't the subject of this heated conversation between Chicago homicide detectives and a small army of sharp-dressed lawyers, all standing in a room draped in crime scene tape. Rick was the only person in the room she knew. The suits were all lackeys for the record label—the most expensive, high-powered legal team money could buy. She didn't care to know their names. All she wanted was for all of them to clear out of her suite.

"I'm going to need to talk to Ms. Davis at the station."

"Ms. Davis will be happy to cooperate with your investigation, but she's not coming to the police station. Tell us what you'd like to know and we'll get you the information."

"Counselor, I think you're forgetting who's in charge here."

"We called you, Detective. Let's not forget our cooperation. Ms. Davis is traumatized by these events and the loss of a good friend. You will ask your questions through us or not at all."

Greer didn't engage in the battle of wills taking place in her suite. She knew Rick would make sure her interests were protected, but she hoped they all cleared out soon. She was scheduled to be at Harpo Studios in less than three hours.

❖

Ainsley leaned back in her chair, a satisfied smile on her face. She'd had to burn several favors, but she'd secured a table for Friday night. She had given up a comp suite for the following weekend, box seats to a Cubs game, and she had canceled a hot date with Francesca, a flight attendant who sometimes shared her bed on occasional layovers. Frank wouldn't appreciate the extent of her efforts. He was a results-oriented individual, but she was still pleased with herself.

"Ms. Faraday?"

Apparently the few moments she'd spent making reservations for dinner with her boss were the only ones she was going to get to herself today. Ainsley looked up at her assistant. "Yes?"

"You might want to turn on the news." The suggestion was delivered with an urgent tone. Ainsley reached for a remote and clicked to the local ABC affiliate.

"Reporters have been confined to the first floor of the Tinsley Hotel for the last hour, but sources report a representative from the police department will be making a statement before noon. For a summary of what we know so far, let's turn to Becky Duncan, live on the scene. Becky, tell us what's happening."

"Thanks, Greg. Here's what I can tell you so far." She ticked the points off on each finger. *"Macy Rivers was found dead this morning in the penthouse of the hotel. She is not a registered guest. The penthouse was registered to Greer Davis. We don't know anything else for sure at this point."*

"Becky, is there any speculation as to what happened?"

"A source within the hotel, who preferred to remain anonymous, did tell us about a party last night in Greer Davis's suite, and now the place is crawling with Chicago's finest. Word is Ms. Davis is still in the hotel and she's being held for questioning."

"Isn't she scheduled to appear on Oprah *this afternoon?"*

"Right, Greg. No word yet on whether the queen of daytime has heard the recent developments, but we'll be on the scene till we have some answers. Reporting live from the Tinsley Hotel, I'm Becky Duncan."

Ainsley clicked the power off and shook her head. "Better make sure we're ready to deal with any spillover from the Tinsley. I imagine there will be plenty of people looking for rooms in a hotel not surrounded by crime scene tape. And tell the chief of security I want to meet with his crew before the night shift. I don't want any parties with dead guests at a Steel Hotel."

❖

"Out of the question!" Rick's tone signaled another temper tantrum was on the way.

"Why not? She's not going to ask about Macy. For God's sake, it's *Oprah*, not *Crossfire*." Appearing on the show was the only highlight in an otherwise laborious press junket. Besides, she could use a dose of Oprah's touchy-feely charm after waking up to find Macy dead in a heap in her beautiful penthouse suite. Why should Macy's downward spiral swirl away her dreams? "I'm the only guest today. I can't cancel with no notice."

"She's a professional. She'll understand a helluva lot better than her viewers would if you're on their TV screens when they expect you to be grieving."

Greer had no independent recollection of any specific words spoken during the few minutes she spent apologizing to Oprah for having to cancel. All she remembered was an overwhelming sense of acceptance and warmth. She understood how Oprah was able to get everyone to open up to her. Rick had grabbed her the minute she left Oprah's dressing room and hustled her out of the building.

"Let's get you out of here."

He had a limo waiting and they dashed from the studio to the waiting car. Greer noticed a large crowd outside the studio, but when she saw many of them were holding signs, she decided they weren't fans, but merely a group gathering for a protest of some kind. The car crept through rush-hour traffic toward the Tinsley. Greer took advantage of the slow commute and poured a stiff drink. She hadn't realized how stressed she was. She settled back in the leather seat and let the warm burn of whisky settle her nerves.

"Rick, how much longer until we get back to the hotel? I'm meeting Ethan for dinner, and I need time for a nice long nap first." Ethan Benavides was one of Greer's oldest friends. He was in Chicago with the traveling production of *Phantom of the Opera*, and tonight was his off night. She knew Ethan from college when they performed campy musical reviews at Hershey Park during the summers to earn tuition money. Ethan went on to perform in Broadway productions, while Greer formed a band that launched her into stardom. Their respective travel schedules made it difficult for them to connect more than a couple of times a year. Greer was anxious to see him.

"Honey, I don't think you're going to want to go out tonight."

"Hell yes, I am. I haven't seen Ethan in months. We have reservations at Charlie Trotter's. Rumor is Charlie himself will be there tonight." She wondered what was behind Rick's conclusion. He knew she was a major foodie and despised the strict diet he insisted on. "I could use a night out after all I've been through. Oh, and I swear I'll work off all seven courses in the hotel gym tomorrow."

"No, dear. It's just…well. You might have an increased number of followers, and I want some time to beef up security. Besides, I think it would look better if you stayed in for a while."

"Seriously? I'm not the one who decided to party my brains out last night. Look, I'm sorry Macy's dead, but why does her decision to let loose get to dictate my every move? Besides, Ethan and I are perfectly capable of slipping away to dinner without attracting a crowd."

Rick shook his head while simultaneously pointing out the tinted window of their car. Greer followed the direction of his hand and gasped. They were down the block from the entrance of the Tinsley Hotel and they wouldn't be able to get any closer in the limo. Crowds hoisting signs thronged the street and lined the steps to the hotel entrance. Greer squinted, trying to figure out the source of this popular protest. Signs were everywhere: "Just Say No," "Get out, Greer," "We Love Macy." The protestors competed for space with dozens of the paparazzi wielding notebooks and cameras as they surged into the street. Greer realized the massive crowd was gathered because of her, and the knowledge made her sick. She grabbed Rick's arm and squeezed. He looked at her and wasted no time responding, shouting to the driver, "Don't stop. Head back up Michigan."

❖

"How is New York?" Ainsley wasn't used to making small talk with her boss, but they were already into the sixth course and Frank had dropped no hints about the reason for his impromptu visit. She had to admit the food was excellent and, except for the pesky crowd of reporters outside, the evening had progressed splendidly. But dinner at Charlie Trotter's was a three-hour event, minimum, and Ainsley was beginning to wonder if Frank was going to wait until the check came to get to the point of his visit.

"Actually, I've been in New Mexico for the past week. I flew here directly from Albuquerque."

Ainsley's mind conjured up visions of desert plains and tumbleweeds. She had trouble picturing the sleek man sitting across from her traversing a prairie in his silk Armani suits. Frank enjoyed life's creature comforts as much as she. She knew many vacationed in the sparsely populated Western state, but she couldn't imagine why. When she vacationed, which was seldom, she preferred city life with all its attendant amenities. Frank looked as if he expected her to remark on his recent trip, so she commented, "I hear it's a quiet destination."

Frank laughed. "You've never been to New Mexico?" At Ainsley's nod, he continued. "It's a beautiful state, a huge draw to tourists looking for rugged vistas. Our research shows those same tourists are increasingly on the hunt for luxurious accommodations from which to appreciate all the state's natural beauty."

Frank droned on for a few more moments describing the beauty of his recent destination. The first two hours of dinner had lulled Ainsley into a food coma. She listened politely to Frank's remarks, but her mind didn't register the idle conversation actually had a specific purpose. When Frank finally got around to the point, she missed it entirely.

"And I need your help."

Ainsley reached for her espresso and downed the scorching tablespoons of black adrenaline. She needed to shake the sleepy haze of the past six courses of extravagant dishes and focus on what Frank had just said.

"Pardon me?"

"I think you'll be a perfect fit. Mergers and Acquisitions has already done most of the due diligence. You'll head up the transition team. The current manager is also one of the former owners, and she'll be staying on. I need you to bring the property in line with our standards. I don't imagine it will take more than a month." He wasn't trying to sell her on the idea. Frank's tone and expression conveyed the deal was done. He expected her to accept her new responsibilities with the same enthusiasm she had accepted every other assignment in her years of employment.

Ainsley cursed her lack of attention. What was he talking about? What property, where? How in the hell did she miss the turn in the conversation? She concentrated on asking a few pointed questions designed to gather information without revealing her inattention. "What's the exact location?"

"Palace Ave. It's just yards from the plaza. You'll love it. Over half the rooms have a view of the Sangre de Cristos. You can walk to some of the best restaurants, galleries, and shops in town."

Sangre de Cristos? For the life of her, Ainsley had no idea what he was talking about. It sounded like a church. Logic told her whatever he was talking about was probably in New Mexico, but she was lost as to any additional detail. Suddenly, she was desperate for dinner to be over so she could Google the answers. She contemplated a trip to the ladies' room so she could use her BlackBerry to gather information, but the restaurant manager suddenly appeared at their table.

"Good evening, Ms. Faraday. Would you and your dinner companion like a tour of Mr. Trotter's studio kitchen?"

Frank's face lit up and Ainsley gave a silent curse. Normally, she would have welcomed the opportunity to impress her boss with the perks she was able to garner in her home city, but tonight all she could think about was filling in the blanks of their dinner conversation. She forced a smile and followed Frank to the inner sanctum of the restaurant, all the while wondering what she had gotten herself into.

❖

"When you invited me for dinner, this wasn't exactly what I had in mind."

Greer punched Ethan in the ribs and wrestled the jar of macadamias away from him. She knew he would never let anyone else see him eating all the junk food from the honor bar, but he would gladly indulge in course after course of hoity-toity food in public. The difference was simple: one was worth hours in the gym, and the other was not. She had to admit she was disappointed at missing their dinner reservations too. "Do you think this is my idea of gastronomic orgasm? I had it on good authority, Charlie Trotter himself was going to be on site this evening. I've had those reservations for months. Some tourist with no taste is probably sitting at the table meant for us, plowing their way through all eight courses. This sucks."

"Please. A superstar like you would be able to get in to Charlie Trotter's on a moment's notice." Ethan ripped open a bag and thrust it toward her. "Pretzels?"

"Is that all you have to say?"

"Doll, what do you want me to say? Beloved Macy Rivers died an infamous death in your hotel suite." He read from the *Star*:

"Rock 'n' roll's bad girl has exceeded all expectations. At least the negative ones. Again. Greer Davis, 32, whom many have compared musically to Joan Jett, served up more of a good time than at least one person could take at her latest wild-girl party. Macy Rivers, the doll of Nashville, fell prey to the lure of Davis's wild side and suffered the ultimate consequence for submitting to Davis's dubious charms.

"You had to expect some fallout." Ethan tossed the copy of the tabloid to Greer, who gasped when she saw the grainy photo on the cover. Poor quality aside, it clearly showed Macy kissing her as the pair stood in the doorway of Greer's bedroom at the Tinsley. The caption read: DEADLY LOVE AFFAIR?

Greer flung the paper to the ground. "She kissed me on the cheek. She wanted to try some coke. I didn't want her using in front of everyone at the party, including those insidious hounds from the press." Greer met Ethan's gaze. "You don't believe we were fucking, do you?"

"No, honey, I don't. But it's a hot story, and it's going to be a while before the heat dies down." He pulled her close. "Is this really the first time you've seen this photo? It's all over the news."

Greer shook her head. Doubtless, Rick had shielded her from the unintended result of his desire to bolster her reputation. Now she was forced to deal with the consequences. "I don't know how I can recover from this." Greer tried to keep the tremor out of her voice, but she couldn't completely hide her fear. She was used to adoring fans, but the angry mob of unfans and hungry press waiting for her outside the Tinsley shook her to the core.

"Here's the plan. You'll hole up here for a couple of days. The press and related kooks will soon find another story to occupy their obsessive tendencies. After forty-eight hours with no new news, they will all have wandered off in search of another victim for their attentions, and you can return to your life." Ethan shook the empty jar of nuts. "I have only one condition to allowing you to share my room." Greer raised her eyebrows. "We must have room service. Now."

Greer laughed and picked up the phone. "It's a deal." She placed a quick call to Rick to let him know she was safe and staying with Ethan for a couple of days, then she ordered half the room service menu to appease Ethan. She was supposed to leave for New York on Sunday for a Monday morning appearance on *The View*. She had no idea if Rick would let her appear or if the ladies on the show would even want her. Maybe Ethan was right; things would surely have settled down by then.

CHAPTER THREE

Ainsley closed her laptop and sighed. Frank was sending her to Nowhereville. She knew Santa Fe was a popular vacation destination, but for crying out loud, the city had a population of only 70,000. Boonies. To top it off, the city was an hour away from the nearest airport of any size. Her morning's worth of Internet research did little to allay her distaste for her new assignment, but she knew Frank expected her to prove herself with the task. If she could turn a small hotel in the sticks into a star of the Hotel Steel line, then she could do anything. Ainsley was up for the challenge. Looking at the wide mountain vistas pictured on the city's Web site, she doubted there would be anything to distract her from the task. Ainsley sighed. No doubt all the women were clad in flannel and heavy boots. She was scheduled on a flight out of O'Hare the next morning, so she had the rest of the day to wrap things up at the hotel and pack. Her assistant manager would be in charge while she was away and, if she did her job right, she might never return. The corner office in New York was becoming more of a reality every day.

She was jerked from thought by the buzzing of the interoffice phone. Punching a button, she answered with a sharp "Yes?"

"Melanie Faraday on two for you, Ms. Faraday."

Ainsley cracked a smile at the formality of the hotel operator and replied, "Thank you. Put her through."

"Hello, little sister, how are you this fine day?"

"Hi, Mel, I'm peachy. What's the occasion?" Ainsley spoke to her sister on birthdays, holidays, and other obligatory occasions. Her busy parents might rate a few additional calls throughout the year, but only if there were important news to relay. If Melanie initiated a call on an average day, odds were she wanted something and she wanted it bad.

"Don't be so tiresome, dear. It's boring." Melanie sighed dramatically. "I'm in town on business. Let's have dinner."

Melanie's career as an account executive at Goldman Sachs was her first love. Ainsley didn't believe her sister would want to take a few hours away from her business to have dinner with a family member. Ainsley sought Melanie's ulterior motive.

"Business, on a Saturday?"

"Look who's talking. Didn't you answer from your office phone?"

"Touché. Will dinner be the two of us?"

"Well, certainly us." A few beats of silence and then, "And one of my clients."

Ainsley could smell a rat even if it was on the other end of a phone line. "Ah, I see. You have someone you'd like me to meet."

"Don't act like you're being tortured. She's smart, beautiful, and witty. I'm certain she'll make a fabulous dinner companion."

Ainsley was used to being used by her family. She had no doubt Melanie had already told her client all about her younger sister and what a good time Ainsley could show said client. While her family didn't pretend to understand what they called her "homosexual lifestyle," they tolerated her. She was, after all, wildly successful, and to her corporate raider parents and highly successful older sister, prosperity was everything. Melanie might not have a relationship in her sights for her, but she wasn't above using Ainsley to help her win an account. Ainsley could hear her now: "You should meet my sister, she's a fox. Quite the catch. She manages a successful hotel. Oh, and she's single." Wink. Wink. Ainsley had been caught unawares on numerous occasions while Melanie was casting her like bait on the end of her line to a business deal. Not anymore. She was done luring clients for her sister.

"Well, I don't want to." Ainsley waited for the simple answer to sink in.

"Well, I want you to," Melanie pouted.

"Seal the deal on your own, big sister. I'm done being your whore."

"Language!"

Ainsley laughed out loud. "Language, my ass. You can call it whatever you want, but the truth is I'm tired of you acting like you accept who I am only when it serves your purposes. This isn't the first account I've helped you land. I've had my fun, but it's over. Why don't *you* sleep with your smart, beautiful, witty client?" Ainsley drew a mock gasp. "Oh wait, I forgot, you don't really approve of same-sex 'relations.'" Ainsley spat out the last phrase as if it were a piece of rotted fruit.

"Oh my. I had no idea you were so bitter."

"Bitter?" Ainsley considered. Was she bitter? No, she was tired of only receiving pseudo acceptance from her family when they wanted something. She got like this every so often. It would pass. It always did. She would slip back into the easy pattern of dysfunctional relations with her family, and Melanie would conveniently forget this momentary zap in the scheme of things. But right now Ainsley felt good about telling her off. For a flicker of a moment, she considered telling Melanie she couldn't have dinner because she had to get ready for her trip. The thought flickered and burned out. Ainsley decided not to dilute her strong stand.

"No, Melanie. I'm not bitter. I am, however, busy, and I need to let you go. Have a wonderful time in Chicago and give my regards to our parents." She clicked off the line, cutting short any argument. Moments after she hung up, she wondered why she hadn't told Melanie she was going out of town rather than burn bridges with her. Melanie did the best she could, considering she was an uptight bitch, and most of the "dates" she hooked Ainsley up with were well worth enduring a business dinner. Ainsley had been so busy over the last few months, she had barely had time for relaxation of any kind. As she thought about her slumbering libido, she told herself it was probably a good thing. She certainly wasn't going to be getting any action in the desert mountains of Santa Fe.

❖

Greer woke up refreshed and ready to take on the day. She had spent all day Saturday watching pay-per-view movies and eating the contents of Ethan's minibar. After sharing coffee with Ethan, she kissed him good-bye and made her way to the lobby to catch a cab back to the Tinsley. Ethan was pouting as she left. He had another day off from the stage production and had tried to talk her into staying with him for a day of Michigan Avenue shopping. Greer was glad for the excuse to leave. She enjoyed Ethan's company, but couldn't handle a day of power shopping with a professional. She also couldn't imagine how they would get any shopping done with a mob on their heels.

A bellman in the lobby greeted her by name. "Ms. Davis, I have your car. Right this way." She was dressed in a pair of Ethan's faded jeans, a T-shirt, and a baseball cap from the Phantom souvenir booth, and was a bit disconcerted to be recognized. She knew Rick had made arrangements for her transportation back to the Tinsley, but it still felt odd to be approached after a full day away from the clamoring crowds.

The uniformed boy led her to a waiting sedan and she tipped him generously for his assistance. The sun was shining, but it was still early enough that the day's humidity hadn't choked off the draw of being outdoors. She doubted anyone on the street would guess her identity and for a moment, she contemplated walking across town, but she realized she wouldn't make her flight if she indulged the whim. Besides, Rick would have a hissy if he found out she was on the street by herself. She slid into the waiting vehicle and told the driver to take her to the Tinsley. Greer found a copy of the Sunday paper on the seat beside her and gasped at the article on the front page, complete with the quarter-page photo. There she was, coming out the doors of Harpo Studios, oblivious to the protestors surrounding her. GREER CONFESSED TO OPRAH? the headline screamed.

She wanted to scream too. Greer was so engrossed in the story, she didn't notice the driver's intense stare into the rearview mirror until he cleared his throat with a loud "ahem."

"Good morning, Ms. Davis."

"Good morning," Greer answered, distracted by the story in her lap.

"I can help you."

Greer responded without looking up. "Excuse me?"

"I can help you with your situation." His voice was quiet but commanding.

"I'm sorry. Do I know you?" Greer locked eyes with the man and was a bit unnerved by his impenetrable stare.

"No, but I know you. I can help you repent." The solid clicks of the automatic door lock punctuated his remark.

Greer shook her head. Surely this wasn't happening. The driver was a kook and she was stuck in the car with him. She decided to ignore him, hoping he would lose interest if she did. "Thanks, but I'm good."

"No, you're not. But you can be. All you have to do is abandon your perverted lifestyle, repent for the death of Macy Rivers, and follow The Way. I can show you how. I will take you to a safe place now."

Holy shit. Greer realized turning the other cheek wasn't going to buy her anything in this situation. She was trapped in a moving car with an extremist kook who thought he was transporting her to salvation. She reached into her bag, opened her cell phone, and started to dial the numbers to reach Rick. As she waited for the line to connect, she almost jumped out of her skin at the booming voice from the front seat.

"This car is plated with armor. Don't expect to get a signal. Trust me, the only signal you need is one from Above."

Greer bit back a comment about how cell towers were above too and at least they could be seen. Now was not the time for humor. Mr. Salvation in the front seat was hell-bent on taking her somewhere. She had to find a way out now. Greer glanced around. She knew Chicago well enough to know they were reaching the outskirts of downtown. Within moments, they would leave the more populated areas and be headed out into the suburbs. She had to act and act now. The light at the intersection ahead was green, but the two cars ahead of them were moving slowly because of tourists lingering their way through the crosswalk. The car she was in was moving, but it was only inching forward. She figured this would be her only opportunity to make a break for it. She lunged over the divider and used one hand to press the button to unlock the doors, then used the other to wrench open the door, and she launched herself from the vehicle. Momentum caused her to lose her footing, and she tumbled out of the car. Fear spurred by the driver's shouts urged her on. She scrambled to her feet and ran the opposite way down the street. The driver, faced with a now-clear intersection, gave in to the honks of the traffic behind him and sped through. Suspicious now, Greer decided Mr. S might very well come back for her, so she zigzagged through the neighborhood, looking for shelter.

She fished her cell out of her pocket and started to dial, but a gut feeling spurred her to snap it shut and go in search of a landline. She had no idea how the crazy car driver had learned where she was staying, but until she figured it out, she was determined to cover her tracks. Greer spotted a diner on the corner and ducked in. The large Mediterranean man at the counter seemed to ignore her request to use the phone and instead spent several long moments surveying her disheveled appearance. After what seemed like forever, he thrust a cup of coffee and a plate of eggs, bacon, and toast her way and grunted, "Eat first. Phone after." Greer resigned herself to the continuing nightmare and ate a few bites. She contemplated her next move, all the while watching the street for signs of the car she had escaped from. Finally, when she had cleared enough of her plate to satisfy the proprietor, she was allowed use of the phone.

"Ethan, I need help."

Big yawn. "You realize it's still very, very early, right?"

"Ethan!"

"Sorry." Smaller yawn. "What's up, babe?"

"I barely escaped from a Jesus freak kidnapper who thinks I perverted and then killed Macy. I'm somewhere in Greek Town. I'm scared to go back to my hotel because if he could find me at a place I wasn't even supposed to be, then surely he can find me where I'm listed as a guest. I have a flight in two hours. I don't know what to do." Greer realized as the words came tumbling out she wasn't making much sense.

"Stop talking." No more trace of tired in his tone, Ethan seemed razor sharp. "Where are you now?"

Greer looked around, finally spotting a corner of a menu with the address. Halsted and Adams. She gave Ethan the address of the diner.

"Don't move. I'll be right there."

"Hurry," Greer said, but Ethan had already clicked off the line. She spent the next few minutes fiddling with the remainder of her breakfast while casting furtive glances at the door. After what seemed like a century, Ethan glided into the joint like he was taking the stage.

"Hi, doll. We're going to get you fixed right up. Where's the restroom?"

Greer was instantly annoyed. "Didn't your mother always tell you to go before you leave the house?"

Ethan grabbed her arm and steered her toward the back of the diner. "You're *hilarious*." He waved a travel case at her. "You are about to become someone else, and I need some room to make it happen. Let's go." He pushed her forward.

"Wait, I need to pay."

"You're this stressed and you ate breakfast?"

Greer jerked her head toward the large man who had force fed her. "He made me. Wouldn't let me use the phone until I ate." She looked frantically away when the man smiled in her direction.

Ethan crinkled his brow. "Interesting." Waving the man over, he called out, "Yoo-hoo, Mr. Diner Man. Do you have a private space we could use for a moment?"

Greer blushed, sure the man would misunderstand Ethan's request. Seconds later she was surprised to find him leading them down the hall to a door marked Office. "Here is good," he said as he left them alone. The room was small and messy. Two desks lined each wall and a tiny TV, mounted on the wall, blared the local early, early morning news show.

"He's a man of few words. Exactly how I like them." Ethan pushed her into a chair and dug a bright red wig, a contact lens case, and a bunch of jars and brushes from his travel case. "You, my friend, are about to become someone else altogether. You'll board your flight and no one will be the wiser."

Greer resigned herself to being made up again. She knew Ethan well enough to know once he made up his mind about something, no one could stop him. As she watched herself transform from a blue-eyed blonde to a brown-eyed fiery redhead, she was once again amazed at his talents. She almost laughed as she watched the transformation. If she stayed in costume, the studio folks at *The View* wouldn't know where to begin when she showed up for the taping, if they even recognized her in the first place.

Greer realized they probably would recognize her, because they would be expecting her. She would be pulling up in the limo the network would send to the airport. Remembering the crowd outside the Tinsley, she wondered what else might be waiting for her in New York. Surely the devastated fans of Macy Rivers wouldn't traverse the continent to fan the flames of tragedy? Even as she had the thought, Greer knew she was being naïve. New York would have its very own throngs ready to display their anger. She shook at the thought.

"Stay still. I'm not used to working in these conditions." Ethan grabbed her chin and peered intently into her now-brown eyes. "What's the matter?"

"Oh, Ethan, I appreciate what you're doing, but it isn't going to work." Greer took a deep breath. "First of all, how am I supposed to get on a plane when I look nothing like my ID? Nine eleven? Hello? Second, I think I may be going from the frying pan to the fire. Who's to say what's waiting in New York?" Even as she spoke these last words, the television echoed her concern.

"Now to our reporter in the field with a human interest story. Nancy?"

"Thanks, Stan. I'm standing outside the Tinsley Hotel, where picketers have been keeping a nonstop vigil mourning the death of Macy Rivers. We have yet to spot Greer Davis, who is probably the only person who knows what really happened to Ms. Rivers, but since she is scheduled to appear on The View *tomorrow morning, we expect to see her exit the hotel at some point."*

Ethan put one hand over Greer's eyes and the other over her ears. "Don't listen."

She brushed his hands away. "Did you hear that? I'm screwed. Not only can I not board a flight looking like this, I'm going to get mobbed in New York."

"So don't go." Ethan reduced the problem to the lowest common denominator.

"I have to go."

"No. You. Don't." Ethan shook her shoulders. "Honey, you are Greer Davis, successful superstar. You're rich, you're beautiful. You're like a superhero except you need a plane to fly. Don't go to New York. Give this thing time to settle down. Then you can face your public again."

Thoughts raced through Greer's head too fast for her to process. Rick would kill her if she didn't show up. Where would she go if she didn't go to New York? She couldn't exactly take up residence in the back room of a Greek Town diner. The food was good, though. *Focus, Greer, focus.*

Ethan, obviously having the same thought, snapped his fingers in front of her eyes. "If you could be anywhere right now, where would it be?"

Greer rolled the question around in her head till it fell into the right slot. Home. She wanted to go home. She didn't really have a home anymore. She had four houses, but she spent so little time at any of them, none of them felt like home. Only one place would ever truly be home, even if she didn't own a house there. She hadn't been there in a long time, but she knew deep down that the length of her absence wouldn't lessen the welcome she'd receive.

"The ranch."

"Then the ranch is where you are going to go." Ethan pulled out a cell phone and punched in a number. "Yes, I'm trying to reach Brad Johnson."

"Who's Brad?" Greer mouthed.

Ethan motioned for her to be quiet and whispered into the phone. After a few mysterious minutes, he clicked the phone shut. "Alrighty then. You are booked on an eleven a.m. flight to Albuquerque out of O'Hare. We need to get you to the airline offices right now so they can process your special permit to bypass general security. For the day, you are an employee of the airlines, which will keep you sheltered from the crowds at the airport." In response to Greer's questioning look, he added "Brad's a friend. A close friend."

He swept up his cosmetics into his bag and started for the office door. "Chop, chop. We have to get going."

"I have to call Rick and let him know what I'm doing."

"I'll call him."

"But, Ethan…"

"No buts. Let's go." Ethan pushed Greer back to the front of the diner and past the large man, tossing out good-byes for both of them. "Thanks for the use of the space. We have to be going."

Greer stopped suddenly. "Ethan, I still haven't paid for breakfast."

The man who had followed them to the door leaned close to Greer. His large head bobbed near hers and she started to shake. Was he crazy too? Was she going to have to make a break for it? With her luck, she would probably be arrested for refusing to pay for her meal when all she was trying to do was save her own hide. Her frantic thoughts almost blocked out his words.

"No charge for you, Miss Davis."

Chapter Four

Ainsley was surprised to see another passenger already in the aisle seat. She would've sworn she was the first one on board. She liked to board first, settle into her first-class window seat and avoid having her personal space invaded by clumsy tourists with snotty-nosed children. She stood in the aisle and waited a few seconds before clearing her throat. Once she did, the woman in 3B jerked upright as if she'd been shot.

"Pardon me," Ainsley said. "I'm in 3A." It seemed like forever before 3B's puzzled expression faded into understanding.

"I'm sorry. Here, let me get out into the aisle so you can get by." She stood hastily and almost fell into Ainsley. As she pulled back to regain her balance, their eyes met. Ainsley was struck by the most beautiful brown eyes she had ever seen. They were an interesting earthy shade and very striking. Her voice too was unique. Sultry tones, low and smooth. Ainsley took a moment to survey everything about the woman standing almost on her feet. She was tall, trim, obviously fit. She was dressed casually in jeans and a royal blue Cubs sweatshirt, which looked very comfortable in contrast with Ainsley's charcoal gray silk suit. The only off-putting feature was her fiery red hair. Ainsley had never favored redheads. Not after a too-long weekend spent with the McFadden twins. She hated to stereotype, but if other redheads had half the tempers of those gals, she didn't even want to know about it and didn't want to get involved. She'd spent too much time refereeing without enough personal fouls to make it worth the effort. No, Ainsley preferred the familiar West Coast staple, the blue-eyed blonde. She knew it was clichéd, but she didn't care. After spending the last five years working in Middle America, who could blame her for wanting to snuggle up to a beach body with hair the color of sunrays and eyes the color of ocean waves?

"Would you like to sit down?"

Ainsley shook away her musings. A line of passengers was threatening to mow her down. Those sultry tones were going to get her into trouble. She stowed her carry-on and slid into her window seat. She spent the next few minutes intently inspecting the runway in an effort to shake the trance of her siren seatmate. It didn't work. She found herself sneaking glances under the guise of making sure her seat back was in the upright position. Yep, 3B was a knockout.

❖

Oh my God, oh my God. Greer could tell 3A was stealing looks at her. She wondered if her disguise was working. After the jolt of electricity she experienced at their brief touch, she almost didn't care. 3A was tall, leggy, and gorgeous. Her sharp features were made prominent because her luscious caramel-colored hair was pulled into a tight braid. On some the look would be severe, but on her it was positively regal. She was tall and not just because of the three-inch slingbacks she was sporting. From where Greer sat, 3A was all leg, and Greer was willing to bet she booked in first class for the extra room. But the most impressive thing about her was her eyes. Hooded baby blues. Not what she'd expect with her light brown hair. Idly wondering if 3A colored her hair, Greer chided herself. She would probably need to color her own if she was going to go out in public again any time soon. This wig thing wasn't going to work for long. She could already feel it slipping like a bad toupee. Bless Ethan's heart. He hadn't had much time to work with his uncooperative subject. Maybe she could get her aunt to help once she got to the ranch.

Even as she had the thought, she hoped someone would be there. She hadn't called ahead. There hadn't been time. She didn't even know how she'd get to the house, since it was a ninety-minute drive from the airport. She didn't want to go through the pain of trying to rent a car with a mismatched ID. Assuming a new identity wasn't all it was cracked up to be. Where was the back-room document forger ready to provide her with any documents she needed if the price was right? *How does anyone even find those people, anyway? Damn.* She should have taken the time to call Rick so he could arrange things. Greer was rambling and she knew it. A sure sign her life was spinning out of control. The only saving grace was the rambling was internal. 3A would think she had lost her mind if she could hear Greer's internal fussing.

"Ainsley Faraday. Nice to meet you."

Greer nearly fell out of her seat. She couldn't muster up enough composure to do anything other than stare at the hand 3A extended her way. Her mind was flooded with Ethan's voice: *The minute you get on the plane, put these earphones on and open this book to the middle and start reading as if your life depended on it.* He had handed her the props, purchased on the airport concourse, and given her a stern look. *Don't talk to anyone.* Well, where was Ethan now, when his advice was worthless? He hadn't prepared her for the friendly seatmate who also happened to be gorgeous. Greer felt the seconds painfully tick away and she finally forced herself to speak.

"Hi. Nice to meet you too." Excellent, she thought. She had spoken, out loud even, and bought herself another second or two to come up with a name. Picking a name shouldn't be hard. She should just pick something. Anything. The more she focused on the task, the harder it became.

"And what should I call you?"

Ainsley was relentless. Name. Name. Name. Greer closed her eyes for a second and vowed she would be inspired by the first thing she saw the moment she opened her eyes. Her eyelids sprang wide and she stared straight ahead. Tray table. Safety Card. Shit. Greer gathered the scattered pieces of her self-confidence and spoke. "Tray, Tray Card...on. Cardon. Tray Cardon." She thrust out a hand and tried not to wince.

"Tray. Interesting name."

"It's a family name."

"Do you have a large family?"

Greer couldn't believe her mixed luck. When she boarded, all she wanted to do was get through the flight without making any waves. But here she was seated next to a ravishing beauty, and she wanted to know more about her. Greer was at a loss, but she couldn't resist the magnetic pull of Ainsley Faraday. Should she stick with facts or invent an entire persona? She could almost hear Ethan whispering into her ear: "Keep it simple. Stick with the truth as much as possible."

"No. I'm an only child. But I'm very close to my aunt and uncle, and they have a daughter. She's my cousin." Greer winced, but carried on. "So I've always felt like I had a bigger family than I really did." *Shut up. Shut up. Shut up.* Greer knew she was sharing too much information. *Toss it back*, she told herself. "How about you?"

"No. I have one sister and we're not close. Both my parents were only children, so no cousins. Are you close to your cousin?"

Greer realized with every answer she gave she was digging a deeper hole. By sharing personal facts, she was doomed to continued conversation. She searched her mind for a logical way out, but could see nothing. *Ethan, where are you?*

Suddenly, she thought of something. A way to shut 3A up without saying something rude. It had to work.

Greer leaned toward the window seat and pulled 3A—Ainsley something—as close as the molded plastic of the armrest would allow and planted a kiss right on her lips.

❖

The kiss took Ainsley completely by surprise, but she recovered quickly so as not to waste it. Her lips parted and coaxed 3B's tongue into her waiting mouth. *Oh. Yeah.* All the doubts she'd developed after hearing her seatmate's ramblings were burned away by the blistering heat of their touch. Tray's lips were soft, but she pressed hard, and Ainsley moaned at the impact. She felt a powerful surge between her legs and stretched her bare muscular calf against the rough fabric covering Tray's thigh. Dizzy waves made her forget everything. The work in her briefcase, the arduous job ahead, the hundred other people surrounding her in the plane.

The presence of others came into crystal focus with a few simple words: "Would you like something to drink before we take off, Ms. Faraday?"

Ainsley reluctantly tore her attention and her lips away from Tray. It took a moment to focus. When she did, she couldn't help but notice the smirk of the dapper young first-class flight attendant. She shot a look at Tray and answered confidently. "Thanks. Champagne." He smiled and turned his attention to Tray. "And for you, Ms. Johnson?"

Ainsley heard Tray let out a pent up breath. "No, I mean, yes. Champagne is good. Thanks." Ainsley smiled to herself. Had their tiny encounter thrown Tray off? No, wait a minute. That wasn't it. Ainsley struggled to focus. Johnson, Johnson. Tray's last name wasn't Johnson. She confronted her. "I thought you're last name was something else, Card something."

Tray delivered a quick response. "Johnson is my middle name. They must be interchanged on the flight manifest." Greer cursed inwardly. She had forgotten Ethan's friend, Brad, had donated his last name to her as a cloaking device.

Ainsley nodded, ostensibly accepting the answer even though she knew it was a lie. Classic signs. Tray hadn't made eye contact, and her tone of voice changed from sultry to a whine. If they were old friends, Ainsley would have called her on it. But they weren't. They were strangers. Strangers bound together by geographic circumstance for the next few hours. Strangers desperately attracted to each other. Ainsley concentrated on slowing the pulse of her heart. As drawn as she was to the pull of Tray's sexual magnetism, she had no intention of joining the mile-high club. Ainsley might be a playgirl, but she wasn't a slut. Besides, she wasn't known for quiet sexual encounters. She was pretty sure the walls of any private space in the plane were paper thin.

Her thoughts were interrupted by the reappearance of the

smirky flight attendant. "Your champagne, ladies." He handed them each a fluted glass and asked if they needed blankets or pillows, this last delivered with a special smile. When he finally left, Ainsley decided to derail the physical with mundane conversation.

"Are you headed to Albuquerque for work or pleasure?" The minute she asked the question, she could see Tray's face morph from control to blankness. These weren't particularly hard questions, but something was making them difficult to answer. Ainsley wondered what the something was. She wasn't going to find out any time soon. Tray merely mumbled something unintelligible, picked up a big fat book, and pretended to read as if her life depended on it.

❖

Greer woke to the sound of the flight attendant announcing connecting gate information. She was positive she had dried drool on her chin and she cast a look at Ainsley while wiping her face. Ainsley was reading a magazine and she had no drool. She looked as perfect as the first moment Greer had seen her. Perfect hair, perfect makeup, perfect dress. Greer decided all the perfection meant she was tightly wound. *She is so not my type. Except for the fact she's a fantastic kisser.* Greer stifled a yawn and straightened her seat.

"Nice nap?"

"Not long enough. I suppose we're about to land?"

"It appears so."

Greer pointed to the window. "Would you mind opening the window shade? We might be able to see the Sandias."

Ainsley gave her a puzzled look, but did as she was asked and went back to reading her magazine. Greer poked her in the arm. "Hey, there they are. Aren't they beautiful?"

Ainsley looked slightly annoyed at being poked, but she glanced out the window. Greer enjoyed watching the expression on her face go from mild disinterest to genuine awe. The Sandia Mountains were indeed a beautiful and majestic sight. "Wow."

Greer laughed. "'Wow' was the only word I could get out the

first time I saw the mountains. Course, I was a kid then and my vocabulary was much more limited."

"So you grew up here?"

Greer bit her tongue. Literally. After a full moment of internal castigation, she found words. "I have family in the area and I spent a lot of time with them."

"Are you headed to visit them now?"

"Yes." Greer figured it was a harmless answer and short too. *Don't ask anything else*, she willed. Then she came upon a brilliant idea. Ask Ainsley questions. Take the focus off herself. Here the plane was landing and she had finally figured out how to control the situation. "Where are you headed?"

"Santa Fe."

"Business or pleasure?"

Ainsley paused before answering. Greer wondered why. It was a pretty easy question. She found it somewhat comforting she wasn't the only one who had trouble with the easy ones.

"Perhaps a little of both." Ainsley's tone was suggestive, and Greer blushed. She willed herself not to respond. No way could she get involved with someone while she was in hiding. Talk about complicated. Besides, she had no intention of keeping this red wig on her head much longer. She planned to hole up at Aunt Ellen's and hide till the press died down. Then she would get back to work. She was scheduled to start a world tour in six weeks. Greer was so distracted by the thought of returning to the real world that she allowed a crucial error to occur. Ainsley asked another question.

"Where does your family live? Are they picking you up at the airport?"

Greer knew the answer to both questions, but Ainsley raised the issue she had been troubled by since she boarded the plane. How was she going to get to her aunt's place? The shuttle only ran to Santa Fe, and hiring a cab was out of the question after her Chicago cabbie nightmare. No way could she fake her way into renting a car. She supposed she could call one of her cousins and hope they could make the run down to Albuquerque to pick her up on short notice. *Quit worrying,* she told herself, *and answer the lady before she begins to think you are both rude and crazy.*

"Um. I will probably—"

"Because I have to rent a car and I could give you a lift."

Greer winced. Not a good idea. Terrible idea. No way should she get into a car with a gorgeous stranger to whom she was hopelessly attracted. Not a chance.

"Thanks. A ride would be great." She heard herself say the words, and while she knew accepting a ride from Ainsley was a mistake, she couldn't help but be excited by where the ride might take her.

CHAPTER FIVE

I appreciate the help navigating," Ainsley said. "This is my first time in New Mexico." Tray murmured an unintelligible reply, and Ainsley wondered what had possessed her to offer her a ride. She had barely said a word since they had left the plane, and they were almost to the exit for Santa Fe. Tray was as jittery as a bank robber on her first heist. Ainsley's thoughts kept wandering back to Tray's evasiveness in response to questions about her personal life and her weirdness about offering up her name. Something was going on with her, but damned if Ainsley could figure it out. Tray's motivation for hedging on the truth was a mystery, but Ainsley was more concerned with finding a solution to the mysterious attraction she experienced in Tray's presence. And it was a mystery. Tray wasn't her usual type. Ainsley shrugged. She knew attraction had been her primary motivation for offering a ride. She didn't have much time before they reached the end of their journey, so she decided to quit trying to figure out anything about Tray other than how to get her in bed.

❖

Greer caught all the lavishing looks Ainsley tossed her way. It took every ounce of restraint she possessed not to reach across the gearshift and accept Ainsley's tacit invitation to touch. She restrained herself. She figured if she could make it through the next hour, she would never see Ainsley again. She needed the complication to be gone.

Ainsley said it was no trouble to drive her directly to Tesuque, but Greer decided as soon as they got to Santa Fe, she would make some excuse for ending the journey there. The relative freedom of the car, compared to the tight quarters of the plane, made her want to do things she knew were crazy. All she could think about were the many secluded places they could turn off I-25 and exorcise the pent-up desire she knew they both were feeling. She envisioned Ainsley's tall, lithe form bent back over the red rocks at the top of La Bajada hill. Her skirt hitched high, granting ready access to Greer's hungry mouth. *Now, what would Ethan say about these visions*, she wondered. She realized channeling Ethan was not going to help in this situation. She knew Ethan would be as torn as she was between lust and sense.

Yep. She planned to get off the temptation train in Santa Fe. She could stop in at her cousin Drew's hotel and hitch a ride with her when she got off work for the day. Besides, she didn't want a stranger, even someone she was currently lusting over, to know where she was staying. She might as well preserve whatever anonymity she could. She had made a quick call to her aunt's house from a pay phone at the airport. No one answered, so she spun a tale as long as the allotted tape time would allow. She was stopping in for a visit, and she would explain the suddenness of her appearance later, her message had said before the beep signaled she was disconnected.

"Do you visit Santa Fe often?"

Greer hesitated before answering. Ainsley's questions so far had been direct and to the point. If she thought she was riding in a car with Greer Davis, or was even curious about it, she would pose a straightforward query. They had a sixty-minute ride in front of them, and Greer knew avoiding casual conversation would be rude. "I grew up out here, but I left after college. I come back for holidays and special occasions." As the words left her lips, she pondered the truth of her last remark. She used to spend holidays at Aunt Ellen's and Uncle Clayton's, but right now she couldn't name the last one she'd been present to help celebrate.

"I'm kind of holiday only with my family too," Ainsley said before resuming her role as inquisitor. "Since this is my first time in Santa Fe, what do you recommend as necessary activity?"

Greer resisted the urge to suggest herself as a "necessary activity" and decided it was time for her to ask some questions. "I get the impression you're here for business. Will you have much free time?"

"Probably not much, but I'd still like some insider scoop on the best spots in case I have time to enjoy them."

"Well, I would suggest hiking, but you don't look like the outdoorsy type." Greer dodged Ainsley's friendly punch. "Seriously, those heels must be six inches tall."

"Three. And, for your information, I'm perfectly capable of enjoying the great outdoors."

She must do something to keep her body in such great shape. Greer feigned indifference. "Whatever. You won't be enjoying many trail hikes in those beauties."

"I assume we're still talking about my shoes?"

Greer laughed. Maybe Ainsley Faraday wasn't so buttoned up after all. "Nope, I've moved on. My second favorite activity out here is eating. Staying in Santa Fe, you'll have your choice of five-star restaurants, but be sure to frequent some of the local dives for fantastic New Mexican food. I hope you like your chile hot."

"I like lots of things hot."

Greer smiled. Definitely not buttoned up at all. She was pleasantly surprised to find that conversation with Ainsley was so free and easy, and Greer contemplated whether she should suggest a detour after all.

"What kind of music do you like?"

Greer's feelings of contentment dissolved, and she shot a suspicious look at Ainsley. What kind of question was that? Was this some clever ploy of Ainsley's to get her to admit who she was?

Ainsley returned her stare and nodded at the radio where her hand rested on the dial. "Radio? Music? Do you have a preference?" They had been listening to NPR the entire drive and now it looked like she was going channel surfing. Greer stifled a groan. Good thing she hadn't voiced her plans for a quickie. She was pretty sure Ainsley thought she was a whack-job. "I'm pretty flexible. I like all kinds of music." She was interested to hear what kind of music Ainsley would choose.

"Our next song is from the latest album by Greer Davis, Escape. *This album hit number one on the Billboard charts last week. Pretty ironic. While Greer's album now has the highest profile in the music industry, she's apparently decided to hide from the limelight after country western star Macy Rivers turned up dead in Greer's penthouse under mysterious circumstances. Escape indeed."*

Greer sat on her hands. It took every ounce of restraint she could muster not to change the station or yell at the dial. *Typical.* What did some two-bit DJ sitting in a booth hundreds of miles away from Chicago know about her or what she had gone through since Macy decided to take a run on the wild side? *Mysterious circumstances, indeed. Macy snorted a little coke, liked it, and didn't know when to stop. End of story.*

Greer tried to focus on the music, but the surreal experience of hearing her own voice growling through the speakers, pining for escape from the pain of lost love, provided a distraction of its own.

"Can you believe her?"

"What?" Greer didn't need to ask the question to know the subject of Ainsley's question. It would be a long time before this story ended.

"That punk, Greer Davis. See what easy success does? Makes you irresponsible." Ainsley waved a hand to emphasize her point. "If she had had to work to achieve the fame she has, she might be less inclined to act out."

Greer was more determined than ever to cut this ride short. Rather than joining Ainsley's criticisms, she pointed to a sign up ahead. "There's the exit you want. St. Francis Drive."

Ainsley reacted quickly and veered to the right. "Is this the best way to get to your place?"

"I need to do a couple of things in town." Greer answered with deliberate vagueness. "I'll let you know where to drop me off and then you can be on your way. I can get a ride to the house later." She studiously ignored the obvious disappointment on Ainsley's face. Hell, she was disappointed too, but the events of the past two days had taught her a stiff lesson in discretion. Concerns about her wig falling off her head at the wrong moment aside, she would be crazy to get involved with someone, especially someone who thought she was completely lacking in moral fiber. Best to cut this little fantasy short before things got out of hand. "Up here you're going to turn right onto Cerrillos. For future reference, it'll take you right into downtown."

"Even smaller than I thought," Ainsley muttered.

"Pardon?"

"Santa Fe's a pretty small town, isn't it?"

"I suppose," Greer replied. "I've seen a lot smaller. Tesuque's center of commerce consists of a combination grocery store/gas station/restaurant." She pointed out a turn ahead while laughing at the round "O" Ainsley's astonished expression produced. "I gather you're a strictly big-city kind of girl."

"Pretty much. Small towns aren't my normal choice of destinations."

Greer searched the side of the road for a distraction. "Pull over there." She pointed to a rail yard on the left. Ainsley maneuvered the car into the gravel-filled parking lot outside of the well-known Tomasita's restaurant. Greer figured she could hang out there, feasting on hot green chile, while she figured out her next step.

"Good food?" Ainsley asked.

"Great food."

"Perhaps I'll join you." Ainsley purred.

"Uh, well, I was…It's just I wasn't going to—"

Ainsley's seductive expression quickly rearranged into nonchalance. "Hey, it was only a suggestion. I have things to do anyway." She stopped the car and pushed the button that opened the trunk. "Need help with your things?"

Greer could read the hurt behind Ainsley's feigned indifference. She would love to share dinner with Ainsley. She would love to share much more. Under different circumstances, she would not have hesitated to take Ainsley up on her offer, though she would have countered with the suggestion they forgo chile and warm up some other way. Under different circumstances.

"Thanks, no. I got it." Greer climbed out of the car. Ainsley wasted no time taking off once Greer pulled her luggage from the trunk. Greer watched the cloud of dust billowing in her wake and cursed her current circumstance. She was certain she had let a good one get away.

❖

Ainsley wasn't hurt by Tray's rejection, but she did question her own prowess. She was confident in her ability to seduce. Maybe it was small-town bad luck or the fiery red hair. Whatever the reason, a tryst with Tray wasn't in the cards. She was there to work anyway, and getting involved with a hot babe was likely to be a distraction.

With her personal navigator gone, Ainsley resorted to plugging the hotel's address into the rental car's GPS device. She didn't plan to stay at the Lancer this evening, but she wanted to at least do a drive-by to get a feel for the place. She and the rest of the acquisition team had rooms booked at the El Dorado. Since a date with Tray was off the table for the evening, she decided to get down to business. She reached for her phone.

"Yes, this is Ainsley Faraday. I'll be checking in shortly, but in the meantime, I'd like to leave a message for several guests who will be staying with you this evening." Ainsley waited a moment while the desk clerk at the El Dorado took down the names she rattled off, then she dictated a message directing the entire team to meet at her suite at seven p.m. sharp. She instructed the desk clerk to order a buffet dinner for the group sent to her room, then she clicked off, determined to locate the Lancer.

Downtown Santa Fe was even smaller than she expected, but it still took several loops around the plaza to locate the Lancer Hotel. She finally located one of the rare parking spots on a side street and got out to walk around.

Most of the shops were closed, but their wide windows reflected a variety of merchandise ranging from original oil paintings depicting adobe buildings and breathtaking sunsets over mountain ranges to row after row of silver and turquoise bangles, with some kitschy T-shirts included in the mix. Each building she passed had a singular aspect in common with its neighbors; they were all finished in one of several shades of brown, with only splotches of color on their signs to mark the differences between them. The Lancer Hotel was no different. A lighter shade of tan, the five-story building was edged on either side by a coffeehouse and an art gallery. The sign was simple and dated. Frank had told her the hotel itself was fifty years old. It housed a tiny lobby bar and café-style restaurant, but its main draw was its location, steps away from the plaza. Ainsley didn't enter the building. She wanted to manage the effect of her arrival. She would get a preliminary report from the team tonight in her hotel suite. Her appraisal of the outside told her everything she needed to know for now. Peeling paint on the window frames, cracks in the stucco, and the old-fashioned sign signaled she would be busier than she had imagined.

❖

"Drew," Greer whispered loudly. "Over here." Greer kept the menu in front of her face, but beckoned with her eyes. Drew walked toward her, but her perplexed expression made it clear she had no idea who Greer was. Greer had been purposely cryptic when she called the Lancer Hotel and asked Drew to meet her at Tomasita's. The crazy details of her last-minute visit were better explained in person.

Greer slowly lowered the menu. She hadn't seen her cousin in several years, but she looked exactly the same. Blond, blue-eyed, and an athletic build from years of outdoor sports. Greer noted, not for the first time, how Drew looked more like a surfer girl than a desert rat. "Don't say anything. It's very important you don't react, okay?"

Drew frowned, and Greer realized if she didn't explain fast,

Drew would walk off, convinced she was being stalked by a crazy woman. Greer leaned in close and whispered in Drew's ear, "It's me, Greer."

Drew jerked back and exclaimed, "What!"

"Shh." Greer ducked back behind the menu. "I told you not to react!"

"What am I supposed to say? Depending on which source you choose to believe, you're either a fugitive from justice or enjoying a life of leisure on a remote desert island. Seeing you here, with flaming red hair, was pretty much the last thing I expected."

"Yeah, me too." Greer placed her hand on her arm. "I know I have some explaining to do, but can we eat first? I'm starving."

Drew shrugged. "If we make it quick. I need to get home. There's a lot going on. You're coming to the house, aren't you?"

Greer noted Drew's words were more expectation than invitation. "Actually, I was hoping you would give me a ride. I'm kinda stranded." Drew raised her eyebrows and Greer added, "It's a long story."

Drew secured a table in the back of the restaurant, though privacy was not guaranteed. Tomasita's was a favorite dining spot for both locals and tourists. A prominent sign on the wall cautioned visitors about the heat of the chile, but the warning didn't deter tourists from the scorch accompanying the generous servings of New Mexican food adorned with both red and green roasted chile peppers.

Greer brought Drew up to speed on the events of the past couple of days.

"Wow, she was lying there dying? Right there in your bedroom?" Her tone implied only a fool wouldn't have detected Macy's condition before it was too late.

"Gimme a break. How was I supposed to know she was there?" Greer knew she sounded defensive, but she couldn't help it. "I told her to take it easy, but last I saw her, she was surrounded by a group of adoring fans blowing whatever she could get up her nose."

"Hey, settle down. I was thinking how weird it must have been to wake up to find her dead. What happened when the cops showed up?"

Greer closed her eyes and recounted the events to Drew. Her call to Rick had set a chain of activity in motion, all of it completely out of her control. A team of guys she had never seen before showed up at her penthouse door within minutes of the end of her call. The men were dressed in black, each carrying a large briefcase. She started to question how they had gotten access to the secure floor, when one of them presented a note from Rick. The message on the note was simple and to the point: *Let them in and leave them alone.* Greer planted herself on the living room sofa and tried to ignore the men who were cleaning the suite with meticulous care. About twenty minutes later, Rick showed up. He checked their work, doled out a stack of large bills to the one who had presented the note to her, and sent them on their way, their briefcases filled with any lingering contraband. Only then did Rick call the police to report Macy's death.

"It was surreal. The cops showed up in the same elevator as a team of lawyers from Chicago's top law firm, hired by my label. They gave the police my version of what happened. I didn't have to say a word."

"Are you allowed to leave the state?"

"The lawyers said there is nothing holding me there. The cops didn't find any evidence of a crime in the penthouse. If they decide Macy's death was the result of foul play, they can certainly ask to talk to me, but the lawyers made it clear the cops would need to go through them." Greer looked hard at her. "I don't know what you've read, but Macy overdosed, plain and simple. I didn't slip something into her drink in an attempt to seduce her into my bed. Macy wanted to go crazy. I tried to help her have a little fun, but she wanted more. I'm not responsible for her going over the edge."

Drew cast her eyes down and whispered, "Sounds like you're trying to convince yourself."

Greer rose from her chair and shook a finger in Drew's face. She almost forgot her disguise and where she was. Her anger boiled over. "I don't need you to judge me, Drew. You haven't lived my life. You don't know what I go through every day."

Drew grabbed her arm and motioned for her to sit back down. "Okay, okay. I don't know what your life is like. You're the one who took off and never looked back. You don't know anything about our lives either. I doubt you even care."

Greer noted the anger that flashed from Drew's eyes. She wondered about the source. She and Drew had been fast friends growing up. Greer's parents were archaeologists and had traveled the world in pursuit of new discoveries, never hesitating to leave Greer in the care of her aunt and uncle. Greer had few complaints about her childhood. Life at her relatives' ranch had been good, but she had always hungered for more. Now she had fame and success. All the more she had ever wanted, but it had definitely come with some sacrifices. Her friendship with Drew and the comfort of family could be counted among them. At first she assumed her relationship with Drew suffered from distance, but the anger Drew exhibited now seemed to come from a deeper source than separation. She forced herself to see beyond her own troubles to find out what was fueling Drew's rage.

"I do care. Sorry, I spent so much time talking about me. What's going on with you?"

Drew didn't seem to know what to say. "I don't think I want to talk about it. Look, I need to get going." She tossed some cash onto the table. "Didn't you say you needed a ride? Where do you want me to take you?"

Greer hid her surprise. She had assumed Drew would take her to the ranch, but it didn't look like Drew was offering that as an option. She wasn't ready to admit she didn't have a place to go. "This was kind of a last-minute trip. I didn't make any plans in advance. I don't suppose you have room at the hotel?"

Drew paused as if trying to make up her mind about something. Finally, she spoke. "We've got rooms, but Mom and Dad would probably kill me if they find out you're in town and I didn't bring you home with me. If you can bear staying out in the sticks."

"I can bear it."

"Come on, then." Drew led the way to her truck and loaded the small piece of luggage Ethan had purchased for her at the airport. As she hefted the bag into the trunk, she remarked, "This feels like air. What's in here?"

"Nothing. Ethan bought it for me at the airport so I'd look like a real traveler instead of a rock star on the run."

Drew grinned. "How is he?"

"Same as usual. I swear he loved the drama of spiriting me away. He's probably made up all kinds of crazy stories about my demise."

As they drove out of the parking lot, Greer put her hand on Drew's arm. "Hey, do you mind driving by the hotel? I'd kind of like to see the old place." She pushed away the nagging thought a drive around the square might net a sighting of Ainsley, the tourist, catching the sights. Even though she was determined to hide out at the ranch and avoid human contact, she harbored some small regret she had seen the last of Ainsley Faraday. Despite the fact Ainsley had seemed quick to pass judgment on a total stranger, Greer was attracted to the juxtaposition of her uptight tailored look with simmering sexiness lurking beneath.

Drew nodded and turned the car from Guadalupe onto Alameda to loop around downtown toward Palace Ave. Greer scratched her head. "Something's been bugging me. When I called earlier to talk to you, the hotel operator said, 'Lancer Hotel, a Steel Property.' What's going on?"

Drew shook her head. "A lot's happened since you were last here."

CHAPTER SIX

"One at a time!" Ainsley raised her hand to silence the group assembled in her suite. "I know we have a big job to do, but we're going to operate in an orderly fashion. Understood?"

The group nodded assent. Frank had assembled the top tier of the Steel Line to manage this takeover, and Ainsley knew he was sending a message. The Lancer acquisition was very important to him. After her drive-by this afternoon, she couldn't for the life of her imagine why. The outside of the hotel showed signs of wear. Some might consider it charming, but in a town that was an attraction for the rich and famous, rustic charm didn't cut it as a competitive destination. Summarizing their mission was simple: turn the Lancer into the hottest new boutique property owned by the Steel Hotel line. It was the execution Ainsley was worried about. One of the contract conditions required the current manager, the daughter of the Lancers, would stay on. She would have an equal say regarding personnel issues, at least with regard to current staff. Ainsley wondered what had possessed Frank to agree on such a major concession. Traditional takeover protocol dictated replacement of the top personnel, or at the very least, the general manager.

Of course, the transition team's off-site housing at the El Dorado was also a total departure from usual Steel procedures, but the smaller Lancer hotel had been booked for months for the days leading up to Las Fiestas in Santa Fe. Ainsley didn't have a clue what Las Fiestas was, but after seeing the Lancer for herself, she was quite happy to be staying at the more modern El Dorado.

Frank didn't do the booking himself, but she was certain he was responsible for her having the roomy and impressive Presidential Suite, which allowed ample room for the entire team to assemble for these planning sessions.

The group in front of her had been on site for several days prior to Ainsley's arrival. Their job so far had been to observe and prepare reports she would use to guide the takeover process. Ainsley would take everything they had to say and prioritize the transition process. She had a meeting scheduled first thing in the morning with the current general manager, and she would have a task list ready to present if she had to stay up all night to get it done.

"Paul, give us a general rundown of the front of the house operations." Ainsley called on the man she remembered from her stint at the Steel's San Francisco property. Paul Garret was the pickiest man she knew, especially when it came to appearances. Even as most of the assembled group sat on the floor, dressed in a random assortment of jeans and T-shirts, Paul was perched on the edge of his chair, decked out in a stylish Prada suit. He had a wealth of experience heading transition teams for Steel, and if the more experienced Ainsley had not been present, he probably would have been in charge of this job. Paul glanced studiously at his leather bound notebook before replying.

"I'm not sure where to begin. At first glance the place is dreadful." At Ainsley's impatient nod, he rushed to add specifics. "The front desk clerk, emphasis on the singular here, doubles as the concierge. The valet stand isn't. There are a couple of guys, not in uniform, who appear to be engaging in the parking of cars when they aren't carting luggage to rooms, but there's no real order to the process.

"I asked the general manager to run a Hotelligence report. She had no idea what I was talking about." Paul referred to the subscription service that allowed management to compare their hotel rates and sales numbers with comparable properties in their market. He shuddered and continued his litany. "There are no dedicated voicemail lines in the rooms, so the front desk clerk takes phone messages for guests, in between making dinner reservations, and writes them down." The last three words were delivered with heavy emphasis, conveying Paul's utter disbelief that such an archaic system existed anywhere in the world.

When Paul finished, Ainsley homed in on the one hopeful thing he said. "At first glance?"

"Don't get me wrong," Paul answered. "All those things, and more, need to be fixed, but the place has a certain allure. The former owner's wife still makes amazing homemade pies for the restaurant and apparently, they are highly sought after by locals and tourists alike. And the restaurant itself offers a, let's call it simple, menu of local favorites."

"Who's the chef?"

"Well, there really isn't a chef per se. More like a group of cooks who take turns working shifts. They all work from old family recipes that feature local favorites."

Ainsley gasped. Steel Hotels were known for their five-star restaurants. Knowing Frank and his tastes, she had never even considered having to deal with replacing what sounded like a diner. Ainsley appreciated culinary expertise, but she didn't give much thought to its origin. The idea of having to build a culinary masterpiece from the ground up wasn't the least bit appealing. She knew from travel literature that Santa Fe was host to many five-star restaurants, but it sounded like the restaurant at the Lancer was more like one of those local dives Tray mentioned. No doubt, with the Steel reputation as backing, they could steal a chef away from one of the finer dining establishments in town. She made her first command decision. "Paul, you're in charge of the restaurant. I'll clean up the rest of the place."

❖

The ranch looked exactly as Greer remembered, but the warm fuzzy feeling she felt at the prospect of nestling into the familiar frosted over the moment she walked through the front door.

Aunt Ellen was in her usual place, the sprawling kitchen, rolling out dough for one of her famous pies. She was wearing an apron and was covered in flour. Her hair poked out in all directions, defying her bandana's efforts to tame her unruly waves. What really threw Greer for a loop was the state of the kitchen itself. Half of the bright copper pans that normally hung from the ceiling were off their hooks and scattered in various states of disarray on the granite countertops. A large trash can was bursting with garbage and streaked with stains. Used dishcloths lay in a heap in the floor. Greer glanced around, looking for the aliens who had obviously invaded her aunt's orderly home. What she saw made her stomach clench.

"Hi, Drew, sorry you had to work late. Did you bring home a new friend from work?" Greer knew the man speaking to Drew was her uncle because she was in his house, but if she had seen him out of the context of this environment, she would've sworn the frail man in the La-Z-Boy was a sickly stranger. She looked back over her shoulder at Drew, half pissed she'd been given no warning before they arrived at the house. Drew shrugged and shot a reproachful look back at her.

Greer strode over to her uncle and extended her hand in welcome, but his eyes were hazy with confusion. She realized he didn't realize who she was. Proximity revealed even more disturbing facts. Thin plastic tubing snaked from each nostril. Clayton was breathing with the aid of an oxygen tank. The sight of the apparatus heightened her awareness of his frailty, and she found herself trying to balance her weight so she wouldn't fall into his lap. She was certain she would crush his birdlike legs if she did. Except for his gentle smile, the man in the chair bore no resemblance to the robust and hearty Clayton Lancer she remembered from her youth. The man she remembered would grab her up like a sack of potatoes and run across the yard with her dangling over his shoulder while she squealed with delight. The man she remembered could carry a newborn calf from the barn to show the kids the wonder of new birth. The man she remembered could do anything. This was not the man Greer remembered, and she wanted to burst into tears at the realization. She had traveled all this way to find refuge in the familiar, and it did not exist.

"Drew, why didn't you tell us you were bringing a friend home?"

Greer nearly jumped out of her skin at the voice from behind her. Before she could recover, Aunt Ellen extended a flour-covered hand in welcome. She looked for Drew over her aunt's shoulder, but Drew was on her way out of the room. She'd have to sort through the changes in the Lancer household on her own.

"Uncle Clayton, Aunt Ellen, it's me, Greer." She watched their puzzled looks for a few seconds before she thought to pull the flaming red wig from her head. Within seconds she found herself wrapped in Aunt Ellen's flour-covered arms. "It was a spur-of-the-moment trip," Greer said. She extricated herself from the tight embrace and motioned at the couch. After they settled in, Greer took a deep breath to steel herself for the story she was about to tell.

"I assume you've heard what happened in Chicago?"

Aunt Ellen spoke up first. "You know we don't pay attention to idle gossip." She looked like she had more to say, but Clayton put his hand on her arm and motioned for her to stop.

"Ellen, let the girl talk." He gave Greer a long, hard look. "We read the papers, but if you have something to say, of course we'd rather hear it directly from you."

Greer screwed up her courage and told them about Macy's death. Other than a couple of random headlines and the snip of footage she'd seen at the diner, she had no idea what the media was saying about her involvement. She could only imagine the worst. The version she told was more gloss than detail. Clayton and Ellen didn't need to know everything, she reasoned. They wouldn't understand her explanation of how drugs were a necessary fixture in her business, and she didn't bother contributing details about her role in Macy's first drug experience. "I guess Macy was not the sweet, innocent girl everyone thought she was." The words fell easily from her lips as she wrapped her mind around their purported truth.

"Well, considering everything, you should probably stay with us for a while." Clayton was the first to speak. "No one knows you're here, right?"

Greer pointed at her carrot-top wig and shrugged. "Would you have recognized me if I hadn't told you who I was?"

"Eventually," Clayton answered with a grin.

Ellen reached out to grab a strand of Greer's wig. "I think we're going to need to work on your look," she said. "Maybe Drew could take you out in the morning to pick out some hair color."

Greer nodded. She needed to do something, but the thought of asking Drew for help wasn't appealing. Something was stuck in Drew's craw, and Greer wasn't sure what it was. She'd have to figure it out soon, because she needed some help and some answers. Something was very, very wrong with Uncle Clayton, but she didn't feel comfortable asking him about it directly. She told her aunt and uncle she was exhausted and headed upstairs to get some answers.

❖

Ainsley was relieved to finally have the suite to herself. She foraged in the minibar and located a tiny bottle of Grey Goose. She added a lime from the buffet remnants and a glass of ice and sipped the cool, smooth vodka while reviewing her notes. Tomorrow would be a busy day. She planned to hit the hotel early and take it by storm. She had a breakfast meeting planned with the general manager, Drew Lancer. Ainsley knew she needed to act quickly to have the upper hand. She had to make it clear to Drew it didn't matter if her last name matched the hotel's, the Lancer Hotel was now a Steel Property and therefore Ainsley's to run as she saw fit. Ainsley poured herself another drink to take the edge off. As she leaned back against the soft, silky pillows, her mind wandered to the soft, silky lips of Tray Cardon. The brief and surprising kiss on the plane had left an indelible impression despite the apparent brush-off Tray had given her at the rail yard. As the flush of vodka warmed her, she imagined how much heat could be generated by a longer embrace with the intriguing stranger.

❖

Drew must have been asleep when Greer headed upstairs the night before. She had either not heard or ignored Greer's loud knocks on her door. But the early light of dawn and a grouchy Drew roused Greer from the few hours of sleep she had managed to grab.

Her thoughts had been full of worry about her future and distracting visions of the gorgeous Ainsley Faraday and musings about where she was and what she was doing. The tiny amount of sleep she had managed to get wasn't enough to fortify her for dealing with Drew's mood.

"Get up. I have to be in town early, and Mom wants me to take you so you can get some things."

Greer focused her sleepy eyes at the form standing in her doorway. Drew was showered and dressed, and was tapping her foot. "What time is it?"

"Time to head out," Drew snapped. "I'll be downstairs waiting. You have five minutes."

Greer used at least two of the allotted minutes trying to wake up. When she finally crawled out from under the covers she found a clean pair of jeans and a T-shirt sitting at the end of the bed. She hurried to get dressed and pulled on her wig. She walked into the adjoining bathroom. She had removed the colored contacts Ethan had given her, but she'd had nowhere to put them so she'd wrapped them in a Kleenex. Now they were stuck to the thin paper and she didn't have the time or the supplies to get them back into her eyes. She'd have to risk showing her deep blue eyes until she could buy some contact solution. The wig looked like rats had nested in it, but it would have to do for now. She tugged it until she was satisfied it wouldn't look any better and then headed downstairs to meet up with her impatient cousin.

The ride to town was full of tension. Drew obviously didn't feel like speaking, and the only sound in the car was Greer's stomach grumbling. Greer finally decided if she was going to find out what was going on at the Lancer household, she was going to have to ask. She dove into the subject concerning her the most.

"What's wrong with Uncle Clayton?"

"He's sick."

"Thanks. You're such a fountain of information. I can tell he's sick. Mind telling me what exactly is wrong with him?" Greer was pissed at Drew's palpable anger. She had her own problems. She didn't need to deal with Drew's pissy self.

"If you bothered to come around more or even call, you might know more about what's going on in our lives."

"Well, it's hard to find time to visit relatives when I spend all my time lying around eating bonbons."

"Don't be an ass. I know you're busy. Hell, it must take all your time to get on the front page of every rag at the check-out stand. I imagine being the center of the world's negative attention is a pretty time-consuming job."

"Fuck you, Drew. Fuck you," Greer shouted. Drew didn't reply other than to shoot daggers her way. Greer took a deep breath. Fighting with Drew wasn't going to get her any information. She didn't know what had gotten Drew so worked up, but she did know something was going on at the Lancer ranch and she was suddenly desperate to know what it was. If she had to suck up to her angry cousin to get information, she would do it. No matter what the rags said, Greer Davis knew how to work her public. She took advantage of the red light to plead her case.

"I'm sorry. I know I barged in on your life, and I realize I haven't been around the last few years. But Clayton looks awful, and I've never seen Ellen let the house get so out of order. I know something's wrong. Please tell me what's going on." The last few words were delivered in her best wheedling tone. She could see Drew's shoulders relax slightly.

"Dad sold the hotel." Drew paused and then delivered the real news. "He has cancer."

Greer hadn't even begun to digest the news about the hotel when Drew's other pronouncement socked her in the gut. Thinking she couldn't have heard her correctly, she grabbed Drew's arm. "What did you say?"

Drew shrugged her off and faced her squarely. "Dad has cancer. Lung. Stage Three. It's painful, it's debilitating, and it's fatal." The light changed, and she drove through the intersection. "Kinda hard to manage a business when you're dying."

Greer was stunned. Clayton Lancer had been like a father to her. He was her only uncle, her mother's brother. She couldn't wrap her mind around the possibility of losing him. Greer was an only child.

She figured she had not been a planned event in her parents' lives. Professors Tom and Kim Davis were world-renowned archeologists. Their fame and the generous financial support they received were dependent on their availability to travel at a moment's notice to the next promising dig or fund-raiser sponsored by a well-heeled patron. When she started high school, her parents had dropped Greer and her belongings at Clayton and Ellen's place and taken off for Egypt on an extended dig. Greer could count on one hand the number of times she had seen them since. The Lancer ranch became her home, and Clayton and Ellen had assumed the job of raising her, a task she was sure had aged them both.

Greer always felt as though she was an afterthought to her parents. She found it ironic. No matter how abandoned she had felt as a child, she had selected for herself the same nomadic lifestyle. Well, here she was, back at the Lancer ranch, and she shrugged off a creeping feeling that she was not so unlike her parents. The number of times she'd been back since college probably didn't add up to much more than her hand could hold. The comparison wasn't flattering.

"But why sell the hotel? You can run it, can't you?"

"Of course I can. In fact, I am running it. That was a condition of the sale."

"Then why sell the place at all?"

"Cancer is expensive."

Greer cringed. The weariness in Drew's voice almost hid the accusation. The Lancers had never wanted for anything, but they weren't wealthy, at least not wealthy the way Greer was. Not many were. Greer was a rock star in every sense of the word. She never gave a thought to the amount of money she had or spent. She had no concept of how much money she actually made. She only knew she had enough to do anything she wanted, have anything she wanted, and have plenty left over for Rick to pay the bills. She wanted to ask why no one had called her to tell her not only about Clayton's illness, but that they needed money. She could probably buy a dozen Lancer Hotels and never notice a dip in her bank balance. Did her family really think she was so out of touch she wouldn't care enough to do something about their troubles? Obviously Drew did, hence the cold shoulder since Greer arrived.

"Is there some reason no one let me know what's going on?" Greer knew her tone carried more anger than she meant to convey.

"Is there some reason why we should assume our problems would be important to you?" Greer started to reply, but Drew held up a hand. "Don't answer, it was a rhetorical question. Seriously, how long has it been since you did more than have your assistant send cards or flowers to recognize a birthday or other special occasion? Sometimes I wonder if you even gave the instructions yourself. Besides, there was nothing you could or can do."

"I have money." Even as she delivered the pronouncement, Greer knew it was hollow and Drew would misinterpret. Before Drew could say anything, Greer pushed on. "If money was what you needed, you know I have more than I can ever spend. I would have gladly given or loaned you whatever you need. All you had to do was ask."

Drew sighed. It was as if she was tired of arguing. "Too late. The hotel's gone. I'm on my way to meet the head of the takeover team. I hear she's a real dragon lady."

"But I thought you were managing the hotel?"

"I am, but it's not our hotel anymore. It's a 'Steel Property,' as I've been told by all the suits from corporate office over the past few days, and it 'must rise to the level of their other boutique luxury hotels.' I have to satisfy the dragon lady or they can exercise an option to replace me as the general manager and assign me to some flunky position."

"Drew, I'm so sorry." Greer placed her hand on Drew's arm and squeezed. "Is there anything I can do?"

"You can keep a low profile. The last thing Mom and Dad need is for you to bring the press down on them, especially now." Drew's tone had gone from wistful, back to snappy.

"Don't worry about me. I'll stay out of your hair." Uttering the word "hair" triggered Greer's memory. Her first order of business would be to do something about the god-awful wig on her head. She glanced in the mirror. She could hide her blue eyes behind shades, but the hairpiece would have to go in favor of something more permanent. She didn't want to risk exposure by having the color done at a salon, so she would need to handle it herself. "Drop me near a drugstore." She checked her wallet. She didn't have any cash, only a Platinum American Express card bearing the name Greer Davis. She had no intention of using that calling card. "Oh, and can I borrow a pair of sunglasses and a twenty?"

Chapter Seven

The distance from the El Dorado to the Lancer Hotel was only a few hundred yards, but Ainsley purposely took a winding amble in order to assess the town square, which she was surprised to find empty. In Chicago or New York hordes of people would be bustling about on their way to work. But here, in the early morning hours in this mountain town, a bare handful of individuals wandered around, seemingly with no specific purpose. She clicked off the tourist spots she had memorized from the brochure in her room. She spotted the Palace of the Governors and finally saw some industry in the sleepy town. Native American men and women spread blankets and arranged handcrafted jewelry, dream catchers, and other works of art in preparation for the daily parade of tourists. Ainsley had a hard time believing tourists would travel to this small mountain town to purchase trinkets from a mismatched group of locals who didn't even try to make an effort at showcasing their wares. Random blankets served as the only background to their work. Ainsley reflected on the shiny displays in the windows on the stores lining Michigan Avenue and thought this place couldn't have been farther away. She recalled seeing a brochure in her room extolling the Indian Market that had taken place on this very plaza a few weeks ago. She tried to reconcile the sleepy square with the pictures she'd seen in the brochure depicting hundreds of stalls and thousands of tourists looking for deals on original works of art. Hard to imagine such bustling energy in this tiny town. Ainsley was so absorbed in watching the vendors prepare for the end-of-summer crowds that she didn't notice the woman heading her way until they collided with a crash.

"Oh my gosh, I'm sorry." Ainsley backed up, but her hand gripped the arm wrapped around hers as both women teetered on the edge of a fall. When she finally gained her balance, Ainsley realized the arm she was holding belonged to Tray Cardon. She had a fleeting thought that Tray must have hurt her head, because her free hand was patting her head furiously as if searching for open wounds. Even with the dark sunglasses, Ainsley would have recognized Tray anywhere. It wasn't the raging red hair, which seemed to have some strange blond highlights poking out around the edges she hadn't noticed before. No, it was the adorable scruffiness about her, a trait normally not high on Ainsley's list of attractive qualities, but she found herself wanting to roll around on the floor, making mad passionate love, and then scoop Tray into her arms and cuddle her. In other words, act completely out of character. *What is it about her?*

Before she could process the thought, her voice acted on its own and she blurted out, "Would you like to get some coffee?"

Tray looked confused and stammered out some unintelligible syllables. Ainsley flashed on the memory of their last parting and quickly backtracked. She had no business going for coffee anyway. She was expected at the hotel. "Never mind. Obviously you have things to do and so do I." She started walking away. "Have a good day."

Ainsley only made it a few steps before she realized her hand had slid into Tray's and Tray had a firm grip. "Wait!"

Ainsley couldn't get far with Tray in tow. She faced her captor, eyebrows raised.

"I have to take care of some things this morning, but I could meet you for lunch. If you're free."

Ainsley couldn't quite read the expression on Tray's face. It was a combination of dread and hope, but she decided to ignore the body language and rely on the words and the spark jumping off the simple touch of their clasped hands. Tray confused the hell out of her, but she was irresistibly drawn to her. She didn't do lunch when she was on site at a transition. She would never finish the long list of tasks she had planned for the first day if she went to lunch. Her team would think she had lost her mind if she took off for a meal in the middle of the day.

"I'm free." The words were out before practicality could stop them. And she was glad. So glad, she decided to keep talking. "I'm staying at the El Dorado. Why don't you meet me there at noon?"

Tray hesitated for a second, then nodded. Ainsley, determined not to risk either of them changing their mind, said, "Great, I'll see you then," and she took off in what she hoped was the direction of her new hotel.

❖

Greer shook her head as she watched the tightly tailored beauty walk through the plaza. She couldn't believe she'd been in town for all of five minutes, and already she'd run into the person she least wanted to be near. She cursed Drew for dropping her off smack in the middle of downtown where all the tourists gathered. Frankly, she'd been lucky to get a ride from Drew at all, considering her grousing about being late to work. To top it all off, now she had a lunch date with the svelte Ainsley Faraday. *Date? Is it really a date?* Greer answered out loud. "It's just lunch." *At her hotel.* Greer's wandering mind had to have the last word.

❖

"Welcome to the Lancer Hotel."

After last night's dish session, Ainsley hadn't expected to be greeted at the door, much less by a hot blonde who epitomized the beach blanket babes of her fantasies. She had to force herself to stop staring. It took a moment, but Ainsley finally recovered enough to introduce herself. "Happy to be here." She didn't try to conceal the sultry undertone. "Ainsley Faraday, pleased to meet you."

The blonde gave Ainsley's outstretched hand an icy stare before turning and walking in the opposite direction. Ainsley was so distracted by the abrupt nongreeting and the tight round ass, she almost missed the words the beautiful stranger tossed over her shoulder. "I'll show you to your office."

Paul was waiting in the office and made the introductions. "Ainsley Faraday, Drew Lancer."

Oh, that explains the cold reception. Paul had filled Ainsley in on the back story the night before. Drew Lancer was the daughter of the former owners and the current manager of the hotel. She'd made it clear to the entire Steel team she opposed the sale of the hotel to a chain with every fiber of her being. Ainsley had encountered similar resistance before and was prepared to deal with unwillingness to change. She hadn't been prepared, though, to be distracted by the drop-dead good looks of the angry party. She could almost feel Paul grinning behind her. They had worked together before, and he knew she had a weakness for stunning women. She shrugged. Paul also knew she never, ever let that particular weakness get in the way of her work ethic. She pushed away the nagging reminder that she had just made a lunch date on her first day at the new site.

Ainsley sucked in her breath and willed her business acumen to the forefront. "Ms. Lancer, it's a pleasure to meet you. Your decision to stay on will prove invaluable to a smooth transition. We're lucky to have you." The words were pleasant and Ainsley didn't mean most of them. It was a pleasure to meet such a beauty, but the pleasure was likely to be short-lived. Small-time property owners didn't take kindly to the changes usually required to make their businesses become viable members of established, successful hotel lines. Ainsley imagined Drew Lancer would be no exception. She would probably fight the Steel team on every suggested change. She might as well plunge in and deal with Ms. Lancer's anger. The sale of the hotel called for them to keep Drew on, but the specifics of her work were within Ainsley's discretion. Drew would learn to deal with the new hierarchy, or she wouldn't. The choice was hers, but no matter what, Ainsley was in charge now and she would do whatever it took to whip this property into shape.

She purposely turned away from Drew and addressed Paul to announce her first decision. "I'd like to go ahead and get started on the list we prepared last night. Why don't you assemble whoever you think needs to be in on the meeting?" Paul left the room and Ainsley took a seat behind the large desk. Drew seemed unsure about whether she was supposed to stay or go, and Ainsley was pleased her directive had had the desired effect. She wanted the young Ms. Lancer to realize she was no longer in charge and to have a measure of uncertainty about her future. Comfort bred complacency, and Ainsley couldn't afford the latter. She was interested to see if Drew would use this moment alone with her to suck up or tell her to go to hell.

"I know more about running this hotel than you ever will."

Ah, the go-to-hell approach. Ainsley didn't care, really. She knew things might go easier at first if the current management fully supported the takeover, but such support wasn't the norm. She was prepared for a challenge. She wasn't scared to tackle difficult projects, and she would rather get the hard parts out of the way. Drew was definitely going to be one of the hard parts.

❖

The tall potted plant was a perfect screen. Greer felt well hidden from the activity in the lobby of the El Dorado, but she still had a perfect view of the entry. She hoped no one would choose that particular moment to water the plants. In her disheveled state, they would probably mistake her for a homeless person and escort her out the door. Then again, this was Santa Fe, the City Different. It would be perfectly normal for superstars like Julia Roberts or Val Kilmer to wander into the nice hotel dressed like they'd spent a day working on the ranch. She would simply be mistaken for an eccentric celebrity. Greer almost hit her head on the pillar behind her as she jerked away from the plant. The last thing she needed was to draw attention to herself by lurking in the greenery. She stood up straight, trying to act normal, as if she knew what normal was. Right now, normal was anything but. Normal would have included a limo driver holding open the door for her and her entourage, and swarms of bellmen vying for the chance to carry her bags while hotel guests hoped she would stop to sign autographs. Normal would have been the finest suite the hotel had to offer, with champagne on ice waiting for her arrival—courtesy of the manager. Normal would have been Greer setting the terms for this date, or whatever it was, and those terms would not have involved waiting behind a potted plant.

Greer mulled over the disadvantages of her current circumstance and decided she didn't have to make things worse by having lunch with a stranger and pretending to be a normal person when she was a rock star. She patted the leaves of her plant shield back into place, firmly grasped the plastic bag containing her new hair color, and started toward the doors. She had enough cash left to grab a sandwich somewhere and take it to nearby Fort Marcy Park, where she could be herself, by herself.

She took two steps and smashed into Ainsley Faraday for the second time that day.

"Tray?" Ainsley rubbed her shoulder. "I'm so sorry. I didn't see you behind the plant. Are you okay?"

Greer shut her eyes and willed herself far away. Was she destined to keep running, literally, into Ainsley? When she opened her eyes she quickly realized sheer will wasn't strong enough to get her out of the situation. She would have to make some excuse and get the hell out. Greer opened her mouth to give some plausible explanation for her departure, but when she started to talk, she realized she had acquired a souvenir from this last run-in. "Ouch!"

"Oh my God, your lip is swelling. Did I hit you in the face?"

Greer looked pointedly at Ainsley's shoulder and nodded. She would have to start watching where she was going. Here she was, standing in the lobby of one of the most popular hotels in a popular tourist destination, with a fat lip and a blazing red wig that was probably off-kilter again. She had to start paying a lot more attention if she was going to stay in hiding until the press died down. Greer mumbled something she hoped sounded like she needed to go and started for the door. Ainsley's hand held her in place.

"Wait." Ainsley paused, took a deep breath, and then rushed out the rest of what she had to say. "Let me get you some ice. In my room. I mean, come with me to my room, and I'll get you some ice for your lip. If you put something on it right away, the swelling will go down."

Greer wavered. No telling how late Drew was going to work. No sense wandering around all day with a fat lip. She might as well kill some time until the swelling went down. She looked at the elegant, strong fingers on the hand holding hers and nodded. Ainsley led her to the elevator and punched the button for the Presidential Suite.

❖

Ainsley was thankful a bucket of ice remained from breakfast. She feared if she left Tray in the room alone, she would probably bolt. Tray had looked ready to bolt from the moment Ainsley had started their first conversation during the flight from Chicago. *I wonder if she's from Chicago and, if so, why I haven't seen her before.* She looked vaguely familiar, but Ainsley was certain if she had seen her out in the Windy City, she wouldn't have forgotten. Tray was definitely part chameleon. Something was different about her even today. As Tray carefully applied a washcloth full of ice cubes to her lower lip, Ainsley tried to figure it out. Finally, it hit her. "You're wearing sunglasses!"

Tray flinched and reached a hand up to feel the frames, but she didn't remove them. "Yes." Long pause. "I'm very sensitive to light."

Ainsley couldn't see her eyes, but the rest of Tray's body language told her what she needed to know. She was certain Tray hadn't been wearing sunglasses when she'd admired the sun-drenched mountain vistas out the window of the plane. Even though she knew Tray was lying, she decided to play the perfect host. She walked over to the tall vertical blinds and pulled them shut, reducing the light to one small bedside lamp. "Better?"

Tray fingered the frames again, but didn't remove the shades. "Um, yeah. Much better. Thanks."

"I'll order us some lunch." With a pointed look at Tray's lip, Ainsley continued, "Would soup be okay?"

"Actually, I'm not hungry." Tray's eyes sought the door. "I should probably get going."

Ainsley resisted the urge to point out lunch had been Tray's idea. It was obvious she would rather be anyplace but there. Ainsley didn't make a habit of chasing women. Normally she would have gladly led the unwilling Tray to the door. But something about this particular prospect pushed her to try harder. Ainsley considered her options. Tray wasn't going to stick around for a meal. What would keep her present and interested? A recent memory surfaced and Ainsley smiled at the quick and sure answer to her dilemma. Careful to avoid Tray's swollen lower lip, she leaned in, placed her hand on the back of Tray's neck, and pulled her in to a soft, warm kiss. A slow, delicious burn coursed down her spine, and she leaned into the flame.

"Ainsley?"

Ainsley jerked her head up at the sound of Paul's voice. Random, urgent thoughts collided in her head: What was he doing here? How in the hell was she going to get the skittish Tray to stick around now? Was she ever going to be able to savor a kiss with her? She grabbed Tray's hand and ignored the wild look in her eyes as she pulled her toward the door.

"Hi, Paul, we're going to dash out and grab a bite to eat. I'll meet you back at the hotel?"

Paul looked at them with a puzzled expression before plunging right into business. "Sorry to burst in, but I have those numbers you wanted."

Ainsley held up her free hand. "Thanks, Paul. I'll be back in about an hour. How about we go over them then?" The inflection she added to the last statement was fake. She was out the door before Paul had a chance to respond.

"Who was he?" Tray's tone carried more than a hint of accusation. Ainsley jabbed at the elevator button as if repeated thrusts could communicate her haste. All she wanted to do was get away from Paul before he asked more questions about her out-of-character actions today. With all her concentration on the immovable elevator doors, it took a hard tug from Tray to make Ainsley realize Paul wasn't the only one with questions.

"He's a coworker."

"Who shares your room? Must make for a fun workplace."

Ainsley was startled at the hint of jealousy. Did Tray really think she would share a room with a man? Ainsley assumed everyone could tell Paul was gay. "He doesn't share my room. There are several of us in the hotel and since my room's a suite, we use it as our work space." The elevator doors finally opened, and she tugged Tray inside. "I haven't had time to get the lay of the land. Where should we go for lunch?"

"I need to get going." Tray's tone was clipped and Ainsley was equal parts pissed and disappointed.

"Hot date?"

Tray shrugged, but didn't say a word.

Ainsley pushed the infernally unresponsive elevator buttons in an attempt to try to accomplish something, anything. "I have a lot to do. I'll walk you out." Ainsley crossed her arms over her chest and took a step away from Tray. She realized the strong attraction she felt was completely one-sided. She was done doing all the pursuing. *Damn, what a waste.*

"Look, I know I'm coming off like a jerk, but I'm stuck here in town without a ride and I need to focus on getting back home."

Ainsley studied her. Business Ainsley would normally launch into a series of questions designed to formulate a plan of action, but she sensed Tray sharing this one piece of information didn't signal the opening of the floodgates of information. When the elevator doors opened, Ainsley grabbed Tray's arm and led her through the lobby. In the short time they had known each other, she'd already learned it was better to ask forgiveness than permission. Signaling to the valet, she requested her car.

"I'll take you wherever you need to go."

"I thought you had things to do." Tray looked like she was about to make a run for it. Ainsley held tighter. She knew she should head back to the hotel to deal with whatever Paul had come to see her about as well as the growing list of issues they had uncovered during the morning. Drew Lancer would require a lot of supervision if Ainsley wanted to make sure things were done the right way, the Steel way. Yet, as she looked at Tray, she realized all she could think about was salvaging her "date."

The valet was waiting with the car door open. Ainsley wasn't about to beg, but she didn't mind heavy urging. She flashed a sexy smile and used a husky tone. "Come with me. I'll make it worth your while." She figured if she could get to the safety of wherever Tray was staying, she might be able to make good on her promise.

Chapter Eight

Ainsely's teasing hand on her thigh signaled plans for afternoon delight. Her touch was tantalizing, and if they weren't well on their way to her aunt and uncle's house, Greer would have found a way to indulge in the attraction.

As it was, Greer couldn't believe she had gotten in the car with Ainsley a second time. She was no stranger to living on the edge, but she had to be more careful, or she was going to blow her cover. Even as she had silently vowed she would make Ainsley drop her at the Tesuque Market, she heard her voice betray her, giving turn-by-turn directions to the ranch. Blame it on the slow burn Ainsley had sparked. As they pulled into the driveway, she prayed Clayton and Ellen would be too preoccupied to come outside and check out the strange car.

No such luck. Ellen waved from the door the minute the car entered the driveway. Ainsley wasted no time getting out of the car and answering Ellen's wave with a friendly one of her own. Greer made hasty introductions, explaining she had run into a friend she'd met on the flight from Chicago who had graciously volunteered to give her a ride back to the ranch. She offered a hurried thanks and good-bye to Ainsley, but Ellen's hospitality was set on super speedy. Before Greer had completely exited the vehicle, Ellen had pulled Ainsley into a hug, and here they were sitting at the big kitchen table eating homemade apple pie and drinking iced tea. Greer wanted to crawl under the table.

"Ainsley. What a pretty name," Ellen said, "what brings you to our corner of the world?"

"Work, mostly, but I can tell I'm going to have to take some time to see the sights." She punctuated this remark with a squeeze to Greer's thigh under the table. "I didn't realize how much natural beauty this part of the world has to offer." Ainsley's observation caused Greer to choke on a bite of pie. Her aunt shot her a questioning look before posing her next question.

"Where are you staying?"

"At the El Dorado."

"Ah, nice hotel, though a bit touristy."

"It's comfortable and close to where I'm working."

"What sort of work do you do, dear?"

Greer cleared her throat loudly. She'd heard enough of the interrogation and wanted to end the conversation before Ellen started volunteering information, rather than merely mining for it. She broke in and addressed Ainsley. "Speaking of work, didn't you say you needed to get back soon? I mean, I really appreciate the ride, but I don't want you to be inconvenienced any more than you have been already." This time it was Greer who did the steering. "Come on, I'll walk you to your car."

"Wait, dear, let me pack you some apple pie to take with you. Most of the hotels in town don't have good homemade desserts." Ellen cut a giant piece of pie and wrapped it carefully. "You should take some time to see some of the local sights while you're here. You've come to town at a great time. Fiestas and Zozobra are this weekend."

"The burning of Zozobra? Seems like I might have read something about it."

"It's a fall tradition. The burning of Old Man Gloom and all your troubles with it. If you've never seen it before, it's spectacular."

Greer chimed in. "Actually, it's kind of spooky."

"Then maybe I'll make sure to go with someone who has gone before." Ainsley grinned. "You know, to keep me from getting scared."

Ellen poked her in the side and Greer stammered, "I suppose I could take you."

"Perfect."

Greer couldn't tell if her stomach was rolling out of fear or excitement. Either way, she had made a date with Ainsley Faraday. She decided the buzzing in her belly was excitement. Mostly.

A few minutes later, Greer held open Ainsley's car door.

"You don't have to take me to Zozobra."

"I want to." Greer was surprised at the truth in her words.

"Good. I'd like to get to know you better."

Greer didn't know what to say in response. She flashed to Ainsley's remark about Greer Davis and counted to ten to silence a sarcastic response. Ainsley wanted to spend a nice evening with Tray, and that's what Greer would give her. The anticipation was exciting.

"Your aunt is very nice."

"She's wonderful."

"You're lucky."

"I know." Greer was struck by a thought. "I've never brought a girl home before. Well, at least not one I was…I mean…"

Ainsley saved her. "One you've kissed? One you want to kiss again?"

"Yes, that's it." Greer glanced back at the house. "May I kiss you now?"

"Oh, you're asking first? That's a change." Ainsley leaned against the car, pulled Greer toward her, and whispered in her ear. "Yes."

"Yes?"

"Kiss me."

She did, and as her lips met Ainsley's everything else faded away. Macy's death, her near brush with a kidnapper, her cousin's anger, her uncle's illness, the fact she was standing just yards from the kitchen window where her aunt was most certainly watching this embrace. Nothing about her current circumstances could pull her attention from the hard strokes of Ainsley's tongue, meeting her lips, tasting her, wanting her. She returned the passion with equal fervor.

❖

Ainsley sped back toward Santa Fe, but she wasn't anxious to return to work. Her blasé attitude about spending the afternoon reviewing hotel policies and procedures stood in sharp contrast to the reluctance she'd experienced the moment she pulled away from Tray's side. The contradiction was unsettling. She was in New Mexico to showcase her talents on Frank's pet project. Her goal was singular: promotion. Wooing a girlfriend didn't figure into the equation.

Girlfriend? Tray wasn't a girlfriend, not even close, but Ainsley couldn't ignore the departure from her usual methods. On a dozen prior business trips, she'd taken her conquests to bed and moved on quickly. She'd had ample opportunity to get Tray naked. Hell, they'd been in her hotel room that very afternoon. Instead, she had yet to see Tray sans clothes, and now she was feeling giddy about a date three days hence. Ainsley didn't understand her altered approach. Indeed, she didn't even try. A part of her worried that closer examination might lead to more questions than answers.

❖

Later in the evening, Greer found her aunt in the kitchen preparing dinner. Ellen looked up as Greer entered the kitchen and said, "Drew called and said to start without her, she's going to be late. Oh, and I put some of Drew's clothes in the closet in your room so you don't have to keep asking to borrow things."

"Thanks. Aunt Ellen, I've been meaning to talk to you about something."

"Sure, what is it?"

"Why didn't you call to tell me Uncle Clayton was sick?"

Ellen sank into one of the kitchen chairs and motioned for Greer to join her. "Honey, I know we should've contacted you, but what would you have done?" Greer opened her mouth to reply, but Ellen shushed her. "You have such a busy schedule and so many demands on your time. You don't need added stress."

Greer shook her head. Ellen was partly right. She didn't need more stress, but her uncle's cancer was an exception. Her aunt's kind intent was more shocking than soothing. Greer hadn't realized the vast distance that had developed between her and her family. She didn't know what to say, what to do to make amends. She settled for enveloping her aunt in a tight embrace. She held her close until Ellen said she had to check the roast in the oven.

As she watched Ellen put the finishing touches on dinner, Greer occupied herself with more pleasant thoughts, like her upcoming date with Ainsley.

"Hey, Aunt Ellen?"

"Yes, dear?"

"I'd appreciate it if you didn't mention Ainsley's visit to Drew. She has a tendency to give me a hard time about...things." Greer had a feeling Drew would give her a very hard time about making a date with a woman she'd just met.

"Of course, dear." Ellen smiled. "It'll be our little secret. Now, go tell Clayton we're ready to eat."

Eating again was the last thing Greer wanted to do. The pie from the afternoon had been sitting like a rock in her stomach while she pondered what in the world she was going to do with herself until the publicity storm blew over. A brief run through the cable channels revealed an endless fascination with where she might be and why she had dropped off the face of the earth. Rumors had spiraled out of control and ranged from Greer killing Macy in a jealous lover's rage to speculation that overcome by grief, Greer had sustained amnesia and was wandering the country, lost. The more tame entertainment news speculated she was in rehab in an effort to avoid legal consequences.

Greer scoffed at the thought of rehab. She used coke on occasion, but she didn't have a problem not using. She knew her limits and never would overdo it, like Macy had. She could use a little something to take the edge off now, but that was perfectly natural after all she had been through. It wasn't likely she'd find any source of relief here, anyway. Rehab was for people who couldn't cope with their lives spiraling out of control. Greer ignored the tickle of recognition her reflection provoked, and she knocked on the door of her uncle's study.

"Come in."

Clayton looked as weak as his voice sounded. Greer wondered if she would get used to the sight of her strong, virile uncle relegated to a chair, covered in blankets, with oxygen at the ready. She visualized him standing up, throwing off his covers, and giving her a mighty bear hug and lifting her off her feet in the process. The vision crumbled as she remembered Drew's words: *He's terminal.*

"Sit down." Clayton pointed to the sofa across from his La-Z-Boy.

Greer hesitated. "Aunt Ellen asked me to tell you dinner's ready."

"Well, I suppose we'll tell her it took me a minute to make my way down there." He pointed again at the sofa. Greer sat. "How long do you plan to stay with us?"

Greer wasn't sure what to say. First off, she hadn't thought far enough into the future to imagine how and when the bad publicity would blow over. Until it did, she wouldn't be able to emerge from hiding and slip back into her star-studded life. She hadn't even considered she might not be welcome here at the ranch. Her aunt and uncle might not want a houseguest when they had so much else on their plates right now. Greer suddenly felt trapped by circumstance. She needed to get out of here and let her family deal with their issues on their own, without the added stress of a houseguest. She started to get up, but Clayton's hand, surprisingly strong, held her in place.

"Greer, you're welcome to stay as long as you like."

She looked at the hand on her arm and then into the face of her strong, kind uncle. She knew he meant his words, but she also knew from the tone a "but" was on its way.

"No drugs and no press." He smiled as if to soften his words. "Your aunt is under a lot of pressure, and I don't want her feeling like she has to make pie for dozens of reporters while they stake out the place hoping to get a picture of you."

Greer sagged with relief. Until that very moment, she hadn't realized how safe she felt at the ranch. The thought of being asked to leave had caused a momentary panic. "Only two people know I'm here, and one of them is Ethan." She returned his grin. Ethan had spent time on the ranch, and Clayton obviously remembered their steadfast friendship. Not even waterboarding would convince him to divulge her whereabouts.

"I hope the other person is Rick. He called here this morning."

Greer wasn't surprised. She had told Rick where she was going because he would need to be able to get in touch with her, and she with him. She had left without taking care of some important details—like making sure she had cash to live on, since using her credit cards would be like having a GPS locator installed in her head. Her cell phone battery was long dead since she hadn't thought to pack her charger. "Rick knows how important it is for me to stay out of the public eye for a while. He has my best interest at heart."

Clayton merely nodded. Greer couldn't quite make out the expression on his face. Greer had hired Rick Seavers as her manager despite Clayton's advice about interviewing more than one candidate for the job. But Rick had discovered her, and Clayton didn't understand how the music business worked. A savvy manager who was willing to give her a second glance before she had ever had a day in a studio was unheard of, and she would have been crazy to risk losing him. She had a whole team now, an agency, attorneys, but she didn't have a clue what they did. She didn't need to know as long as Rick wore his dual hats as her business and personal manager. He took care of all the details so she could focus on her music.

"What are you going to do with yourself while you're here?"

"I haven't thought about it. I suppose I could start reviewing tracks for the next album, but I'm too stressed right now to focus." She paused. "Looks like I have a date Thursday night. I met her on the plane. Her name is Ainsley Faraday. She's here on business—I'm not sure what. Anyway, I ran into her downtown today, and she drove me back here so I wouldn't have to wait for Drew. We're going to Zozobra Thursday night." As soon as she finished delivering the rush of words, she realized her uncle would probably think she was insane for planning to go out to a public event, and he didn't even know Ainsley had no idea who she really was. She wasn't, however, the least bit prepared for his next words.

"Greer, I've never pried in your private life, but I have to ask you something." His pause seemed to last years. "Were you involved with Macy Rivers?"

She didn't have words adequate to express her shock. Never in a million years would she have expected her no nonsense uncle to buy into the mindless gossip spewed out by *TMZ*, *E! News*, and the *National Enquirer*. This place wasn't safe after all. She had to get out of here and find another place to stay. She would call Rick and have him make the arrangements. She stood and shrugged off his grasp. "Aunt Ellen's going to be upset if you don't head down to dinner. I'll see you later. I've lost my appetite." Without waiting for a reaction, Greer stalked from the room.

Within moments she was on the phone to Rick. Her message was fast and clear. "Get me out of here."

"Slow down. I thought you were staying with your family for a while."

"It's been a long time since I've been here. Things aren't what I imagined them to be." Greer had expected a warm welcome from everyone, Drew included. She had also expected to be treated like the baby in the family and to hide away in spoiled comfort. She did not expect to receive rules, ultimatums, and prying questions about her personal life. She'd be better off hiding away in Ethan's hotel room. All she could think about was getting away from this place, and she told Rick her desire in no uncertain terms. "I'm stuck here with no money, no clothes, and no car and driver. My cell phone is dead, and I'm too scared to use it even if it wasn't. I want my life back." She didn't bother to tone down the escalating volume as she continued. "I want you to fix things. Now. Do you understand?"

"Aw, honey, everything's going to be fine."

Greer gritted her teeth. She recognized the placating tone Rick used when he sensed she was getting out of control and needed to be handled. She didn't want to be handled right now, she wanted some action. "Don't patronize me. I want you to fix things now! Get the good-for-nothing publicist to leak a story saying Macy was begging me for drugs, that she was desperate. So desperate, it's clear to me she had used before and was an addict. Tell the public I didn't have anything to do with her out-of-control behavior and, if Macy had some kind of latent crush on me, I had no idea and I certainly didn't encourage it. Can't these idiot reporters get it through their heads I have plenty of women falling at my feet? I certainly don't need to try to lure supposedly naïve young country girls into lesboland. Got it?"

The other end of the phone was silent. Even as she had her fit, Greer realized Rick knew from experience her anger would pass. Well, she was sick and tired of no one taking her seriously. "Dammit, Rick, answer me!"

"I hear you, honey. I'll get right to work on things and I'll be in touch." A dial tone signaled he had ended the call, obviously choosing to endure Greer's increased wrath rather than listen to her any longer.

❖

"I'm ready. Let's get everyone in here." Ainsley sighed as Paul opened the door and signaled in the executive team of the Lancer Hotel. She had spent the last two days making her own observations about the property and its personnel, and it was time to take action. Even though she purposely cultivated her bitch on wheels reputation, she would always dread this part of the transition process. She watched as the hotel management filed in, a much smaller team than she was used to working with, consisting of the guest services manager, the engineer, the controller, the concierge, and the general manager, Drew Lancer, who also doubled as director of sales. Their expressions were grim. Industry practice usually dictated a clean sweep during a transition. Sure, the management team was always told they could stick around and re-interview for their positions, but everyone knew their hopes of rehire were dim. The only team member assured of her position was Drew Lancer. As the daughter of the former owner, she would be the one most likely to be resistant to change. So why did Drew look as depressed as the rest of the group? Oh well, she thought, they were all in for a bit of a surprise.

"Thanks to everyone for welcoming us during what is always a difficult part of the process," Ainsley lied easily. She figured if she acted like they had been welcoming, they might start acting like they could more than tolerate her presence. "I've worked with the Steel Hotel Corporation for a number of years, and I can assure you the changes you are about to see will be exciting. As you know, Drew Lancer, a major force behind the hotel's current success, will be staying on as the GM." Ainsley nodded toward Drew and forced a smile, which Drew did not return. *Lovely.* Drew needed to get on board if they were going to have any chance at a smooth transition. Based on her team's reports, all the Lancer employees had a strong sense of loyalty to the former owners, which meant keeping Drew on could cut both ways.

Now for the surprise. Ainsley decided to cut to the chase. "How many of you have your desks packed?" Everyone began inspecting something on the floor. "Hopefully no one. For the next two weeks, you'll remain in your current positions working side by side with a member of the transition team." She could feel the air in the room lighten with her announcement. This approach to transition was highly unusual. Normally, following an acquisition, corporate management would have hand-selected personnel for many of the key positions at the new hotel and job interviews were pro forma—but nothing about this acquisition was normal. Frank had made the decision to purchase this property on the fly. Probably due to altitude sickness, Ainsley could only imagine. Apparently, the family who previously owned the hotel had been slick negotiators since it was unheard of to include a contractual provision requiring the new owners to keep the current general manager. In any event, Ainsley and Paul decided, considering the circumstances, it would be better to keep the original team in place for a few weeks before they made any snap decisions. If the current personnel measured up, they would be spared the chore of finding replacements.

"Consider this time a lengthy interview. We'll revisit the situation in two weeks. Now, does everyone have the status reports

I asked you to prepare?" Her swift transition from impending termination to regular business didn't dissuade the Lancer team from sharing barely concealed smiles with each other. Ainsley studiously avoided giving in to the lightened mood. They had a lot of work to do, and these people better show they had the right stuff to get the job done.

❖

Greer had spent the last two days holed up in her old room, watching cable and eating the supply of energy bars Ethan had packed the day she left Chicago. She was dressed in a pair of Drew's sweats she had found in the closet, and sitting next to her on the bed was her first love.

The moment she pulled Betty, the Martin D-28, from the back of the closet, the memories of the first time she had held the guitar in her hands came flooding back. She'd worked her ass off that summer, saving for a brand-new acoustic Fender dreadnought she'd seen at Grandma's Music & Sound in Albuquerque. One Saturday, Drew dragged her out of bed super early for a trip to the Tesuque Flea Market to look for some funky new art for the hotel. Greer had griped the whole time. She'd worked a double shift the night before, and she was enjoying the opportunity to sleep in before heading back to the hotel for another late shift. Greer strolled the dusty dirt aisles of the market, more focused on the coffee in her hand than on unique trinkets Drew kept pointing out. When she first laid eyes on Betty, she almost dropped her coffee in surprise. She'd seen other Martins at Grandma's but had never given them a serious look. She could work double shifts all year long and still not be able to afford to call a Martin her own. Yet here was a beautiful specimen, sitting upright in its case, mere inches away from the dusty ground.

"She's a D-28, circa 1967." The elderly man spoke in loving tones. Greer groaned. This baby was so out of her reach. They might be standing in a dusty outdoor flea market, but the atmosphere did nothing to devalue the gorgeous guitar.

"You play?"

Greer pulled her attention away from the instrument and back to the man. "Yep. She's beautiful." Way to bargain, she thought, then she realized she couldn't afford this guitar. Brazilian rosewood and mahogany combined to make this the most beautiful guitar she had ever seen. She longed to feel it in her arms, make those strings come to life. As if he could hear her thoughts, he picked up the Martin and handed it to her. "Why don't you try her out?"

Greer wanted to take it from him, but she knew once she held the Martin, no other guitar could measure up. "Thanks, but I better not. I'm saving for a new guitar, but she's out of my league."

The man smiled and pushed the guitar into her arms. "Play something." Greer didn't resist. She cradled the Martin and spent a moment exploring the feel of the classic guitar before building to a riff. She reveled in the growl of the Martin and didn't even notice the knot of observers who paused to watch her get acquainted with her new friend. When she finished, she reluctantly handed the guitar back to its owner. The man shook his head. "She needs you. She needs to be played."

Greer shook her head. "She's worth way more than I can afford."

"Give me what you've saved and promise me you'll always play her like that." The man would accept none of her arguments, and Greer finally decided she wanted the Martin more than she wanted to resist. She wrote a check for $300, the money she'd saved for the Fender, and walked away with Betty, her first real guitar.

Years later, Greer broke her promise to the man. When she signed with Rick, he insisted she play the guitars provided by her promoters. She couldn't really complain since she always had the latest, greatest acoustic and electric guitars on the market, but seeing Betty tucked away in the back of the closet in her old room, she felt a tinge of guilt. And longing. She wouldn't have survived her first paying gig without Betty in her arms. The smoky bar had been scattered with patrons more interested in their next beer than the lyrics of the tunes she belted out. Lyrics and tunes she had penned herself.

Like Betty, her songwriting was a distant memory. She protested at first when Rick told her the record company insisted on first rights to select the tracks for her albums, but he finally convinced her the company's producers were paid to know what would sell and what wouldn't. If she wanted to make it big, she couldn't be so personally invested in every detail of her music. She had made it big on Rick's advice, but she couldn't help but wonder what would have happened if she had found her own way.

Greer had pulled the guitar out of her case and cradled it in her arms, but she couldn't manage to play. She wasn't ready. She probably wouldn't be until she could put her latest calamity behind her and get the hell out of this place. Greer made a silent promise to Betty: next time she took the stage, the Martin would be right there with her.

She hadn't heard from Rick since her call to him on Monday. She had a wallet full of credit cards she didn't dare risk using, no car, and nowhere to go even if she had a way to get there. She thought, more than once, about calling the El Dorado and asking for Ainsley, but she wasn't sure what she would say. *Hi, can I come stay in your room for a few days till I get my life straightened out? Oh, and can I borrow some cash? See, I'm really rich, but I can't use my own money because I don't want my real identity to be exposed because lots of people don't like me right now.* Greer grimaced as she remembered Ainsley was one of those people.

Up until last week she would have told anyone who asked that she loved her life. Ostensibly, she had everything she could ever want. She was rich and wildly successful. Every time she entered a crowded arena, thousands jumped to their feet and cheered. In a single twenty-four-hour period, her tower of success crumbled. Rick always said all press is good press, but he didn't have to live her life. She spent her days kissing up to sponsors, watching her weight, and checking off items on the rigorous daily schedule Rick planned out. The decision to come to New Mexico was the first one she had made on her own in as long as she could remember. As out of control as she felt about her life now, at least she was out of the watchful eye of the media, Rick, and her personal trainer.

"Mom wants to talk to you. Downstairs. Now." Drew's entrance interrupted her assessment. Greer tried to see around her, but Drew was determined to block the TV. She would rather watch another infomercial than converse with her sullen cousin. "Leave me alone."

"I'd love to leave you alone, but Mom doesn't. They've given you a place to stay, the least you can do is talk to her."

Greer ignored the jab like she'd ignored everything else since her conversation with Clayton on Monday, but Drew wasn't done.

"Mom's never done anything to you. She loves you like you're her own daughter. Can you manage to put aside whatever's going on with yourself and give her five minutes of your precious time?"

Greer refused to meet her stare, but she stood, straightened her clothes, and followed Drew downstairs to the kitchen. The smell of dinner cooking did her in.

"Greer, sweetheart, you look thin as a rail." Ellen ushered her into a seat and set a large sandwich in front of her. "Dinner will be ready in about an hour, but eat this snack before you blow away." Greer tackled the monster sandwich and saw Drew roll her eyes. Ellen settled into the seat beside her. "Your agent sent this package for you today."

Greer choked. "He sent a package addressed to me? Here?"

"No, Ms. Secret Identity," Drew responded. "He sent it to Mom at the bank. She had to drive into town to pick it up for you. Try to act a little more grateful."

Greer stuck her tongue out at her. "Sorry, Aunt Ellen. I was only concerned about your privacy." She tore into the envelope and dumped the contents on the table. Several bundles of hundred dollar bills were accompanied by a tiny note. *Greer, here's some cash to help you out. Still think it's a good idea for you to stay put for now. I'll be in touch. Rick.*

"Not what you were expecting?" Drew asked.

"Not exactly." Greer wasn't in the mood to talk about her predicament anymore. She had a date with Ainsley tomorrow, and even though she had absolutely no idea how she was going to get to town, she was determined to have a great time. "Drew, I'm tired of hiding out in my old room. Can we have a truce?"

Drew glanced at the piles of cash on the kitchen table and flashed a grin, which Greer reflected was an increasingly rare event. "Might cost you," Drew said.

Greer laughed and waved a stack of bills. "Can you give me a lift into town tomorrow afternoon?"

"Ask for something else. I won't be able to get away tomorrow. Fiestas starts and tomorrow night's Zozobra. I've got the dragon lady from corporate and her team of minions on my ass twenty-four/seven, and I can't cut out to be your chauffeur."

"Chill, it was just a question. I haven't been to Fiestas in forever and I thought it would be fun to check it out." Greer shot a glance at her aunt, hoping she would remember to keep their little secret.

Ellen piped in. "I'll run you into town if you don't mind getting there around four. Clayton has a doctor's appointment, and I can drop you off on the way. You can get a ride home with Drew when she gets off work."

"Great. Thanks." Greer flashed back to the waves of pleasure she experienced from the last kiss she'd shared with Ainsley and secretly hoped she wouldn't need a ride home.

CHAPTER NINE

She had no business taking the night off, but Ainsley was determined nothing was going to get in the way of her date with Tray. The Lancer was booked solid with the strangest mixture of guests. A large contingent of somberly dressed characters, bibles in hand, had appeared at the front desk, asking a lot of questions about the burning of Zozobra. Luckily, Ainsley had read up on the subject after Tray's aunt had suggested she take it in. Based on what she'd learned, she wondered if this curious band of Quaker-looking folks knew what they were in for. A local artist had started the tradition over eighty years ago as a private party in his backyard. In the sixties, he assigned the rights of the popular event to the local Kiwanis Club, and they spent months out of every year building a forty-nine-foot-tall figure out of wood, wire, and muslin to represent Old Man Gloom. On the Thursday before Las Fiestas was to begin, they posed the carefully constructed man on a local hillside and set him on fire before of an audience of around thirty thousand people. The act was supposed to symbolize the burning away of everyone's troubles, but Ainsley thought the whole process sounded downright morbid. She could imagine a thousand better date activities than sitting on a blanket in a park, watching some fake person burn to the ground, but if this was the only way she was going to get Tray to herself in the dark, she was all for it. She hadn't expected to crave companionship while on this trip, but ever since she'd met Tray, she couldn't be responsible for her cravings.

"Paul, I need to get out of here at five."

"Hot date?"

"I want to check out all the fuss about this Zozobra thing."

Paul arched his eyebrows. "Really? I wouldn't have pictured a big burning man to be your cup of tea."

"Well, you know…" Ainsley's voice trailed off. She couldn't think of a plausible explanation that didn't include divulging her real intentions. Paul, apparently, wasn't going to let her off the hook.

"Tell all or I'll create a diversion to keep you here for hours."

"Aren't you forgetting who the boss is? You're treading on dangerous ground here."

"Darling, I forget nothing. Let me guess. It's the spicy redhead I saw in your suite." Paul tsked. "Not really your type, as I recall."

Ainsley cursed his elephant-like memory. She had certainly made the rounds while working at the San Francisco property and, as much as he liked to gossip, Paul had kept her confidences. She would probably be better off trusting him with the truth now. "It is the redhead. I met her on the plane from Chicago, and we hit it off." Ainsley almost choked on those last words since the chemistry between her and Tray could scarcely be summed up as "hitting it off." But she felt sparks between them, and she was determined to fan them and see what happened. "We're going to this crazy Zozobra thing tonight."

"Do tell. Nothing like a big bonfire to get things heated up. I imagine you'll want us to stay away from the suite tonight?"

"You can handle anything, and Drew will be here all night."

"Speaking of the lovely Ms. Lancer," Paul said, "I had her pegged as your type. Definitely more so than the redhead."

"If you haven't noticed, she spits nails whenever I'm around. Besides, I don't like mixing work with pleasure."

"Except for getting a little something-something on a business trip."

"Smart ass." Ainsley didn't mind Paul thinking she was a bit of a playgirl, but she didn't want him to think she wasn't taking her position as team leader seriously. He wasn't likely to rat her out to Frank, but she wasn't so sure about the rest of her team. She had worked like a woman possessed her entire career in anticipation of making it to the top at Steel, but the last few days the motivation behind her hard work was laser focused on a singular goal—time off for her date with Tray.

"Have a great time and don't worry about us. If anyone asks, I'll let them know you're researching the locals." Paul spoke as if he could read her mind. "Oops, sorry, I meant the local sights."

❖

"Is that what you're wearing?"

"Nice to see you too." Ainsley looked down at her clothes and then back at Greer. "What's wrong?"

Greer surveyed her attire. Ainsley was wearing crisp white linen pants and a pale blue sweater set the color of her eyes. Her sleek strappy sandals were low-heeled but still not well suited for hiking up the path to the park. Parking at the event was nonexistent, and they would have to walk to the grounds. They were standing in front of Ainsley's hotel, so it wouldn't be a big deal for her to go back inside and change. Greer glanced at her own outfit—jeans, hiking boots, and long-sleeved polo, all borrowed from Drew—and decided she looked like a lumberjack escorting a princess to the event. "Well, you look like you fell off the page of a designer catalog, those shoes look like they'll fall apart after a few steps, and this," she held up a blanket, "is the only thing you'll have between you and the ground."

Ainsley's expression was suggestive. She said, "I kinda hoped there might be something, I mean someone, else between me and the ground."

Greer felt her cheeks flush and knew she was rapidly turning red. The sensation was strange. She was used to careless, flirty banter. Hordes of grasping fans delivered all the endearments she could ever want. Her exchanges with Ainsley were different, but she couldn't put her finger on exactly why. Maybe the difference was this evening she wasn't the famous Greer Davis, and Ainsley wasn't some adoring fan offering up whatever was necessary to get her attention. Every bit of Ainsley's attention had been genuine, which was a completely new experience for Greer. It was almost overwhelming.

"Did I say something wrong?"

Greer realized she'd let Ainsley's suggestion thud for lack of a response. She shook her head and smiled. "No, baby, you said exactly the right thing." Greer looked pointedly at Ainsley's shoes. "If you're game, let's go."

"I'm game."

Greer led the way. She strode the familiar streets with confidence, partly due to her newly dyed hair. The home hair job wasn't perfect, but she didn't have to worry about her wig being knocked askew by the jostling crowd. Downtown was already thick with locals and tourists. The next day marked the start of Las Fiestas, the annual celebration of Don Diego de Vargas's peaceful occupation of the city of Santa Fe in the late 1600s. Since the early 1700s, residents of the city had celebrated La Fiesta de Santa Fe with a spate of parades, religious ceremonies, and celebrations. Nowadays, most tourists saw only a large street festival, kicked off with the burning of Zozobra, with vendors selling everything from fry bread and roasted corn on the cob to handmade jewelry, and cultural performances in the square. Las Fiestas was a much more commercial event than it started out to be, but its redeeming grace was its ability to draw huge crowds of tourists to the city.

As they passed a line of food vendors, Greer asked, "Are you hungry? I know some of this stuff looks cheesy, but the fry bread tacos are to die for."

Ainsley hefted the huge Prada bag on her shoulder. "I didn't want to take a chance on scrounging something on the street. I had the hotel pack us dinner." Greer realized her expression must have given away her disappointment because Ainsley immediately backtracked. "We don't have to eat what I brought."

Greer didn't really care either way. Hell, if Aunt Ellen hadn't suggested this little outing, she herself would have preferred to spend the evening at a five-star restaurant, especially since she was out from under Rick's watchful eye. She couldn't blame Ainsley for seeking out the creature comforts of big-city life. Had she not felt the tug of childhood memory conjured up by the delicious smells, she would never have suggested they buy messy tacos sure to drip grease all over Ainsley's snow white slacks. Greer leaned in close and took the opportunity to kiss Ainsley lightly on the neck. "Actually, I'm sure whatever you have in your gorgeous bag will be perfect." She hesitated for a brief moment and then added, "To go with whatever else we can find to eat." There, now she was feeling like her confident heartbreaker self again. She could already visualize the rest of the evening. Firedancers, moaning, groaning Old Man Gloom, fireworks, and then back to Ainsley's suite for more fireworks.

With the end of the evening in mind, Greer found a place for their blanket along the edge of the park. Once they had enough watching the old man burn, they'd be able to make a quick getaway. While Ainsley spread out the dinner the El Dorado had packed, she snagged a fry bread taco from a vendor. The pungent smell of roasted green chile was irresistible, and Greer polished off the local delicacy in a few quick bites.

"Need help licking your fingers?"

Greer blushed. "I don't usually eat like this."

Ainsley gave her body an appraising look. "I can tell."

"Rick would have a fit if he saw me right now." Greer waved at the lavish spread in front of them.

"Who's Rick?"

Greer scrambled to recover, silently chastising herself for being careless.

"Just a friend." *More like a bossy diet and exercise Nazi.* "He's always after me to watch what I eat."

"Sounds like a fun guy."

"Oh, I'm sure he has my best interests at heart." Greer heard the question buried in her words. She hated being so careful about how she looked, but Rick had spent years drilling her on the importance of image. She pondered the irony of having a great body while the world saw her as a reckless drug addict.

Ainsley handed her a piece of pastry. "I think it would be in your best interest to try this blue cheese tart. It's amazing."

Greer groaned as she chewed. "That is amazing. Almost makes me wish I hadn't eaten that taco." She rubbed her stomach. "Almost."

"You shouldn't deny yourself. You can obviously afford to indulge. What do you do, after all?"

"Do?" Greer knew exactly what Ainsley was asking, but the timing of the question caught her off guard.

"For a living."

Greer wasn't used to answering questions about her occupation since anyone with access to radio, television, magazines, or the Internet had at least a passing familiarity with her music, if not her antics. Greer wanted to know what Ainsley did too, but she had purposely avoided asking Ainsley the same question in an effort to dodge a reciprocal grilling. She should have spent more time figuring out Tray's answers for routine questions. What she really wanted was to be Tray. Honest and uncomplicated.

Greer settled on a half truth. "I work for a production company." No one could argue Greer Davis, Inc. was in the business of production. She resisted the urge to ask Ainsley the same question. The last thing she needed was to turn the topic of their respective careers into an extended conversation. She pointed to the stage. "Look, the fire dancers are here." Greer pulled Ainsley into her arms and held her close. "Things are just getting started." Indeed, they were.

"I'm a little creeped out." Ainsley was way more than a little creeped out, but she didn't feel like she should lay all her cards on the table. She had actually enjoyed the firedancers who opened the festivities, but morbid was the only word she could think of to describe what happened next. Each dancer finished out their act by using their torch to light the long white robe of Old Man Gloom. As he started to burn, large speakers located at each end of the stage came to life with the sounds of his wailing demise. Burning against the darkened sky, Mr. Gloom was staged like a marionette, and somewhere, someone was pulling his strings so he moved in grotesque convulsions as the flames climbed his form. Ainsley thought this spectacle was the spookiest thing she had ever seen. She leaned back into Tray's arms and whispered, "When does this end?"

"In a bit, he'll get pretty crispy and then they start shooting off fireworks over his head. The wailing will get pretty intense."

"As if it isn't already?"

Tray squeezed her close. "Had enough?"

Ainsley didn't want anyone to think she couldn't handle a little local flavor, but frankly, she didn't see the point in waiting out the inevitable. This guy was done for. She could watch the ashes pile up or she could start a fire of her own. Much as she enjoyed the excuse to cuddle up to Tray in the dark, she decided her skills of persuasion were powerful enough to convince Tray they could get more out of this closeness back in her room.

"I was thinking we could leave now and beat the crowd back downtown."

Tray's tone conveyed her smile. "Excellent idea. Lead the way."

After they crossed Paseo de Peralta, they heard the loud popping of fireworks. Ainsley leaned into Tray's arms and turned back to catch the show. "Now, that's more like it."

"Like fireworks, do you?"

"All kinds." She pressed as much meaning into the words as possible. Tray pulled her close. Ainsley held her breath as Tray leaned in. She could feel her breath, warm and close, and she almost missed the words "me too," delivered on the cusp of the kiss. Her lips met Tray's and then opened quickly to invite her in. Their tongues danced and Ainsley forgot she was standing on the street, in wrinkled pants, fresh from a fiery display that had sent shivers up her spine. The only shivers she felt now were from the way Tray held her, commanded her, and turned her on. In the moment, she couldn't imagine not being in Tray's embrace forever.

"Pagans must repent!"

"Revelers will burn in hell!"

The shouts broke the trance. Ainsley looked up to see a mass of black-robed individuals carrying signs and chanting. As if the night hadn't been spooky enough. "What the hell?"

Tray was frantically looking around and Ainsley couldn't catch her eyes. Ainsley grabbed her arm and shook it. "Tray? Who are all these people?"

Greer ignored the question. All she saw was a wall of blackness. Her world began to shrink into the small spot of earth on which she stood. The wall came closer and her eyes focused on squares of white floating in the air. She flashed back to Chicago, outside Harpo Studios, outside the Tinsley. *Protestors.* Greer knew they were there for her, but she couldn't answer Ainsley's question. To do so would reveal her true identity. She expressed her immediate need instead. "I need to get out of here. Now."

Despite her pronouncement, Greer was rooted to the spot. A large man, one of the sign-toting crazies, was headed their way. He looked as if he was going to walk right through them. Greer squinted, trying to focus on the sign he held. She could swear the angry words were directed at her, but she couldn't make them all out before he was right beside her. — *MUST DIE!*

ABANDON YOUR PERVERTED LIFESTYLE.

REPENT FOR THE DEATH OF MACY RIVERS.

Greer flashed back to the man in the limousine at Ethan's hotel, and she panicked. She could hear the car doors locking again, but this time it sounded like a gunshot and this time, instead of running, her fear paralyzed her in place. Sweat ran down her back and she smelled the sour scent of her own fear. She knew instinctively Ainsley was still beside her, murmuring in her ear, but all she saw was the row of black-suited protesters and all she heard was the dull roar of reproach: "We love Macy." "Greer's a killer."

Good girl wants to let her inner bad girl out for the night?

I have what you want.

Come to my room and try it there.

Her own words, sharp and castigating, shouted reproach.

She moved her head from side to side, looking for an escape route, but all paths were blocked. She felt a rush of air as the hulking man beside her swung his sign through the air. Her breaths came quick and hard, and her knees locked as she braced herself for the consequences of her actions.

❖

Ainsley watched the panic play out on Tray's face. Her first instinct was to protect her. She looked around. Fort Marcy Park was starting to empty and a crowd of revelers was approaching from behind. They could sink back and hope the force of the masses would get them past these protestors, or they could try to cut around. She looked at Tray again. Her face was white as a sheet, and she didn't look like she was in any condition to fight a crowd, friendly or not. Ainsley made a snap decision. She wielded her big bag like a shield and shoved past the man standing practically on top of them and then sidestepped his followers. Pushing Tray in front of her, she walked them parallel to both crowds until they reached the small convention center. After a bit of searching, she found a safe path, cutting down side streets, and finally wound her way back to the hotel. When they finally reached the room, she gently urged Tray onto the love seat and pulled a selection of liquor bottles from the minibar. She started to ask Tray what she would like, but it was clear from the expression on her face that she was in no condition to talk. Ainsley poured a vodka for herself and a bourbon for Tray. She eased the glass to Tray's lips and urged her to drink.

Tray didn't need much urging. She drank it down like it was long-awaited medicine, then spoke for the first time since they had encountered the pandemonium. "Another?"

Ainsley poured another of the tiny bottles into the glass and handed it to Tray. She picked up the phone and placed an order with room service, then slid into the love seat alongside Tray. Something was definitely wrong. She didn't have a clue what it was, but the alcohol seemed to be doing the trick. After the second drink, Tray's shoulders finally relaxed, and Ainsley hugged her close. She didn't usually fancy herself in the role of comforter, but something about Tray's demeanor called out to her. It was almost as if the man with the sign had struck Tray with the wooden stake he carried. Ainsley might have been scared of Zozobra, but Tray was absolutely terrified after their encounter with the black-suited protestors.

A knock on the door signaled the room service steward had arrived. Ainsley took the full-sized liquor bottles and bucket of ice and arranged them in the room herself. She could tell Tray wasn't up for a stranger in the room. She almost laughed. She was a stranger to Tray. She knew her name and she knew Tray had a family who lived several miles away. Otherwise, she didn't know a damn thing about her. She assumed she lived in Chicago, but she didn't know for sure. She didn't know what she did for a living or why she was in Santa Fe. She did know she was inexplicably attracted to Tray, and Tray seemed to be drawn to her as well. Ainsley had visualized a perfect ending to their pleasant evening. This wasn't it.

"I'm sorry." Tray's voice was small, but it still startled Ainsley since she was lost in thought. She poured another glass of bourbon and walked back to the love seat and waited to see if Tray would make room. She did, and Ainsley curled up next to her. Tray drank the liquor in one swallow and pulled Ainsley close.

"Are you okay?" Ainsley resisted asking what had happened. She figured Tray would share what had triggered the reaction if she wanted, but she wasn't going to push.

"I'm perfect." Her short answer didn't hide the slur. Ainsley was about to offer her the couch in the other room to sleep it off when she felt wandering hands palm her breasts. The touch was scorching and she leaned into the fire. Tray pulled her close and urged, "Kiss me."

Ainsley complied and dissolved into the soft lips she remembered. The kiss deepened while Tray continued to lavish attention on her now-hard nipples. Kneading, tugging, her hands drove Ainsley to the brink of madness while her lips and tongue threatened to push her over the edge. Within moments, Ainsley's sweater was lying in a pile on the floor. She had no recollection of Tray breaking their connection in order to undress her. She only knew she was held by strong arms, stroked by knowing hands, and plied with an insistent tongue. The shy, reticent woman she had met on the plane was gone, replaced by a tigress bent on domination. Something about the way Tray exerted her power caused Ainsley to tender herself to the tangle. She didn't mind being topped, when she chose. She hadn't picked her current role, but she seemed to relish it more because it was being thrust upon her—a totally new sensation. When Tray ripped her pants down, she didn't fight, but she didn't help either. Ainsley enjoyed a strange sense of pleasure in this unfamiliar role as submissive.

Tray didn't ask what she wanted, didn't even seem to care. She wasn't an attentive lover, but she was focused. On what, Ainsley couldn't be sure. It almost felt as if she could have left her body in place and Tray would have exorcised her desires without noticing Ainsley, the soul, was no longer present. The strange thing was, Ainsley was present and felt every touch as if it were the most intense sensation she had ever experienced.

They moved from the love seat to the bedroom. Tray positioned Ainsley on the large bed, making her more accessible with every move. She pinned Ainsley's arms over her head with one hand and spread her legs with the other. Ainsley writhed against the restraint, but desire quickly replaced resistance. Her body rose to meet Tray's tongue, her fingers, her thighs. Tray was everywhere and Ainsley couldn't keep up with the source of her own sensations. Her only awareness was that each touch lit a new fire that burned her to the core. Each time Ainsley came, Tray waited mere moments before bringing her quickly back to arousal again and again. When Ainsley no longer had the energy for her own release, she rallied to please Tray, but Tray wasn't interested in being touched. She pushed away Ainsley's advances and curled into a ball, racked with sobs.

Ainsley didn't know what to do. Nothing about this evening fit her usual script. She was tempted to suggest Tray leave, but Tray's tears weren't conducive to conversation. Perhaps she should try to comfort Tray. This was new ground, but Ainsley was determined to dig in. As competent as she was at handling any situation the hotel might throw her way, surely she could provide a little TLC to Tray, who had spent the night bringing her to orgasm again and again. Ainsley slid close and gingerly drew Tray into her arms. The closeness of their still bodies rivaled the pleasure she'd felt earlier. New ground indeed.

CHAPTER TEN

Where the hell am I? It wasn't anything new for Greer to wake up in a hotel room with cotton coating her tongue. But through the fog of her hangover, she knew this wasn't her room, and the last time she'd felt like this she had woken to find Macy Rivers dead on the floor. The memory tore through her, and she grabbed her stomach to quiet the rolling waves of nausea it provoked. Greer leaned back on the pillows of the bed and tried to sort out her surroundings. Her thoughts were interrupted by a knock on the door. Seconds later, Ainsley appeared from somewhere in the room. *Ainsley.* Oh shit. Greer knew she had better start remembering what had happened, and fast. Looking down, she noted she was fully dressed in last night's clothes, and Ainsley looked like she was ready for a business meeting. She was sporting a well-tailored skirt, soft silk blouse, and tall heels.

Ainsley didn't look at Greer as she walked to the other end of the suite and opened the door. Greer heard a softly spoken exchange and the sound of a cart being rolled into the room.

"I ordered breakfast for you." Without a sound, Ainsley had reappeared in the bedroom. Greer watched her pull on her suit jacket and head to the door as her mind scrambled to process what was happening. Ainsley paused with her hand on the door handle. "Stay as long as you like."

"Wait!" Greer had no idea what she was going to say if Ainsley did wait, but she couldn't let her leave without puzzling out the pieces of what had happened between them. Ainsley stood in place, still facing the door.

"I think I've done something to make you angry with me."

Ainsley laughed, but it was clear she was not amused. "I'm not angry."

"Or something else, then." Greer fought hard to find the right words, a difficult task since she knew she was walking through a minefield. "I lost my head last night."

Ainsley faced her then and Greer knew she had hit her mark. Ainsley's expression was hard, but sadness lingered in her eyes. Whatever had happened, Greer knew she had definitely lost her head. For once in her life she was sorry about the lack of control. She chanced casting another line. "I want to see you again."

Ainsley's expression stayed cool, but the tone underlying her words betrayed her desires nevertheless. "Stay as long as you like." And she left.

❖

When Greer woke up again, the omelet and coffee were cold, but she ate them with heavy doses of fiery green chile as if it were the only way to warm her soul. Several times, she started to leave the room, but knew if she left before Ainsley returned, she would never see her again. Memories of the evening before had finally cued up and played like grainy porn shorts in her mind. She saw herself, grasping for control, taking Ainsley over and over in her quest to dominate something in her out-of-control life. She shuddered at her shameful display of aggression and wondered why Ainsley had been so gracious this morning. She had to find a way to make it up to her.

She decided to start by staying. Her habits leaned more toward writing off past embarrassments by moving on to new opportunities. She didn't want to reflect too much on whether she had wasted most of those opportunities. The events of the previous night might be hazy, but significant memories included Ainsley shielding her from the crowd and guiding her safely through the night. Greer's embarrassment at how she had handled herself was not greater than her desire to make the most of the opportunity to get to know more about Ainsley Faraday.

❖

"What in the world happened here last night?" Ainsley pointed at the boarded-up glass door panes on either side of the bell stand, as if it wasn't readily apparent to everyone within earshot what she was referring to.

"I'm not sure, Ms. Faraday." The young man who spoke was unfortunate enough to be right in Ainsley's line of sight. "When I came in this morning, Drew sent us to buy boards so we could keep guests from getting cut on the shards of glass."

"Well, of course," Ainsley roared. "We wouldn't want our guests to slice open their skin while looking at the new jagged glass design of the front door! Where is Drew?" She spat out her name and watched him step back from the force of her words. He didn't move. "Find. Her. Now."

"Looking for me?"

Ainsley whirled. Drew Lancer was dressed casually in jeans and a polo shirt. Her only deference to business attire was a lightweight blazer. She wasn't tall, but the western boots she was wearing gave her height. Perched in high heels, Ainsley was uncomfortably conscious of how uptight her sharply tailored wardrobe made her appear. Her discomfort spilled into her attitude and she snapped, "Any particular reason you think a plywood façade is acceptable for a Steel Hotel?"

Drew strode slowly over to the busted doors and glanced at the make-do repair. "Simmer down, corporate lady. We had some broken glass and I had the guys board it up until it can be fixed. They did a good job. No need to get your panties in a wad." Drew seemed intent on getting a rise out of her.

"We don't mask our problems with tape and string, we fix them at the source." Ainsley wondered if Drew got the message. "You should have called a glazier."

"Uh—looked outside lately? Fiestas?"

Ainsley wondered if Drew had lost the ability to speak and reason. "Yes, what about it?"

"People here don't work during Fiestas unless they're selling food or rooms. We'll call someone to fix the glass on Monday."

Ainsley wondered if she'd suddenly been transported to another country where people took naps in the middle of the day and went on holiday for months at a time. No, she was still here in the good old capitalist US of A, and if a glazier lived within a hundred-mile radius of this godforsaken place, she knew she could convince him to get these panes replaced. Before lunch.

❖

"Any luck, boss?"

"Are you trying to get your ass kicked?" Ainsley threw the phone book on the desk and slumped into a nearby chair. Paul picked up the discarded volume and offered to assist. "Don't bother. I've called every glass shop, handyman, you name it. Either I get a message saying they're closed for Fiestas or they don't answer at all. What kind of business doesn't have an answering machine with at least some kind of outgoing message?"

Paul shrugged. "They do things a little differently out here."

"In the middle of nowhere?"

"Darling, we're not exactly in the sticks. Have you not driven around this city? You're surrounded by some of the most expensive real estate in the country. This mountain town is a playground for the rich and famous. This town has some of the best restaurants and galleries in the country. Not to mention a world-class opera."

"I know, I know. We're in a mecca for the highly cultured. I flew here from a world-class city and so did you. You know what this place is lacking?" She didn't wait for a response before answering her own question. "Tall buildings, real mass transit, people who are on call twenty four/seven for whatever you need. Like having a broken window repaired. What kind of city completely shuts down for a street festival?" Ainsley continued her rant. "And seriously, why would anyone pay top dollar for the houses around here? How many shades of brown could there possibly be? The architecture is all early American mud hut."

Paul laughed. "Easy, girl. Frank bought a rather large one of those 'mud huts' when he was last out here." He poked her in the side. "What did he bribe you with to get you to come out here?"

It was Ainsley's turn to shrug. Frank's promises were implied. If she did her job, she would be rewarded. She wondered how much of her sour mood was a hangover from the strange night she'd spent with Tray. She had woken up feeling used, like she had spent the night as a vessel whose only purpose was to catch Tray's powerful emotions and hold them in check. Though physically satisfied, she was mentally battered from the experience. Ainsley knew her feelings were affecting her attitude on the job. Part of her wanted to return to her hotel room and take Tray as hard and fast as she had been taken the night before, but the sensible side of her knew she would be better off working here long enough to ensure Tray would be long gone from her room. Ainsley was nothing if not sensible, and she imagined Tray had already left her room. Surely Tray had better things to do than hang out in a hotel room all day, and it wasn't as if Ainsley had left a key. All she needed to do was make it through the day and then she would hole up in the room with a bottle of champagne and the oversized bath to keep her company. The heated jet spray would soothe her aching muscles, and the bubbly would relax her busy mind.

In the meantime, the task list for the hotel transition grew. "I need you to talk to Drew Lancer about her wardrobe."

Paul raised a hand in protest. "Slow down. We have a lot of other things to accomplish before we start playing fashion police." He continued in the face of Ainsley's glare. "I know you two didn't get started on the right foot, and I know you're in charge." Paul paused.

"But?"

"Well, I've done a lot of wandering around the city, and Drew Lancer definitely reflects the local flavor."

"Local flavor?"

"This is a casual place."

"Are you staying at the same hotel I am? Everyone working at the El Dorado is dressed for business, from the uniformed bellman to the desk clerks in tailored suits."

"Maybe, but hear me out on this. People here are pretty eclectic."

"We're not catering to the rich has-been hippies who live here. Our business comes from the rich tourists who come to ski, buy art, and visit the spas."

"And I'm saying those rich tourists could go anywhere to spend their money, but the reason they choose to come here is the offbeat charm of this place. This is the City Different, after all. Why can't we offer them something a little different?"

Paul's words resonated, but she wasn't ready to let go of her strongly held perceptions about what constituted an acceptable addition to the Steel line. She'd had something different the night before. She wasn't prepared for more of the same.

Chapter Eleven

It was the longest day of her life. Greer had exhausted every possibility for entertaining herself. Well, she conceded, not *every* possibility. Probably the highlight of the day had been the difficult task of trying to get the room service waiter to accept cash instead of billing the room for the elaborate dinner she had ordered.

Greer had taken Ainsley at her word that she could stay as long as she liked. She'd spent the day in bed watching TV in between naps. She was surprised at how well she was able to sleep considering the sounds of Fiestas on the street below. Last night's run-in with the protesters had thoroughly drained her. She had only hazy memories about what she and Ainsley had done once they reached the room. The mostly empty bourbon bottle explained why her memory was faulty, but on some level she knew Ainsley had paid some price for the fear Greer felt. When the large man came toward her as they left the park the night before, she could have sworn the sign he held said something about Macy Rivers. She supposed she had imagined the connection. For years, religious fanatics had protested the burning of Zozobra as some sort of pagan ritual. No one besides her family and Rick knew she was here. She knew it was vain to think the crowd of protestors had anything to do with her.

But last night the fear was real, and it drove her to excess. Her memory hadn't returned in full, but snips here and there had played back during the day and she was embarrassed at her drunken

Neanderthal display of power over Ainsley. A fierce desire to create a better impression forced her to stay the day in this place to which she knew Ainsley would return.

The ice shifted in the champagne bucket, masking the sound of the key in the door. As much as she wanted to see Ainsley again, she was totally unprepared to see her standing in the doorway, wearing an expression that was part surprise, part shock.

"Hi." It was all Greer could manage.

"Hello." Ainsley strode across the room, kicked off her shoes, and shrugged out of her suit jacket. Glancing at the elaborate cart of food and champagne stand, she raised her eyebrows. "Did you have a good day?"

"No."

"No?"

"I missed you." Greer was tentative. Sticking around and dealing with antics of the night before was new ground. She flashed back to her Chicago hotel room crawling with police but shrugged off any comparison. She was there in Ainsley's room because she wanted to be. "I ordered dinner. Not on your tab."

"Thanks, but I'm not very hungry."

Greer looked away to hide the disappointment on her face. What had made her think some bubbly and a bunch of expensive food would make up for her behavior? *Because it always has before.* She should have known Ainsley was different than the adoring fans who would forgive anything for a chance to be with the famous Greer Davis.

She stood and grabbed her jacket from the chair by the door. "Okay, well, I suppose I'll be heading out." The door wasn't as close as it seemed. The silence accompanying her progress to it made the journey seem even longer. She had nothing left to say. It was her fault she hadn't made the most of their night together. She wasn't capable of something more anyway. *Face it, you want to replicate what happened in hopes you'll remember this time.* Greer knew memories didn't work that way. The chemistry Ainsley had felt the night before had apparently fizzled out. The only thing left between them was ashes and residue. She shut the door behind her and leaned against the wall outside Ainsley's room, forcing her mind to process her next steps rather than the missteps that had derailed what she had planned for the evening.

"Tray?" Ainsley stood in the doorway of her suite. "Are you leaving?"

"Seemed like you wanted me to."

"I'm too tired to know what I really want. Dinner doesn't sound good, but I see you ordered champagne." Her smile was genuine. "Are you up for something besides dinner?"

Greer flashed a grin. This was familiar territory. "I'm always up for something."

Ainsley slid her hand seductively down Greer's arm and clasped her hand. "Why don't you come back in, then?"

❖

The oversized bath was perfect. Greer enjoyed being held even though she wouldn't have chosen the position. Ainsley's mile-high legs demanded she sit in the back of the tub. The lavender oil Ainsley had added to the water had a relaxing effect, and the champagne was doing its part as well to take the edge off. Greer was surprised to find herself leaning into Ainsley's embrace, welcoming her tentative touches. Ainsley took her time, gently massaging her breasts, lightly pinching her hard nipples, and nipping at her neck with kisses, both soft and firm.

As Ainsley's hand drifted from down her stomach and teased the curls between her thighs, Greer resisted the urge to turn and top her again. As much as she wanted to control the situation, her instincts told her Ainsley had the same need. If she wanted to be with her, she needed to make up for her power grab the night before and cede control. Greer opened her legs, signaling her surrender, and Ainsley's hand moved deeper to stroke her willing sex. She hooked her own long legs over Greer's and held her wide open. Greer's head rolled back as she gave in to the rush of sensation: Ainsley's hands moved against her breasts and the folds around her clit in slow circles, urging her into heady oblivion. Within moments, she could no longer pinpoint the exact source of her arousal. Ainsley's expert touches swelled into a blurry, mind-blowing sea of pleasure, and Greer was content to ride the waves. Within moments, she bucked with orgasm and Ainsley held her, murmuring soft kisses against her neck until she was finally spent.

❖

"Darling, I hate to disturb you, but I fear we'll both catch pneumonia if we don't get out of this cold bath." Ainsley rubbed Tray's shoulders and was pleased at the soft groan she elicited from the simple action.

"I don't mind moving out of the tub if you can figure out a way to do it without breaking contact." Tray turned her head so she was half facing Ainsley. "You were amazing. Can we do it again?"

The praise and question were so simple and earnest, Ainsley laughed and matched Tray's tone. "Please, let's! But on dry ground." Tray started to get out of the tub, but Ainsley tightened the hold around her waist. "Wait a sec."

"I thought you were done with bath bubbles."

"For now, but I'm not done with you." She tugged her even closer and rested her chin on Tray's shoulder. "Can we talk about last night?"

Greer stiffened. She'd been foolish to think she wouldn't have to answer for her aggressive display of control. Obviously her actions hadn't driven Ainsley completely away—otherwise she wouldn't be pressed up again her naked body—but apparently it was time for ground rules to be set. She braced herself for the specifics. "Sure."

Ainsley took a deep breath. She hoped broaching the subject while they were naked and dripping wet would minimize the chance Tray would bolt. "Something scared you last night. Severely. I realize you don't know me very well, but I wanted to let you know if you need someone to talk to, or even if you just need someone to listen, I'm here and I'm willing." Ainsley released her grip and waited. Would her words scare the skittish Tray off? Chances were good. Hell, she was scaring herself. Second chances and tender conversations were not part of her usual skill set when it came to romantic encounters. As she waited for Tray's response, she realized how much she wanted Tray to confide in her, as if her decision to disclose was a litmus test for whatever might come next between them. Contemplating a future of any kind was another new development.

Greer wasn't used to her sexual partners asking questions outside the realm of what other celebrities she knew or the size of her bank accounts. She didn't have a gauge for how much she should share, or even could share without revealing her well-guarded identity. She wanted to tell Ainsley everything, but caution tempered her response. "That guy who came toward us last night?" Ainsley nodded. "He reminded me of someone. Someone who threatened me once. I freaked out." Ainsley's arms circled back around her, squeezing gently. "I'm sorry for how I behaved." Greer felt a tinge of guilt for her less than forthright disclosure. She opened her mouth to add more, but Ainsley reached around, tilted her head back, and delivered a mouthwatering kiss.

Ainsley sensed Tray's story was skinny on detail, but she didn't want to push the point at the risk of pushing her away. They would have plenty of time to get to know each other better. Right now, she wanted to continue what they started in the bath. She rolled over Tray's smaller body, stood, and pulled Tray to her. "Come on, I'll stick close." Ainsley pulled a robe from the nearby rack and offered it to Tray, hoping she would decline to put it on. She was amazed at the beautiful body standing before her and was grateful the increased intimacy of this encounter gave her the opportunity to appreciate Tray's beauty. Baggy jeans and sweatshirts didn't do Tray's lithe frame justice. She obviously worked out enough to be fit, but not enough to create definition where soft curves were more attractive. Ainsley stared until she felt Tray start to squirm. She murmured, "I'm sorry," and looked away to give her a moment of privacy. Ainsley stepped out of the tub and started to towel herself dry when she was interrupted by a tap on the shoulder. She met Tray's gentle gaze. "May I have a towel instead? I don't think I'm quite ready to cover up." Ainsley smiled at the words. She grabbed another towel, but instead of giving it to Tray, she handled the task herself, lightly brushing the soft towel over every inch of Tray's lovely body. Within moments, the towel was on the floor and they were rubbing against each other, glad to be rid of any barrier between their flaming skin.

Ainsley led Tray to the bed and gently pushed her down. She · took her place on top, but was careful to set a gentle tone. Ainsley wanted Tray's arousal to spiral slowly this time, and she planned to wind herself within it. But the sensation of their skin touching, every inch from head to toe, foiled her plan to protract their pleasure. Ainsley slid down from hungry lips to swollen breasts. Tray reacted by rising up from the bed, seeking the lost contact. She didn't have to wait long. Ainsley took first one taut nipple in her mouth and then the other. Her tongue lashed between Tray's breasts as she bucked her wet center between Tray's open legs.

The dynamic had changed drastically from the night before. She had no doubt they had both received pleasure from their raw encounter, but now it was clear they both craved the tender intimacy they were about to share. Through the night they shared power, giving and receiving, with equal measure. Ainsley reveled in it, but even as she realized they now knew how to evoke each other's pleasure, she realized there was so much more to Tray. She wanted to know it all.

❖

"Well, look the prodigal daughter makes another return. Need something?" Drew was sitting at the kitchen table as Greer tried to tiptoe into the house Saturday morning. Any thoughts she might have been able to slip in unnoticed went up in smoke.

"Why are you always in such a rotten mood?"

"Want a list?" Drew started ticking off her reasons. "My dad has cancer, our family business now belongs to a bunch of heartless corporate hacks, and I spend my days explaining my life's work to a dragon lady from the big city who thinks we all live in the sticks. Meanwhile, my cousin drops in for a visit, which consists of her borrowing rides and money, coming home whenever the hell she feels like it, and not lifting one finger to help out."

Greer hadn't realized the level of Drew's frustration with her. She was too busy basking in the glow of the wonderful time she'd spent with Ainsley to appreciate the strain of her very presence on her already stressed-out cousin. "I'm sorry. I could arrange for you to have some help around here. You know, to clean the house and help Clayton get to his appointments." As she spoke, she saw Drew get apoplectic, but she didn't have a clue what she had said wrong. "What?"

"Is money your solution to everything?"

"Geez, chill out. I was only offering to help."

"Where did you spend the last two nights?"

Greer was thrown by the subject change. "What?"

"How did you get home? I waited for you yesterday, but you never showed up."

Greer had completely forgotten she had told Drew she would let her know if she needed a ride home after Zozobra Thursday night. No wonder Drew was so angry. "Sorry, I stayed with a friend. She gave me a ride home."

"Maybe you should move in with your friend permanently, and leave us alone." With her pronouncement, Drew huffed her way out of the room.

"Bitch." Greer made sure the word was soft enough not to cause her to turn around. Her empathy for Drew vanished. She was in no mood for anyone to rain on her parade. Her goal for the day was to rest up and figure out a way to get back to town in the morning for brunch with Ainsley. She reflected on Drew's words and wondered why she should have to bum rides and money. Everything she could ever want was only a phone call away. She dialed the number from memory.

"Rick, thanks for the money." She waited a beat before continuing. "I need a car." She listened to him harangue about how she needed to stay put before she cut in. "I'm not leaving the area, but this isn't Chicago where I can get a cab at every corner. I'm tired of relying on my relatives every time I need something from the store. It doesn't have to be anything fancy, but have someone deliver a car out here today. Understood?"

As much as Rick liked to manage her life, they both knew Greer's money and fame meant she was the boss. He had ditched the rest of his clients years ago and hitched his wagon to her rising star. Every dime he made was a piece of her action, and ultimately, she ruled his life, not the other way around. Rarely did she exercise her veto power, so she was sure he understood she expected him to give in to her demand.

"Car. Today. No problem. Anything else?"

She could almost hear him holding his breath and she waited through the silence. "No. Wait, yes. Send me a cell phone. I pitched mine. Also, can you tell me how much longer you think I need to hang out here? I seem to be wearing out my welcome pretty quickly. Besides, it's cramping my style to act like I'm someone I'm not."

"Another week ought to do it."

Greer wondered how long Ainsley's work would keep her in town. If she was going to be around, another week might not seem so long, especially not if she could come and go as she pleased. "Great. Thanks, Rick."

"Don't I always look out for your best interests?"

❖

"You look beat."

"Thanks, Paul."

"Hard night?"

"Not exactly." Ainsley worked hard to mask the appearance of the dreamy smile she had seen in the mirror that morning. The night had been both hard and soft by turns. All in a good way.

Paul shoved her with his hip. "You must have a woman in every city. You make it seem so easy. Any tips for a good-looking gentleman like myself?"

Ainsley knew Paul was teasing, but she couldn't help but be offended at the implication. She had opened or transitioned seven properties for the Steel company in various cities, and Paul had been on the team for five of those. She had no doubt he was right, despite the fast pace of these working trips, she always managed to find time for extracurricular activity on the road. It was the perfect arrangement. She got to spend a couple of weeks playing with a complete stranger and both of them knew the terms. All play, no strings. She didn't keep in touch with any of these women, not even in the event she might return to their home cities. There were plenty of women in the world; if she came back, she'd meet new ones.

So why did she even care to know more about Tray? Ainsley would be back in Chicago soon, and she certainly wouldn't be returning to this outpost. Maybe that was the problem. If Tray was from Chicago, perhaps Ainsley had a latent fear she would see her there in the future, thereby ruining her no repeat out-of-town-fuck rule. She shrugged. Deep inside, she knew that wasn't the issue. She had no problem keeping even in-town dates at a distance since her work was the only relationship to which she was willing to commit. Tray was different because she didn't want to share. Ainsley was skilled at fending off a companion's desire to go deeper, to get to know each other beyond the bounds of what pleased their bodies. Now the roles were reversed and, though physically satisfied, she found herself wanting more of an emotional connection.

"Are you ignoring me?" Paul huffed.

"I guess I am," Ainsley said. "You don't need to go trolling around for dates. Stay focused on your work."

Paul gave her a knowing look. "Are you talking to me, or to yourself?"

Ainsley silently cursed him for knowing her too well.

❖

"Uncle Clayton, aren't you hungry?" Greer paused with the large bowl of mashed potatoes in her hand. She never ate like this. She would have to stop eating like a cow if she was going to fit into any of her clothes when she got home. Wherever home was. Funny, she had closets loaded with clothing in every house she owned, and here she was, dressed in Drew's cast-offs. She couldn't wait for the promised car to be delivered so she could do some shopping. So far her disguise seemed to be working. She'd been into town twice and no one recognized her on either occasion. Of course, she spent the majority of one of those trips in Ainsley's bed. Who was going to see her there? Greer felt the blush creep up her neck and brushed away thoughts of Ainsley, nude.

"Dad had chemo this morning. If you'd take the time to learn anything about his condition, you'd know he's feeling the aftereffects right about now."

Clayton placed a hand on Drew's arm. "Drew, honey. Try to get along with your cousin. You hardly ever see her. All you've done is fight since she got here."

"Not my fault she never comes around. We're way too backwoods for Miss Bigshot Rock Star to visit." Drew seemed to notice Clayton's increasing discomfort. "Sorry, Dad." Flashing a hard look at Greer, she softened her tone. "I'm sorry. I'm frustrated. This transition has been harder than I thought it would be."

"But things are working out well, right?" Clayton's tone told everyone at the table what he needed the answer to be.

"Sure, Dad. After we get through the adjustments, everything will be okay." She paused. "Most of the people from Steel are nice and understand we don't always do things at a big-city pace, but the manager of the team is...well, she's unreasonable most of the time."

"She'll come around," Clayton said.

The doorbell rang and they stared at each other. They weren't in the kind of neighborhood where people dropped in to say hello. Greer, on the other hand, practically leapt from the table in her excitement. "I think I know who it is, or what anyway." Without further explanation, she ran to the front door and yanked it open.

"Ms. Davis?"

"Um, who's asking?" Greer was disconcerted at the use of her real name. She hadn't expected Rick to give the delivery service any information about who they were there to see.

"Mr. Seavers sent me. I have a delivery for you."

Those welcome words whisked away any uncertainty. Greer

stepped outside and smiled at the sight of the sleek black Corvette Z06 sitting in the driveway. Perfect. "Where do I sign?"

The young man handed her a clipboard and then tore off a receipt. She waved it away. "Send it to Mr. Seavers."

"Yes, ma'am." He handed her the keys and a bulky envelope that contained her new cell phone.

Greer watched him walk to a waiting Jeep and step inside. She waited until the Jeep was headed down the driveway before opening the door of her shiny new prize. Even in the evening dusk, she could tell it was brand new. As she slid into the driver's seat, she saw a flash of light in the nearby trees. Glancing overhead, she could tell it was a clear night, but it wasn't unusual in the desert for there to be a lightning show even with no rain in sight. The smell of new leather drew her attention away from the weather. Greer turned the key and relished the roar of the engine. Greer had several cars at her various residences, but she rarely had the opportunity to drive any of them. She couldn't wait to pick Ainsley up in the morning. They would drive to Taos for brunch. This baby was too sweet not to share. Morning couldn't come soon enough.

Chapter Twelve

G o away!" Ainsley shouted from the bed. She was determined to catch the last few minutes of sleep before getting ready for brunch with Tray. She thought spending the night alone would allow plenty of time for recharging, but in reality she had tossed and turned, frustrated by the absence of a certain redhead. The memory of the morning before sparked a smile and she rose to answer the door.

"What on earth is so important?"

Paul pushed his way into the room and ordered, "Sit down."

Ainsley stared at him. "What in the hell's the matter with you? Shouldn't you be at the hotel?"

"Sit." His tone brooked no argument. Ainsley sat. "Look at this." Paul shoved the thick Sunday newspaper into her hand and jabbed at the front page.

❖

"Good morning, everyone." Greer was so excited about what the day might hold, she didn't notice at first that no one in the family returned her greeting. She grabbed a mug of coffee and joined them at the table. She had no intention of eating, but she could be social for a few minutes before heading out to pick up Ainsley in her new toy.

Clayton spoke first. "Greer, honey, I don't think you're going to want to go into town today."

"Sure I am, Uncle Clayton." She flashed a smile that faded fast as she took in the newspaper someone had left covering her place at the table. "What…what…where did this come from?"

"Usually a high school kid delivers it."

Greer was too dumbstruck to rise to Drew's sarcasm. "Is this today's paper?" Without waiting for an answer, she hefted the large volume. There were actually two papers stacked in front of her, the *Santa Fe New Mexican* and the *Albuquerque Journal*. She placed them side by side and stared at the front page of each. She went numb.

"When were you going to tell me you're fucking my new boss?"

"Language!" Aunt Ellen finally contributed to the conversation.

Drew's profanity was so jarring, used as it was in front of her parents, it took Greer a moment to process the content of her question. "Your boss?"

"Dragon Lady, a.k.a. Ainsley Faraday."

"Ainsley is your boss?" Greer knew her questions were focused in the wrong direction. *Who really cares if Ainsley is Drew's superior?* Greer realized she hadn't asked a single question about the hotel since Drew told her about the takeover. She hadn't even been to visit, which was fairly unusual since she'd spent many a summer doing odd jobs around the Lancer Hotel.

"What are you going to do about this?" Drew pointed at the papers in front of Greer. Drew was angry, and Greer knew her reasons included more than the mere revelation Greer was doing Ainsley Faraday. Drew had warned her not to draw attention to herself. She didn't want paparazzi around the ranch. Hell, for once Greer agreed with her. She'd gone to great pains to hide out here; the last thing she wanted was to be cornered here in the sticks with none of her usual buffers to protect her from the prying eyes of reporters.

Greer looked at the front page of the Sunday edition of the *Santa Fe New Mexican*. The photos were grainy, but she was unmistakably in both of them, kissing Ainsley the night of Zozobra in one, and climbing into her new Vette in the other. The headlines dispelled all doubt.

LOCAL STAR COMES HOME, FINDS NEW LOVE IN THE CITY DIFFERENT

Greer Davis, top ten recording artist, was spotted in downtown Santa Fe celebrating Fiestas and an apparent new love interest. Despite lots of speculation when she first disappeared that she was trying to avoid publicity, it appears from the photos above she is ready to return to the limelight and even has a new paramour. The woman kissing Ms. Davis has been identified as Ainsley Faraday. Ms. Faraday is a hotshot in her own right, but opening top ten hotels is more her style. She arrived from Chicago last week and, according to sources, has been spending most of her spare time with Ms. Davis.

Many speculated Ms. Davis had more than a passing friendship with Macy Rivers, the young country star who was found dead of a drug overdose in Greer Davis's hotel suite in Chicago. However, Ms. Faraday is from Chicago, and Ms. Davis apparently traveled here directly from the Windy City. Insiders are speculating about whether this new relationship is a destination romance or whether the bond between the two women goes deeper.

Greer didn't read the remaining blurbs summarizing her past successes. She threw the paper down, grabbed her keys, and ran out the door, ignoring her uncle's call to stop.

❖

"At least it says you're a hotshot." Paul folded the paper and tossed it on the table.

"Shut up, Paul." Ainsley rubbed her temples. Her relaxing Sunday morning had exploded. She felt the blast still reverberating in her head. Her first instinct was to call Tray, Greer, or whatever her name was and get some answers. She reached for the phone but stopped, realizing she didn't know her phone number. She grabbed the phone book from the drawer of her nightstand, but stopped when she remembered she didn't know Aunt Ellen's last name. She did know where she lived, however, and maybe a face-to-face was in order. Good thing she had the morning off.

"I have to run an errand. Is this all you needed?" She struggled for nonchalant. As much as she trusted Paul, she didn't trust anyone to know her feelings right now, since they might get her indicted for something. Maybe by the time she saw Greer she would have cooled down.

"Uh, Ainsley, I don't think you're going to want to go anywhere today." Paul walked over to the window and peeked out. All Ainsley could manage to process was he was missing her hint he should leave. No problem. She could be direct. "Paul, I appreciate you bringing me the papers, but I need to get ready. I have somewhere I need to be."

Paul beckoned her over to the window and pointed down. "See those guys with cameras?" Ainsley looked at the array of TV cameramen. They were probably in town to get some footage of Fiestas for the local news. "Yes, local news."

"No. National news. Every major network with an entertainment reporter is huddled outside waiting for a story. There are a lot more like them in the hotel lobby."

"Paul, I really have to be going."

"They're here for you. Well, you and Greer Davis. I heard them harassing the desk clerks, trying to get your room number. Every rag magazine and entertainment show has someone here in this hotel lobby, staked out and ready for you to walk through."

Ainsley sank into the nearest chair. Greer was supposed to pick her up in an hour. They had planned to have brunch. Ainsley had hoped Greer wouldn't mind if they ordered room service and had a naked brunch, with food as the second course. Now all she could think about were the choice words she would have to say when Greer showed up at her door. *Oh shit! She can't show up here, she'll be mobbed.* Ainsley's first instinct was to warn her, but again, she didn't have a way to contact her. Torn between wanting to see her for sex and wanting to see her for punishment, she rocked in the chair, paralyzed.

The ringing of the phone was piercing. Ainsley reached over to answer, but Paul beat her to it.

"Hello." It was more growl than greeting. "Who's calling?" Ainsley noted his expression change from confident to uncertain. "I'm going to need you to give me some more information in order for me to know it's really you on the line." After what seemed like a few minutes, Paul finally handed the phone to Ainsley. "It's Frank. You made the national news."

Ainsley had always considered Paul a friend even though they only saw each other a few times a year during hotel openings. She figured they got along so well because they were both family. But Paul's willingness to quiz their boss, making him prove his identity, spoke volumes about the depth of his loyalty and friendship. She resolved to pay him back in spades. After she dealt with what had to be an angry Frank.

"Frank?" Ainsley braced herself for the lecture about her poor judgment. "No, I haven't seen the reports...I swear I had no idea...I don't keep up with entertainment gossip, but I always thought she was a blue-eyed blonde, and Tray, well...she wasn't." Frank rambled on and Ainsley resisted the urge to ask him to repeat himself. She couldn't believe what he was saying. "Yes, I understand...No, I won't...Rest assured I will be careful. Thank you." She shoved the phone at Paul. "He wants to talk to you."

After Paul took the phone, she leaned back and shut her eyes. She had been totally unprepared for Frank's reaction, which wasn't surprising since she hadn't much time to let the entire situation sink in at all. It was almost laughable. She was dating a rock star. Not just any rock star, but a bona fide top ten recording artist whose name was captured in tabloid headlines on a weekly basis. No wonder Tray, make that Greer, had seemed familiar at first. Ainsley didn't buy the rags at the checkout counter, but like everyone else, she couldn't help but read the covers while waiting in line. And Greer had so many top ten singles, Ainsley should have recognized her famous rough-around-the-edges voice despite the distracting red hair and funky brown eyes.

"We have a lot to do today." Paul's voice was a welcome interruption to her self-flagellation.

"I know." Ainsley had expected Frank to yank her off the job and send her to someplace even less palatable, like one of their properties in the Northwest. She had been shocked to learn he was almost gleeful about the attention her love life had generated, and he planned to keep her right here in the eye of the publicity storm. Despite her own worries, Frank expressed no concern about her ability to maintain authority in the face of her professional gaffe. He did insist she move to the Lancer so they would have more control over access. The press was camped out there as well, but at least at one of their hotels they could decide who came and went. He must have told Paul to take charge of the move. She didn't have a clue how they were going to get out of the El Dorado without being mobbed.

Paul was already on the phone again, giving instructions to someone. Ainsley was content to have a passive role. She wasn't prepared to deal with her own calamity.

"Here's the plan." Paul outlined how he planned to spirit Ainsley out of her room and into the Lancer.

❖

Greer drove on autopilot. Her only plan was to get as far away from her troubles as quickly she possibly could. The Vette burned up the road faster than she could have hoped for and within moments she had navigated the twists and turns of Tesuque and found herself back on Highway 285. The engine roared even while idling, as if impatient for her to select a route. South would take her to Santa Fe, where Ainsley was presumably waiting on Tray to pick her up for brunch. Her former excitement about showing Ainsley her new car was doused by the realization Ainsley, like everyone else in the world, probably read the morning paper. She hadn't a clue how to explain her recent masquerade. Her rationalization made perfect sense in her head, but every time she practiced saying it out loud, she sounded like a fake, a phony, a…what had Ainsley called Greer? An irresponsible punk. She felt like exactly that. Maybe a little worse, but she wasn't ready to try to make nice. Greer pointed the car north and let it fly.

❖

"I'm not hiding under a room service cart. It's the height of cliché."

Paul delivered his best wheedling tone. "Aw, come on, Ainsley. It's only for a few minutes."

"Right. And then your brilliant plan is to have me dress up in coveralls and masquerade as a repairman."

"It won't be easy. We'll have to bulk you up a bit." Paul eyed her critically. "Put your hair up so it won't hang out of the hat." He dodged her punch before it connected. "Hey, don't kill the messenger. It's the best I could do."

Ainsley sighed. Paul had used all his gentlemanly charm to convince Drew to use her connections to find a repair firm to come out on a Sunday to fix the glass doors at the Lancer. He then devised an elaborate scheme to sneak Ainsley in as one of the repairmen, but first he had to get her out of the El Dorado. The room service cart, still in the room from the evening before, was central to part A of the plan. She was resistant to the idea such elaborate measures were necessary, but a call from the manager of the El Dorado, a Mr. Giraldi, had clinched their plans. He hadn't exactly told her to leave, but his hints were clear. He expressed his concern that the other guests weren't too keen on being trampled by entertainment journalists who were a unique breed willing to do anything to get a photo or story to launch their career to the next level. No one was looking for a Pultizer here; instead, they wanted something, anything, to satisfy the gossip-hungry public's desire for more news about Greer Davis. Today Ainsley was news. Mr. Giraldi let Ainsley know he would do everything possible to assist her in making a smooth transition to another property. He'd even gone so far as to comp her weekend room service bill and arrange for a maid to transport Ainsley to the waiting van via her room service cart. Ainsley appreciated the difficult position he was in, but she was too concerned about her own dilemma to make his job easier. She'd ride out tucked beneath the skirt of the room service cart, but before she did, she would make someone pay. "Paul, order up the most expensive meal you can find. I'm going to need to fortify myself before you roll me out of here."

❖

Greer made it to Española in record time. She imagined all the local cops were in town for Fiestas and none were patrolling the roads or she would have been the recipient of a ticket sure to land her in the local lockup. The Vette was a monster, but its powerful engine gulped gasoline in large doses. She chose one of the local casinos to make a pit stop. She figured most of the people inside would be paying too much attention to the cards in their hand or the whir of fruit on the slot machines to notice a scruffy rock star dressed in a T-shirt and jeans enter the building. First order of business was to add to her disguise, and she made her way directly to the casino gift shop to pick up a few items. She had forgotten her sunglasses in her haste to leave, and she wanted a hat to cover the now well-known red hair. She selected a decent pair of aviators and the least touristy baseball cap she could find. She ripped the tags from both items and arranged them on her head. At the register, she grabbed a handful of candy bars and a pack of gum and tossed the items along with the tags from her headgear on the counter. The cashier rang up her purchases without ever looking up. Forty dollars later, she was out the door.

Greer slid into her car and unwrapped a Hershey's chocolate bar with almonds. The endorphins from the chocolate hit, and she spent a few minutes regrouping. She considered her options and decided to head to Taos. She hadn't been to the small town since high school and she found herself craving the rugged terrain. For a split second, Greer considered doubling back and taking the high road. She hadn't driven the scenic byway since she was in high school. The idea evaporated quickly. The last thing she needed to do was act like a sightseer, especially considering what had happened on her last tourist outing. A flash of the fear she'd felt when she saw the protestors after Zozobra was all the motivation she needed to stay on the main road and find a place to hole up, far away from the public eye. Greer eased the Vette back onto the highway and punched the gas, letting the supercharged V8 take her away.

❖

Ainsley was relieved Drew was nowhere in sight. She felt ridiculous enough in the coveralls and hat bearing the logo for Zia Doors & Glass; she didn't need the added embarrassment of Drew's comments about her predicament. All Ainsley wanted to do was get out of her silly getup and take a long hot bath. Paul figured reporters would be watching all the exits for a covert operation, so his brilliant idea had her riding in the van carrying the work crew Drew had hired to replace the broken glass. She walked right in the front door and no one noticed. Within moments she slipped away from the group, and Paul whisked her away to a room located behind the manager's office.

"Is this all we have available?" Ainsley looked around the room. It was appointed with the same features as the rest of the hotel guest rooms except the door that would normally lead to the hallway connected her directly to the main office.

"At least for the rest of weekend," Paul answered. "And even if we have some rooms open up tomorrow, I'd prefer you stay here anyway. It'll be much easier to control access."

"So, I have to walk by Drew Lancer every time I come and go?"

Paul shuffled his feet. "Yeah, I realize that could be a problem. It may take her a few days to simmer down."

Ainsley realized Drew didn't like what she represented—loss of control and a complete change in the way the hotel was operated—but she didn't think she'd given Drew any reason to be so angry with her. "I don't get it, Paul. Why is she so angry with me? Surely she knows this is all just business."

"You didn't read the whole article in the paper this morning, did you?"

Ainsley couldn't figure out what Paul's question had to do with hers. She tried again. "What did I do to her?"

"You did my cousin." Drew suddenly appeared. Her blue eyes flashed with anger.

"What in the world are you talking about?" Ainsley's confusion was fast becoming anger. She hadn't done anything to merit the constant scathing looks and overall bitchy attitude of Drew Lancer. Ainsley was tired of walking on eggshells. If Drew wanted a power struggle, she was going to get one. Ainsley was certain about the outcome. She stepped toward Drew. "Look here, I'm tired—"

"You? You're tired?" Drew was in her face now.

Paul stepped between them, but Ainsley pushed him out of the way. She was in charge and it was high time Drew Lancer respected her authority. "If you have a problem with me, say it now and then get the fuck over it. I was sent here to make this the next premier Steel property, and I will. You're welcome here as long as our goals are the same, but if your attitude gets in the way of our progress, I will show you the door."

"Ainsley, can I talk to you for a minute?" Paul grabbed her arm and pulled her into the adjoining room, motioning for Drew to wait in the office. He kicked the door shut and pushed Ainsley into a chair. "I know you've been through a lot today, but you need to lay off Drew."

"Come on, Paul, I'm not treating her any differently than I would the manager of any other property we've converted."

"Maybe you should."

She started to respond, but he held up a hand. "Hear me out." She settled back in the chair and resigned herself to hearing what he had to say. "Drew is Greer Davis's cousin."

"Oh my God!"

"Yep. Apparently, after the flap in Chicago, Greer showed up at Drew's family's house, looking for a place to hide out. I get the impression there's no love lost between them."

Ainsley's mind raced. Tray's, no Greer's, Aunt Ellen must be Drew's mother. She shared pie with her, for crying out loud. Obviously Drew didn't get her grouchy disposition from her mother. Still, she could understand why Drew might be extra grouchy learning Ainsley had been sleeping with her cousin. She probably thought Ainsley knew who she was all along. She needed to take another shot at getting off on the right foot with Drew if this transition was going to work at all. *Well, after a nap.* The stress of having to escape from her own hotel room and the impact of the news about Greer Davis was starting to take its toll. Paul was still talking, but his words were fuzzy. She stood, intending to go into the bedroom to lie down, but she didn't quite make it. Paul caught her as she fell, and he eased her back into the chair.

"I need to lie down."

"I know. Let me help you, since it's not in my contract to pick my lady boss up off the floor." He placed an arm under hers and eased her up. She leaned heavily against him, and he walked her carefully into the room adjoining the office and sat her on the edge of the bed. "Take off your shoes." She complied and then rolled onto her back. She was still wearing the coveralls, but she didn't care anymore. All she wanted to do was sleep. She closed her eyes and watched as a parade of memories of Tray kissing her danced on the inside of her eyelids.

Chapter Thirteen

Greer pulled into a run-down ten-room motel on the outskirts of Taos. *I think I need to hole up for a day or so. Let the crazy news stories die down.* Greer knew the reporters wouldn't completely go away. At least not until she appeared and said something, anything, to address the mess she had left back in Chicago. The lawyers had expressly forbidden her from making any statements, but this was becoming a PR nightmare, not to mention it was choking her ability to live her life. She was going to have to talk to Rick and figure out a plan. She needed to say something, shed this silly red hair, and walk the streets like a normal person again. Well, as normal as possible for someone whose photo was constantly featured in celebrity magazines. And maybe, if Ainsley heard an explanation, she might revise her opinion of Greer. *She liked Tray well enough, and except for the physical features and name, Tray and I are exactly the same.* A nagging sense her comparison was not entirely accurate forced Greer to take her reasoning to the next step. *Both of us have lied to her. She probably doesn't have a clue what to believe about what kind of person I am.*

Cash bought her a room for the night and, she hoped, some measure of anonymity before she drove off to visit one of her favorite sights. Greer took her time on the drive, drinking in the high mountain air through the open window of the Vette. The bridge over the Rio Grande Gorge was a popular tourist spot, but she hoped most of the weekend vacationers were on their way to the airport to catch flights home. Greer was happy to be far away from the crowds.

The rising mountain lines in the distance were all the company she wanted right now.

Within about twenty minutes Greer pulled into the parking lot on the west side of the bridge. She straightened her cap and looked in the rearview mirror. She was dusty from the drive. No one would mistake her for a rock star, which is exactly what she wanted. She climbed out of her car and walked through the parking lot. A small group of tourists clustered around the open tailgate of a pickup. When Greer looked closer, she could see a short, round Native American woman stoically exchanging wrapped smudge sticks and turquoise trinkets for dollar bills. Greer used to have a whole box of handmade trinkets, rings, bracelets, and fetishes purchased from roadside stands like this one. She wondered how much money the tribal vendor made and if it was worth the hours spent creating these one-of-a-kind pieces tourists haggled over. When the cluster of tourists finally moved on, she approached the pickup.

Greer looked at the simple blanket spread across the tailgate. The large number of items still remaining told her everything she needed to know about tourist traffic on the bridge that day. She was surprised at the variety of items and guessed the selection included items from various members of her pueblo. Greer spotted a group of fetishes. "Zuni?" The woman nodded. Greer recalled the Zuni Pueblo was a couple of hundred miles south and wondered if she had traveled for the day to sell her wares. "May I handle?" She nodded again. Greer carefully selected a small bear crafted from onyx. She was surprised at the level of detail, from the inlaid turquoise heart line to the intricate bundle of gemstones secured on the bear's back. Usually roadside vendors carried the simpler designs. The fetish in her hand was worthy of the finest Santa Fe galleries. Greer searched her memory but couldn't recall the various meanings assigned to each design feature. She started to ask, but before she could get the words out of her mouth, the woman plucked the bear from her hand and replaced it with a different fetish.

"The wolf is better for you."

"It is?"

"Yes."

Greer looked at the fetish in her hand, which in her opinion didn't really look like a wolf. She studied the detailed alabaster carving, including the onyx arrowhead and tiny amethyst nuggets that were secured to the wolf's back with a thin strip of leather. The piece was unique and Greer appreciated the use of materials other than the usual turquoise and coral present in much of the Southwestern art outside of exclusive galleries.

"Are you the artist?"

"Yes."

"How much?"

"Do you want to know what it means?"

Greer was going to buy the fetish no matter what she said. It was a beautiful piece and likely to be a bargain in this not very busy parking lot, but she didn't want to be rude, so she nodded. She knew the artist wasn't going to quote her a price until she was ready.

"The wolf is a teacher. Pathfinder. You," she pointed at Greer, "you have lost your way. The wolf. He will help you find the right path." She held up the fetish and pointed out the arrowhead. "See this? Arrowhead will give you safe journey. The purple stones are amethyst. Healing." She finished her presentation by closing Greer's palm around the carving.

Greer pulled a wad of cash from her pocket but the woman vigorously shook her head. "It's for you."

"And it's beautiful. I'm happy to pay for it."

"No. It is for you." She smiled. The first real expression Greer had seen her share. "You can buy something else, though, if you want."

Greer returned the smile and purchased a couple of bracelets. She handed over the bracelets to be wrapped, but she slid the fetish into her pocket. Bag of bracelets in hand, Greer walked the trail to the bridge.

The Rio Grande River Gorge Bridge was a cantilever truss bridge, the fifth highest in the U.S. Greer knew from high school field trips that the drop from the bridge to the bottom of the gorge was close to seven hundred feet, but the number alone was meaningless. She paused at the overlook before entering the bridge, and looked down. The view made the height seem every bit as significant as it was. No one would survive a fall. Rafters looked like ants, and the smashed-up automobile on the wall of the gorge was a sharp testament to the relentless terrain. Until you reached the edge of the gorge, it looked as if the desert terrain stretched for miles to the nearest mountain range. Greer idly wondered if, before it was discovered and a bridge was built, explorers heading west had plunged to their deaths, having no idea the ground would open up in their path. It sure looked like giant hands had pulled the earth apart and poured a stream of water in, enough to cover the ground at the bottom, but not enough to break a fall.

She walked along the bridge and leaned closer to the edge. The last week's headlines smeared her reputation in a way she had never experienced, and she knew this was just the beginning. She'd gone from harmless rowdy playgirl to drug-addicted, homicidal predator in less than a day. Now they were saying she was a heartless bitch, and all because she was finally trying to live her life below the radar. They didn't know anything about her. She was no stranger to being maligned by the press, but for the first time in her life she cared what everyone said and thought about her. She was trying to reconnect with her family, and she had finally found a woman who was interested in her, and not because she was a superstar.

It wasn't like Ainsley made a choice. She didn't know who she was kissing.

The thought stopped her cold. Greer had savored the knowledge Ainsley liked her for who she really was, but the truth was Ainsley didn't know her at all. All Ainsley knew was a scruffy redhead named Tray, who seemed shy because she rarely answered a question directly. Greer wasn't anything like Tray. She was bold and brassy, not meek and mild. She might be scruffy in real life, but it was designer scruff, not hand-me-downs from her cousin. Greer knew she had done more than change her looks since she left Chicago. At least when it came to Ainsley, Greer felt like she had become a completely different person. *So, what are you going to do about it?* Tray would shuffle away in embarrassment over the cluster, but Greer would call Ainsley out and see where things stood. She looked deep into the canyon gorge and considered her choices. *Maybe it's time for Ainsley to meet Greer Davis.*

Chapter Fourteen

T here's a woman at the front desk who says she knows you.
She insists you handle her accommodations personally."
Ainsley was startled. This was the first time Drew had spoken
to her since she'd sneaked into the hotel the day before. Ainsley
wondered if the scowl on Drew's face was for her or the pesky
customer at the front desk. Drew clearly thought one of them was
a bitch. *Probably me.* She started to ask if Drew had asked more
questions to find out who the woman was before disturbing her,
but the deepening scowl kept her quiet. Ainsley had avoided any
contact with the lobby since her arrival. The guys who slacked
through their bellman duties actually made decent bouncers and had
escorted numerous clever reporters disguised as tourists from the
premises. Ainsley figured the press would become more clever with
every passing hour, so she chose to stay behind the scenes for a
while. Her mind churned to formulate an excuse for making Drew
handle whatever it was this guest wanted, but Drew's expression
made it clear she should deal with the situation herself if she wanted
a chance at Drew's respect. Ainsley stood and walked to the door,
but couldn't resist a parting comment. "I didn't know she was your
cousin, and I had absolutely no idea she was the infamous Greer
Davis."

"And if you did?"

"I would have sent her packing."

For the first time since they met, Drew gave Ainsley a big
smile. She opened the door and said, "I'll walk ahead to make sure
the coast is clear."

Ainsley didn't have time to wonder about the abrupt change in Drew's attitude. She could already hear a familiar voice haranguing the front desk clerk. "Look, I know she's here, so you can stop pretending. She's working here, and I wasn't under the impression it was undercover, though she's not above going there. If you get my drift."

Ainsley interrupted her laughter at her own joke. "Dammit, Melanie. What are you doing here?"

Melanie Faraday, complete with luggage, couldn't have looked more out of place. She, like Ainsley, was dressed in an expensive tailored suit and designer heels. She looked like she was used to being waited on, and her tapping foot demanded service. "Waiting for you, silly. And a room. Who does someone have to know around here to get some attention?"

Ainsley glanced around the lobby and noted the stares. "Apparently you're doing splendidly in the attention-getting department all on your own." She pulled Melanie to the side of the front desk. "In case you haven't heard, we've had a little bit of excitement around here." She took a deep breath and was about to ask again what she was doing in Santa Fe, of all places, but Melanie launched in.

"I did hear. *Everyone heard*. Why else would I be here? To check on you, of course. Are you seriously involved with Greer Davis?"

Ainsley ignored the expectant expression on Melanie's face as she struggled to find an answer to her sister's question. Even as Ainsley's rational, intelligent mind sent the word "no" to her lips, memories surged in and halted her response. Tray dressed in ragged jeans and a Cubs sweatshirt; Tray smacking her with a kiss midflight; Tray wet from the bath and their sex play. All day yesterday she had held out hope Tray would call and offer some plausible explanation for her identity issues. The call never came. Ainsley realized she needed to face the truth. Sweet, vulnerable Tray didn't exist, but thoughtless, heartless Greer was alive and well. Ainsley was glad to be rid of her. The last woman Greer had romanced in a hotel room was dead.

She faced Melanie squarely. "No, I'm not involved with Greer Davis, but I don't want to talk about it here." She swept her hand in the air. "If you seriously want a room, I'll get you one. We can talk when I'm not working."

"You're such a stick in the mud, Ain. After all, I came all this way to see you."

"Totally wasn't necessary."

"Whatever." Melanie huffed. "I'll take a room now."

"I'll take care of it."

They looked up to find Drew standing in front of them. Ainsley wondered how much of their conversation Drew had heard. She was still trying to sort out Drew's odd reaction earlier, but she wasn't entirely convinced dissing her cousin was prudent to their already tenuous professional relationship.

Melanie handed Drew her bag. "Finally, someone who cares about making people happy." She tapped her foot until Drew got the hint and led her to the elevator. Ainsley watched them go, wondering about the real reason for Melanie's impromptu cross-country visit.

❖

Greer looked at the blinking envelope on the screen of her new cell phone. She had completely forgotten she had renewed contact with the outside world, but apparently no one else had. When she had returned from the gorge the night before, she had suffered from a strange combination of anticipation and exhaustion. She had considered driving directly to Ainsley's hotel and declaring her feelings, but she had convinced herself to spend the night in hopes the media frenzy might die down a bit. Now it was almost noon and she was ready to hit the road. When she climbed in her car, she heard a low buzzing from the glove compartment and discovered the forgotten cell phone.

She flipped open the cell phone and punched the power button. The parade of messages was overwhelming.

"Greer, It's your Uncle Clayton. Rick Seavers, came by looking

for you. I promised him I'd pass along the message he was here, so now you know. If you want my opinion he's not worth the price of a phone call. I threw him out on his ear. Give us a call and I'll tell you what he had to say for himself."

"Greer, baby, it's Rick. Where the hell are you? Your uncle's a mean sonofabitch. Practically tossed me off the place with his bare hands. I don't have a clue what I did to offend him, but when I mentioned all this publicity you're getting will sell more records, he came unglued. Call me, rock star. We'll figure out damage control."

"Hey, doll, it's Ethan. Leave it to you to have an adventure without me. I saw you on the Internet in a hot lip lock with a smokin' babe and I thought to myself, man, she works fast. I think your red hair is working wonders for you. I called Rick to check on you and he acted kinda weird. He gave me this number and asked if I could convince you to call him. Are you okay, sweetie? We have our midseason break soon. If you need me I'll be there in a heartbeat. Oh, but you still have to make up for the whole Charlie Trotter's episode."

The last message was from Drew:

"I don't want to talk to you, but Mom and Dad are worried sick. Could you find it within yourself to have a shred of decency and give them a call to let them know you're okay?"

Greer clicked the phone shut. *Fuck you, Drew.* Greer didn't need to be reminded how much Drew resented her. Drew had reminded her at every turn. As she drove the familiar road from Taos back to Tesuque, she wondered when their relationship had taken a wrong turn. Until she'd arrived in town a week ago, she hadn't talked to Drew in weeks. Well, make that months. Greer scrunched her brow. It might even have been a year. She honestly couldn't remember the last time she had been to visit. Although she considered the Lancers her primary family, she had probably missed dozens of holidays, birthdays, and anniversaries. No wonder Drew acted like she was the prodigal daughter. No one had called to tell her Clayton had cancer. Greer realized she had been acting like an ass. She had some serious groveling in her future. First on the list was the person who had suffered the most from her recently antics. She dug the wolf fetish from her pocket and nestled it into a groove on her dash. She pointed the Vette in the direction of the arrowhead. *Show me the right path.*

❖

Drew's change in attitude was refreshing. In a twenty-four-hour period she had gone from sullen to civil. Whatever the reason, Ainsley had one less obstacle to getting her own work done. If Drew would start working with instead of against her, her plans to implement all the changes necessary to bring the Lancer up to Steel standards would have a better chance of success.

She picked up the office phone and asked the front desk clerk to locate Paul and ask him to come see her. While she waited for him, she reviewed recent numbers. Apparently Frank knew a good investment when he saw one. The hotel had been booked to capacity the past weekend and for several weeks before. She realized the last few weeks had been chock full of touristy events, but if she could leverage the Steel name with the loyal following the Lancer already had, she might be able to make a smashing success out of this little place. *Listen to me. I'll be gone in a few weeks, never to return. What do I care?* She had to admit the mountain views were breathtaking, but she was already feeling suffocated by the smallish tourist town. Tourist trade was always welcome in the hotel industry, but Ainsley was used to more of a balance with the bread and butter of the business travelers. They were in and out with a minimum of fuss. They rarely traveled on their own dime, so they didn't act like every detail had to be perfect, unlike the family of four who'd spent their nest egg on the trip. Ainsley was all about excellent customer service, but the understated kind. Business travelers to Santa Fe were rare. After all, what business would people have in this out-of-the-way place?

She couldn't help but smile at her questionable logic. After all, she was here on business. And so were the hordes of national media personnel camped outside the hotel. She wondered what Greer was doing right now. She overheard a couple of the front desk clerks talking about the silly morning news shows. Greer's appearance in Santa Fe after almost a week of being missing apparently was news worth broadcasting about on three major networks during the prime a.m. slot. It was hard to believe it had only been two days since she and Greer—would she ever get used to using her real name?—since she and Greer greeted the early morning hours with their own special show. Friday night had stretched into Saturday morning with only turn-by-turn climaxes to mark the passage of time. Ainsley had never felt more special, cherished. Greer had been both gentle and fierce, delivering exactly what Ainsley needed and what she feared. Tender love from a strong lover. Love? No, the feeling they shared hadn't been love, but she couldn't conjure another word to describe what she felt when she lay in Greer's arms. Ainsley didn't have a benchmark for the feeling. She didn't want to. The aftereffects of those tender moments with Greer were ripping her up inside. Definitely not worth her time or emotion. Greer had Ainsley convinced the feelings behind her actions were genuine, but Ainsley knew now that Greer's emotions were a farce. Maybe Greer should go into acting.

Ainsley was startled from her thoughts by the knock on the door. Thinking Paul had finally arrived to work on their project, she called out, "Come in." She heard the door swing open, and she looked up from the desk. Her breath was sucked dry. She was completely prepared to take on the world, but she was completely unprepared to deal with Greer Davis, standing right in front of her.

❖

Greer had driven full throttle directly from Taos to the El Dorado looking for Ainsley, only to be disappointed to learn she was gone. The young couple who answered the door of Ainsley's room professed to know nothing about a Ms. Faraday having occupied the suite. They seemed alarmed at the camera-toting man in dark sunglasses who popped out of nowhere to flash pictures of Greer as she stood in their doorway. Greer beat a path away from the reporter and made her way to the front desk, where a team of desk clerks steadfastly refused to tell her a thing. After Greer ventured threats, the manager of the hotel came out and asked her to leave. Greer was glad no reporters were in the lobby to catch the exchange, but she had no doubt one of the desk clerks who professed to be so very concerned about their guests' privacy would sell the story of her outburst or post it on the Internet within the hour. She didn't have a lot of time to process the thought before she was surrounded at the valet station. The El Dorado might have cleared the lobby of press, but they were still camped in droves outside the hotel. When Greer handed her ticket stub to the valet, she was instantly thronged. Apparently a week out of the public eye had lowered her defenses. The flashing bulbs blinded her and the barrage of questions made her head spin. *Where the hell did they park my car, anyway, Spain?* The few minutes seemed like forever, but she forced herself to recover. She forced herself to appear relaxed. She smiled for the cameras, waved off questions, and when the Vette finally arrived, she resisted the urge to run over the paparazzi who ran alongside in pursuit. She had driven the streets of Santa Fe as a teenager and not much had changed, at least on this side of town. She used her memory and the power of the Vette to her advantage and finally shook loose the press who pursued her in their own vehicles.

She pulled over in a residential neighborhood off Hyde Park Road and got out of the car to assess her strategy. Looking for Ainsley would be like looking for a needle in a haystack. She was willing to bet Ainsley was still at the El Dorado, but in a different suite. She was definitely not going back there. She hoped Ainsley was still in town. At least if she were still in Santa Fe, Greer had some hope of finding her, but if she'd gone back to Chicago it was hopeless. She thought about item two on her list, talking to Drew. As much as she dreaded a confrontation with her, at least she knew where Drew was.

Greer glanced at the Vette. The press had probably figured out she was related to the Lancers by now, and she wasn't likely to get off on the right foot with Drew if she showed up with reporters in tow. She decided to leave the car where it was and walk down the hill, back into town to the Lancer Hotel. Before she left, she reached in and snagged the wolf fetish from the dash and slipped it in her pocket. *Safe journey.* She knew the way, but she could use as much help as she could find to get there undetected. As she approached the door, she spotted a few out-of-place characters who were probably reporters. She was glad she had remembered her casino cap and sunglasses. She waited till she was sure they weren't looking, pulled her cap low, and ducked in the side entrance. She started toward Drew's office but was abruptly pulled back by strong arms. "Where do you think you're going?"

"Wherever the hell I want," Greer growled, despite knowing she didn't have the muscle to slip out of the grasp of the gorilla who held her. *What is it with me and hotel lobbies today?*

"I'm going to need to see your room key and identification," the gorilla said. He turned Greer around, keeping a tight grip on her arms. The minute she saw his face, which was not gorilla-like at all, she laughed. She had wrestled with Joey Vega before, but they'd been crazy teenagers back then. Joey was a freshman when Greer was a senior at Santa Fe High School. He had professed to be in love with her and followed her around like a lovesick puppy. Greer felt sorry for the kid who didn't seem to get the hint. She finally told him in no uncertain terms why he had absolutely no chance at a lifetime of wedded bliss with her, but assured him that if he would stop dogging her, they could be friends. After graduation, Joey actually joined Greer's tour as a roadie. He had eventually stopped working for her, but she didn't remember why. Something about him having to move back to Santa Fe, no longer being able to travel.

She saw by his facial expression that he finally recognized her, and she put a finger to her lips to keep him from voicing his reaction. She motioned to the storage room by the bell stand and they both ducked in.

"Joey Vega! I haven't seen you in forever. How's your family?" Greer instantly knew she'd said something wrong by the way Joey shifted his feet and wiped away the trace of a tear. "Hey, what is it?"

"Mom died last year." The words triggered memories. Greer cursed her own stupidity. She now recalled Joey asking for leave from the tour to take care of his mother. She thought he would eventually return, but he never did. She never asked or even wondered why. She hoped against hope someone on her staff had at least sent flowers. Greer gave him an awkward hug before she plunged into a discussion of her own drama.

"I'm looking for Drew. Is she around?"

"Isn't she always?" Greer didn't hear any judgment behind Joey's question, but rather a sense of pride. Drew had always worked hard. She had probably expected this place would be hers to run as she wished someday. No wonder she was in such a foul mood lately. Greer was more determined than ever to clear the air. Hell, she'd buy Drew her own hotel if she would cut her some slack. "If you'll let her know I'm here, I'll wait for her in the office." Greer started to walk out of the cloakroom, but Joey grabbed her arm.

"Be careful, there's press everywhere."

Greer shrugged. "Actually, I think they may be chasing their tails looking for me in Hyde Park. Matter of fact, I could use a favor." Joey nodded, and Greer pulled a car key from her pocket and handed it to him. "I can find my way to the office, but I left my car parked in Hyde Park, on Los Altos. It's a black Vette. Would you mind getting it for me? I'll need it to get back to the ranch later, but feel free to take it for a spin if you want. I think you might attract a few camera snapping chase cars, but she's supercharged so you should be able to lose them."

His face lit up like a kid at Christmas. "Sure, Greer. I'll have it back here and ready for you in no time. The office is in the same place. Drew will be glad to see you."

Greer flashed a smile at Joey's optimism and made her way across the lobby to face her angry cousin. She started to barge in, but decided she should knock if she wanted to start off on the right foot. A familiar voice called out for her to come in, but it wasn't until she actually entered the room that she realized whose voice it was. Ainsley Faraday, seated at Drew's desk, looking for all the world like she owned the place. At least until her face registered the same shock Greer was feeling. They stared at each other, jaws slack, unable to speak.

Greer finally recovered from her initial shock to flash a broad smile at Ainsley. It was time for them to be properly introduced.

❖

No freaking way. Ainsley had looked up expecting to see Paul and instead, standing in front of her, smiling like she hadn't a care in the world, was the infamous Greer Davis. Ainsley stood, nearly toppling her chair. She needed her full height to deliver the scathing message she was about to impart. She started to speak, but Greer beat her to actual words. "Hi, Ainsley, I don't think we've been properly introduced. I'm—"

Ainsley shot out her hand, palm out. Like magic, Greer stopped talking. *As if I don't know who the hell you are, you scheming tramp. How dare you think you can skulk around town in your scrubby little outfits, playing the role of regular girl about town, playing me for a fool! You must have known all the while I was working at your cousin's hotel. I bet you and Drew had a few laughs about how you were bagging the boss lady.* The rational part of Ainsley's brain knew that last wasn't true, based on Drew's obvious dislike of Greer, but rationality wasn't winning the battle raging between her thoughts and emotions. Ainsley was furious, too furious to actually speak the curses flowing through her head. She stared daggers at Greer as if the force of her gaze would send her screaming from the room. Finally, realizing her mind-bending powers were lacking, she mustered two words and hoped they would do the trick. "Get out."

It didn't work. Greer Davis was still standing in front of her desk. Her eyes sparkled, but she shuffled her feet in a strange combination of confidence and contrition. Ainsley's resolve sagged. She knew she was seeing a glimpse of Tray, and she struggled against the urge to go to her and brush her hands through Tray's wayward, mussy, adorable hair. *Damn it, Ainsley, Tray doesn't exist.*

"Why are you still here?" Ainsley shook off her double vision. Greer Davis was standing in front of her, not Tray Cardon. Whoever she was, Ainsley was done with her antics. Whoever she was, she was getting tossed out right now. "Never mind. I don't want to know. I want you to leave. I don't ever want to see you again."

Greer moved, but toward Ainsley, not the door. "Come on, baby, you can't mean that." *Tray's sultry voice.* She circled her arms around Ainsley and pulled her close. *Tray's gentle touch.* She nuzzled Ainsley's neck, her warm breath sending waves of heat to melt Ainsley's resolve. And then she kissed Ainsley, deep and long. *Tray's masterful lips and tongue.*

Ainsley succumbed. Unable to resist, she returned Greer's intimate kiss and lost herself in the tangle of touch. Locked together at the lips, both of them used their hands to consume what they could without breaking contact. Ainsley grabbed Greer's ass and pulled her close with one hand while running the fingers of her other hand roughly through the short spikes of Greer's hair. She couldn't get close enough. She jerked up Greer's shirt and shoved her hands inside, molding her breasts against Greer's naked flesh. Still not close enough. Still pressed hard against Greer, she lifted her own skirt and shoved Greer's hand into the band of her thin panties, holding it in place while she ground against her. She couldn't get any closer, and still it wasn't enough.

Tears rolled down Ainsley's face as she realized she couldn't meld the woman she craved with the one she despised. Only one of them really existed, and it wasn't the one she had fallen for. Greer Davis was bigger than life, but she was standing right here in front of her. Cute, sweet Tray was nowhere in sight. Ainsley was done mistaking chemistry for something more. This little experiment had resulted in sharp burns. She disentangled herself from their intimate embrace.

"Ainsley, baby, why are you crying?"

The voice was Tray's, but Ainsley knew better. Greer Davis

didn't give a shit about anyone but herself. Ainsley leaned her head back and stared at her. She looked like she really cared about Ainsley's feelings, but Ainsley knew it was a mask. Greer was merely trying to get Ainsley past her issue and back into a lip lock. Ainsley felt the anger swell and rush up from her core. She concentrated all her power on containing the rage, but it crashed against her resolve and shot to the surface. *Well then, you can find someone else to use, Ms. Davis. I'm not your flavor of the week.* She opened her mouth to deliver her scathing good-bye, but Greer, apparently oblivious to the raging volcano Ainsley had become, dove in for another kiss. It was too much. Ainsley abandoned the power of speech and slapped the shit out of the approaching face. Before either one could recover, the office door burst open.

"I've been wanting to do that for a long time," Drew said in a dry tone. Ainsley was paralyzed, her hand still in the air. Greer held her reddening jaw and looked like she'd seen bats fly out of the top of Ainsley's head. In contrast, her sister Melanie was standing next to Drew looking like she had just seen the funniest thing ever. Ainsley focused on the familiar and barked at her sister, "What the hell are you smiling about?"

Melanie's smile graduated to a full-on chuckle. "You, dear sister. You're always so composed, so particular, even when you're playing the field. Too good to be an ambassador for your older sister, but here you are, not only getting it on with this infamous bad girl, but apparently you like it rough. Who knew?"

"Fuck you." Ainsley spat the words at her.

"Language," Melanie gasped.

"I'm not a bad girl." Greer was petulant.

Drew barked, "Tell it to Oprah."

"I meant it as a compliment," Melanie offered.

"Shut up!" Ainsley yelled. How in the hell did her confrontation with Greer disintegrate into this free-for-all multifamily feud? She returned her focus to Greer. "Leave." All her will was forced into the one word, and she hoped it was enough.

It wasn't. Greer was nothing if not persistent. She shot a glance at Drew and Melanie, then leaned in, out of slap reach, to whisper, "Ainsley, honey. Come on, you know what we had was special. Tell them to go away. I'm sorry for everything. Let me make up for all this craziness." *Why is she still talking?* Ainsley heard the words, but they were empty, coming as they were from this stranger who didn't look like she was going anywhere. *Why is she still here?*

Ainsley summoned all her inner strength. "Let me be clear. I want you to leave. Now." Ainsley watched Greer shoot a look at Drew, as if asking her to override the order. Drew shook her head. Defeated, Greer made her way to the door, but Ainsley wasn't going to be satisfied till she cleared the room. She shot a pointed look at Drew and then Melanie.

Drew answered. "I'm going, I'm going. Your sister wanted to see you, and I came in to tell you I'm going to be late for our afternoon meeting. I have to pick up my dad from the doctor."

Ainsley noted Greer, who was almost through the door, paused for a second. To her utter disbelief, Greer walked back into the room. "Hey, cuz, I can pick him up."

"No, you can't."

"Yes, I can."

Ainsley felt like she was in the middle of a three-ring circus. The most puzzling part of the act was the third ring. What was Melanie, her stuffy, corporate sister, doing there? Not only here in New Mexico, but here in this room. She didn't believe for a minute Melanie had flown to a city with no major airport or metropolitan banking center for the sole purpose of checking on her only-on-special-occasions sister. Melanie was dressed like she was on a business trip, but Ainsley couldn't imagine this tourist town had much to offer in the way of securities trading. Melanie caught her glance and delivered a sly smile. No doubt she was up to no good. It was time to clear the lot of them out of the office if she planned to get any work done. Paul had probably heard the commotion and taken cover somewhere far away.

"Drew, for God's sake, let her take care of your dad. We have a lot to do this afternoon and I need you here. Melanie, I am working here, so why don't you enjoy your stay in the parts of the hotel meant for visitors." She focused on Greer. "Don't you have somewhere to be?"

Ainsley watched Greer and Melanie shuffle from the room. She heard Melanie whisper, loudly enough for Ainsley to hear, asking Greer for her autograph. Had Drew not been in the room, she would have thrown the heaviest object from the desk, and damn the consequences.

CHAPTER FIFTEEN

"Greer, your car's safe and sound," said Joey.

"Is it here?"

"Yes, ma'am." He leaned closer and whispered, "A few of the cars following me were hard to shake, but your wheels go from zero to one hundred in about five seconds. Those reporters are on their way to Raton by now. No way they could have seen me double back." He rifled through his pockets and produced a key. Greer waved it away.

"Keep it. I need a favor."

"Whatever you need, ma'am."

"First of all, what's with the 'ma'am'?"

Joey looked embarrassed and muttered something about her being a big star and all. Greer would have laughed out loud except she didn't want to draw attention to herself. "Drop the pleasantries, buddy. It's me, okay? Now, is your car here at the hotel?" He nodded. "I need you to take the Vette and drive it to St. John's. I'll meet you there in your car and we'll switch. If you feel like you're being followed, call me on my cell and we'll pick another place. Okay?"

Joey's expression was a mixture of excitement and angst. "I'm supposed to be on duty till four."

Greer gave him a hug and flashed her superstar smile. "No worries. Drew won't mind. Hell, we're almost like sisters."

Within moments Greer was on her way to St. John's College in Joey's beat-up Chevy Cavalier. She had no trouble sneaking out of the parking garage in the nondescript vehicle. Greer used the short drive to reflect. She understood Ainsley's anger. She'd expected Ainsley would not be happy when she found out Greer had lied about who she was, but she was totally unprepared for Ainsley's resistance to her charms. Greer Davis was used to fighting women off, not fighting to win them over. *Punk. Irresponsible.* Ainsley's words echoed. Whatever impression Tray had made was quickly eclipsed once her true identity was revealed. *Well, not entirely.* Greer flashed back to the lascivious embrace she and Ainsley had shared moments earlier. The physical attraction was still electrifying, but it wasn't enough to revive their emotional link.

Greer shook her head. She realized her usual methods weren't going to work with Ainsley Faraday. Successful in her own right, Ainsley wasn't impressed by her fame and fortune. Any chemical attraction they shared wasn't enough to overcome Ainsley's impression that Greer Davis was an irresponsible punk. Not the kind of woman Ainsley would want as a lover. For the first time in her life Greer wanted someone to want her for more than the image she projected. She wanted someone to want her for the person she hid behind her rock-star persona. And she wanted that someone to be Ainsley Faraday.

Within moments she arrived at the campus. She parked in back near the hiking trails that led to the Santa Fe National Forest. Joey called to say he had to take a detour to shake his press followers, but was confident he could rendezvous at the designated spot. Greer climbed out of the car to stretch her legs and took a deep breath, filling her lungs with the scents of sage and pine. Both smells evoked memories of days Greer had spent mountain biking on these very trails when she was in high school. Not much had changed in this town. Sure, new development was scattered around, but it was all still done in the same adobe with nothing to block the beautiful mountain views, Sangre de Cristos to the north, Sandias to the south.

I should call Rick and have him send me a bike. She wondered if Rick was still speaking to her. She hadn't spoken to him since he left the whiny message on her cell. Her problems were big enough without having to smooth his ruffled feathers. He'd said something about her uncle tossing him out. *Wait a minute. Rick is here.* Or at least he had been in New Mexico as recently as yesterday. Nothing short of a sold-out show would get Rick out of promotion tour mode, but he'd obviously thought something was important enough to make the journey. Greer wondered if the police had found drugs at the hotel, if they planned to charge her with something. Of course, then it would have been the local sheriff who showed up knocking, not her micromanaging agent. The simple answer was probably Rick needed her to do her job, kiss the ass of every reporter in the country so they would take the focus off her recent troubles and put the focus on her music. As if they ever did.

A dust bowl signaled the arrival of Joey and the Vette. Greer almost laughed at the kid-in-a-candy-shop expression on Joey's face as the car barreled into the parking lot. It was a slick car. Greer traded keys with him and forced herself to drive at a regular clip the additional distance to the medical offices at St. Vincent's Hospital. The last thing she needed was to draw more attention to herself by burning up the roadway.

Even at a slow pace, she quickly found the right building. Greer consulted the slip of paper Drew had given her and negotiated her way to the appropriate suite. Clayton wasn't in the waiting room, so she approached the glass window and waited for the receptionist to finish her phone conversation.

"May I help you?"

"I'm here to pick up my uncle. Clayton Lancer."

"And you are?" The question was delivered in a kind tone, but the implication was clear. This battle ax manning the desk wasn't going to acknowledge Clayton was a patient without addtional intel on the stranger standing at her counter. Greer fished her memory for what Drew had told her so she could have something to offer besides her name.

"My aunt, Ellen, was supposed to be here, but she's stuck at the ranch waiting on the plumber." *Or was it an electrician?* "Anyway, I wasn't doing anything so I told her I'd pick him up."

"Usually Ellen or Drew are here with Mr. Lancer."

Greer's patience waned. At least she knew she was in the right place. "Well, *I'm* here now. I'd like to get my uncle, if that's okay with you."

She didn't waver. "Tell me your name again?" Her half-smile didn't hide the steel resolve behind it. No way was Greer getting through the magic gate without a revelation.

"You want to know my name so badly? I'll tell you my name." Greer resorted to behavior she could count on to get her what she needed. Her eyes swept the table in the middle of the room till she found what she was looking for. She stalked over, snatched a magazine, and stomped back to the window. She shook the well worn issue of *People* magazine in the gatekeeper's face. "I'm Greer Davis!" She shoved the magazine through the open window and tossed it on the receptionist's desk. "Here's my I.D.!"

The woman's face froze. Greer couldn't tell if she was paralyzed by the announcement or the delivery, but Greer didn't stick around to find out since she spotted her uncle making his way slowly through the magic gate. Greer cast a withering glance at the receptionist and hurried over to him. The cheery nurse standing with him was the polar opposite of crotchety gatekeeper.

"Hi, hon, you're right on time." The nurse handed Greer a sturdy canvas bag. "Here's his bag. Today was a bit of a nasty day. He'll be glad to have your help. Let us know if he has any unexpected symptoms." She smiled at Clayton. "See you Wednesday, Clayton."

Greer took the bag and slid her free arm around her uncle's waist, her thoughts cascading. *When did he get so thin? How am I supposed to know what an unexpected symptom is when I don't even know what symptoms to expect? If this is treatment, then why does he look so terrible? What the hell are they doing to him?*

"Greer?" Clayton sagged against her.

She shook herself and channeled her energy on getting them away from the watchful eyes of the gatekeeper and the curious onlookers in the waiting room. When they reached the parking lot, Greer realized Clayton would have to practically sit on the ground to get into the Corvette. *I should've kept Joey's car.*

The feel of the road didn't interfere with Clayton's drowsiness.

Greer was simultaneously relieved and disappointed. She had hoped to use the time it took to drive back to the ranch to mend at least one of the relationships in her life. Uncle Clayton was her rock. When Aunt Ellen worried about the out-of-control teenager Greer had been, he could be counted on to intervene and play down Greer's boundary-testing ways. He had calmly accepted every detail of her life from poor report cards to tabloid headlines with nothing more than a shrug, as if he knew none of those outward judgments defined the Greer Davis he knew. His question about whether she had been involved with Macy Rivers was out of character with his live-and-let-live outlook. It meant he believed at least some of what he had read. Greer knew it was a slippery slope from there. Soon, he'd start to think she needed a trip to the Betty Ford Clinic, celibacy, and to be taken down a few notches by the public who supported her lavish lifestyle.

"I love you, Greer."

Startled, Greer nearly drove into a ditch. "I thought you were asleep."

"I wasn't. Just tired. And weak."

"Sorry the car is so rough."

"Isn't it supposed to be?"

Greer managed a grin. "Yep."

"Then what're sorry for?"

Greer gave the question more weight than it called for. "A lot. I'm sorry for a lot."

"Don't be." He shifted in the seat. "I meant what I said, honey. I love you. Exactly the way you are."

Tears pooled in Greer's eyes. She knew he meant the words, but knew it was she who didn't see the logic behind the emotion. She'd started down the slippery slope herself, doubting her own worth and redeeming value. Maybe she did need to step out of public life for a while, shed some of the fame and fortune she used to cloak her ability to be someone worthy of simple, pure love like the kind her uncle was offering now. The kind she wanted from someone like Ainsley. Could Ainsley ever see the person her uncle saw? How could she when Greer herself couldn't?

"Clayton, you don't look so good."

He responded with a chuckle that quickly dissolved into a coughing fit. Greer started to pull over, but he waved her back onto the road. "I don't feel so good, but I'm getting used to it. It's my own damn fault. All those cigars." He coughed again. "Didn't think it would happen to me."

"How bad is it?"

"Not so bad." Greer's hope soared at his words, then crashed as he continued to speak. "But even if the treatment goes well, I probably only have a year or two. At the most."

Greer couldn't give a specific date to the last time she'd seen her uncle before this trip, but she'd always relied on him to be a constant in her life. She couldn't digest a reality with him not in it. Her first impulse was to beat the dashboard with her fists and wail about the unfairness of it all, but a glance at the combination of fear and strength in his eyes made her realize her impulse was selfish. This was Clayton's battle. Her wailing about the futility of the fight wasn't going to help him survive. Greer seized on something positive she could do.

"I'll make a few calls when we get back to the ranch. We can get you into the Mayo or the Cleveland Clinic. Aren't those the top-of-the-line treatment centers in the world?" She didn't pause for an answer. "I'll charter a private jet. You'll be perfectly comfortable during the trip. We'll arrange for accommodations for Aunt Ellen, and I'll hire someone to look after the ranch while you're gone." She finally stopped talking, pleased she'd covered all the details and ready to execute her plan.

Clayton merely shook his head.

"What?"

"Honey, I have good doctors. I've had second, even third opinions. Believe it or not, Drew reacted the same way when she learned my prognosis, so I've been shuffled around from doctor to doctor only to find out they all agree. This treatment will prolong my life, but it won't save it. Nothing will."

Greer wanted to argue, but the expression on her uncle's face told her he was resigned to his fate and wouldn't be persuaded otherwise.

She was surprised at how calmly he discussed certain death. She decided as long as he was willing to have a frank discussion about his prognosis, she would ask some pointed questions.

"What were you at the doctor's for today?"

"I was having radiation treatment."

"What does that involve?"

"They put me on a table, line up the emitter to tattoos on my chest, and blast the hell out of the cancer cells."

"Oh my God, it sounds awful. Does it hurt?"

"Burns. Not like a stove burn, but like sunburn. My skin's all scratchy and cracked where the radiation stream hits it. Your aunt keeps trying out different lotions, but they never seem to help." Greer could tell by his tone that he thought the application of lotion was another indignity he'd rather not suffer.

"I can tell you don't feel well now. Is it because of the radiation?"

"Not really. I wasn't feeling well when I got up this morning. I have good days and bad days. Today is not one of the good ones," he said matter-of-factly.

"The nurse said you have to come back Wednesday. More radiation?"

"Chemo."

"Both?"

"Yep."

"For how long?"

"Wednesday's the end of this round. Then they'll check me out and see how I'm doing." Clayton leaned his head back and closed his eyes. Greer decided to hold off on the dozen other questions she still wanted to ask and let him rest for the rest of the drive. She could Google what she needed to know as soon as they got back to the ranch.

❖

Drew kept looking at her watch, and the not-so-subtle action drove Ainsley insane.

Ainsley was accustomed to handling the interview and selection process for the new GM herself, and Drew was not the type of manager she would have chosen. Despite their differences, she had to admit Drew had a lot of good qualities. The hotel wasn't up to Steel standards, but it had been doing well enough for Frank to consider it a worthy acquisition. Her primary concern was that Drew wasn't authoritative enough. The employees treated her like a buddy, not a boss, and as far as Ainsley was concerned, Drew's chummy method of management kept her from achieving maximum effectiveness. On the other hand, a strong sense of loyalty permeated the staff. Ainsley had no doubt if Drew asked them to go above and beyond their regular duties, every one of them would comply.

And then there was the issue with her famous cousin. Ainsley found it interesting neither Drew nor anyone else at the hotel had mentioned the connection to Greer Davis. Especially since Greer's name had achieved Britney Spears–like status over the past week. Today Drew made it perfectly clear she didn't care for Greer, and Ainsley was dying to know why. Sure, she was mad at Greer herself, but she didn't have the bonds of family to temper her anger. Ainsley almost laughed out loud. It wasn't like she placed much stock in so-called family ties. Melanie had flown across the country, declaring her worry for Ainsley, and the only feeling Ainsley could conjure up in response was suspicion. Still, she was anxious to know what caused the obvious rift between Drew and Greer even as she refused to acknowledge the why behind her curiosity.

"Drew, do you have somewhere you need to be?"

"Would it make a difference if I did?"

Ainsley felt the daggers aimed her way. Catching a sharp look from Paul, she tempered her response. "We have a lot of data to review. It would help if your head was in it."

"I have a lot on my mind."

Ainsley wondered how much the recent antics of her famous cousin factored into Drew's preoccupation. She empathized, but she wasn't in the mood to cut anyone any slack. "I understand, but we have a lot to do and I need you on board and fully plugged in." Ignoring Paul's cautioning stare, she continued. "Until we're done with this process, I'm in charge and your position is largely dependent—"

"Ainsley," Paul interrupted, "May I speak with you for a moment?"

"Not now."

He matched her commanding tone with his own. "It's important. For a moment. Alone." He spoke to Drew. "Could you give us a moment?"

Drew stalked out of the room and the moment the door closed behind her, Ainsley barked, "What are you thinking? She has absolutely no respect for me, and you're not helping."

"Have you tried to get to know anything about her?"

"Paul, we're not here to make friends, we're here to make a successful venture."

"Maybe there are more paths to success than you're willing to admit." He raised his hand as she started to protest. "Hear me out. Maybe Drew is a little too chummy with the employees, but have you noticed how they do anything she asks? Granted, she may not ask them to do everything she could or should, but there's potential there. Your method works for you, but you're not staying around. Drew is. You've got to figure out a way to blend her style with yours to get the best result."

Ainsley wasn't used to being schooled in management styles. She had a style and it worked. Well, she made it work. She ran her own hotel with precision and control, and she had always assumed because the hotel was successful, her style was the right way. She was almost embarrassed to admit she had never considered other methods of achieving the same result. Although she wasn't entirely convinced she wasn't right, she knew Paul was a smart guy and decided to give his idea the benefit of the doubt.

"Suggestions about what I should do?"

He smiled, careful not to signal too much self-satisfaction. "You don't have to become her best friend, but it wouldn't hurt you to get to know your new GM."

"You mean I need to know something other than she has a famous cousin?" Ainsley displayed a reluctant grin.

"Yeah, boss. A few more details couldn't hurt."

"I suppose I can give your way a shot."

Paul nodded. "I'll give you guys some space. I need to meet with the restaurant manager anyway." He paused at the door before exiting. "Ain, trust me. This is a good idea."

Ainsley tried for a smile. She was reluctant to admit the major reason for her concession was her desire to learn more about Drew's cousin than about Drew herself. She didn't have a clue as to why she was still obsessed with the mystique of Greer Davis. She, like everyone else in the world, had seen Greer's name headlining music charts and tabloid rags for the past several years, but unlike adoring fans and gossipmongers, she had never given Greer's personal life a second thought. But then Tray had entered her life and she was suckered in. Who was the real Greer Davis? Was she the cocky woman who lived a devil-may-care lifestyle or was she the sweet, adorable woman who had cuddled up next to her on the plane? Ainsley tried to reconcile the vastly divergent personas, but she was left with only a jumbled mixture of feelings swirling in her gut. A single cohesive thought emerged from the confusion. Greer Davis was bad news, and she planned to keep her distance.

CHAPTER SIXTEEN

Rick was sitting in the same seat Ainsley had occupied a few days ago and he was drooling his way through a slice of Aunt Ellen's homemade strawberry rhubarb pie. Greer wished she could blink her eyes and have Ainsley appear in his place. She started to say hello, but her uncle got the first word.

"Young man, I thought I told you to leave."

Ellen opened her mouth, but Rick beat her to a response. "Why hello, Mr. Lancer. I stopped by to give Greer some important papers. Your wife was kind enough to offer me some pie." He paused to wave his fork. "Greer, sit down, let's talk."

Greer felt her uncle's tight grip on her shoulder. He was angry with Rick, and she didn't have a clue why. Hell, she was angry with Rick half the time, but he took care of every detail of her life and made her lots of money, so she usually kept her displeasure to herself. So what if he was a control freak, insisting she keep up an incredibly strenuous schedule designed to maximize her fame? With his help, she had become an extremely wealthy, successful superstar. His philosophy was simple: no press is bad press. Every time she read a scandalous headline with her name in it, she had to remind herself how successful his philosophy had made her. She imagined her uncle was feeling protective, but he didn't understand the path to fame and fortune would always be a bumpy ride.

"May I have a few minutes with Rick, alone?" She could tell Clayton didn't want to leave, but as weak as he felt, he would feel better once he was off his feet. Ellen cut Greer a slice of pie she wouldn't eat and then ushered Clayton from the kitchen. Greer pushed the pie over to Rick, who wasted no time digging in.

"What's so important you came all this way to talk to me?"

"No distance is too far to travel to see my number one star," Rick managed to say between bites.

"What did you say to my uncle when you came by, was it yesterday?" Greer paused to calculate. Had it really only been yesterday when all hell broke loose? Her world had fallen apart for the second time in two weeks and, yes, she could arrange total disaster in mere twenty-four-hour cycles.

"I tried to have a little man-to-man talk about the best way to spin your latest calamity. He's got a short fuse."

Greer could only imagine how Rick's slick style had clashed with Clayton's down-to-earth approach. He measured success in units of family, friends, health, and happiness. Those measurements wouldn't compute to someone like Rick who tallied only money, sales, and headlines in his success calculation. Greer reflected on a time in her past when she would have thought a paid-off car, a steady girlfriend, and a modest crowd of fans at the Paolo Soleri would equal total success. When had she started using Rick's method? Now platinum records, sold-out stadiums, and a half dozen paid-off cars and houses were mere stepping stones on the way to real stardom. Using that yardstick, would she ever achieve true fame?

Greer shrugged. She didn't always like Rick's style, but he got results. She might as well hear what he had to say. Staying here was out of the question. Clayton didn't need her problems on top of his own, and she had her answer about Ainsley's reaction to meeting the famous Greer Davis. She could still feel the heat of her slap. "What's the plan?"

He tossed several brochures on the table. "A little vacation. For a few weeks. Pick one and I'll make the call. We can get you in today."

Greer picked up the pamphlets and began browsing. Each one offered a beautiful unique setting: gorgeous mountain vistas, bountiful gardens, natural springs kissed by bright sunshine. But as Greer read further, she realized they all had one thing in common.

"You're sending me to rehab!"

"Calm down. These are top-of-the-line places. They're used to catering to famous guests."

"What does that mean? They have great turn down service?"

"I can make arrangements for your new arm candy to visit you once you get settled in."

Greer ignored Rick's reference to Ainsley, but she was pissed. As angry as she was at Rick's characterization, she didn't want to discuss anything about Ainsley with him.

Greer tossed the brochures back at him. "I'm not going to rehab, Rick."

"Yes, you are." His tone had a level of authority he didn't often use so early in their tussles. It didn't foster submission.

"No," Greer paused for emphasis, "I'm not."

He resorted to wheedling. "Greer, honey, you need to. Everyone thinks Macy died because of you. It's a simple equation. Good girl meets bad girl. Bad girl gives good girl drugs. Good girl dies. Bad girl must atone or never sell another record. All the big stars go to rehab at some point in their career. I've already got *People* lined up for an exclusive."

All Greer heard was, "Everyone thinks Macy died because of you." It wasn't enough she was responsible for all her own bad actions, but now she was responsible for sweet innocent Macy's as well. She had considered Macy her friend and wouldn't have done anything to hurt her. She'd warned her about overindulging, but was she also supposed to babysit Macy to keep her from the grip of vice? Did everyone really think she had essentially killed Macy? Did Rick? Only one way to learn the answer.

"Do you think Macy's death was my fault?"

Rick obviously didn't expect such a direct question. "Don't worry. I have it on good authority the police have closed their investigation and have ruled her death an accidental overdose. They'll issue a press release sometime this week which, combined with your interview in *People,* will paint you in the best possible light."

"You didn't answer my question."

"Huh?" He could play dumb all he wanted, but Greer wasn't

buying it. She knew how much Rick hated confronting her, but he had come here today ready to send her off to twelve steps of retribution. She was determined to hear if he thought she deserved it.

"You heard me. Do you think Macy's death was my fault?" Greer carefully enunciated each word, determined not to let Rick off the hook until he acknowledged and answered her question.

Rick refused to meet her eyes. "Greer, it doesn't matter what I think."

He did. He thought Macy Rivers would be belting out her signature heart-melting ballads right now if it weren't for Greer. Greer's heart sank at the realization that the one person she relied on to manage all her affairs and she trusted her future with thought she had been so careless, so indifferent to another person's life that she had caused an overdose, or at the very least done nothing to prevent it. Hell, if Rick, who played fast and loose on a regular basis, thought so ill of her, then no wonder Ainsley, consummate perfectionist, didn't want to have anything to do with her.

As if he could tell she was upset, Rick gave his response another go, but there weren't a whole lot of ways to vary his conclusion. "Seriously, kid, all that matters is improving your image."

"Her image is not the issue here."

Greer didn't know how Clayton managed to recapture the boom in his voice, when his body still looked so frail. But there he was, leaning against a chair, sounding like he could pick Rick up and throw him out on his ass. Rick didn't get the message.

"Actually, it is."

"What's at issue is my niece's well-being. How she *is*, not how she appears." Clayton delivered a withering stare. "Has it even occurred to you she lost a friend in a tragic circumstance and no one," he shook his finger at Rick, "I mean no one, has the guts to stand up and say Macy Rivers was an adult, responsible for her own actions?"

"Uncle Clayton." Greer stood up. "It's okay, Rick didn't mean anything." She pulled out a chair. "Have a seat. You don't look so good."

"Oh, he didn't, did he?" Clayton shook his head at the offered seat. "Why don't you ask Mr. Seavers how the press found out you were here?"

"What?"

Rick spoke up quickly. "She was probably followed from Chicago. Greer made her own arrangements getting out of the city, so I didn't have a chance to take all the usual precautions." Greer felt her uncle bristle, and she could feel her own blood pressure rise in response to Rick's scolding tone. She started to respond, but Clayton beat her to it.

"And the hungry press waited an entire week before they reported the missing star's whereabouts? Do you expect us to believe they didn't have an inside track?" Clayton coughed and it took him a moment to regain control of his voice. "Or is it more likely they had no idea where Greer was until someone tipped them off? Someone who knew exactly where she was. Someone who needed his meal ticket back on the front page before the starving media took their feeding frenzy elsewhere." Clayton finally sat down, seemingly exhausted from the unanswered interrogation.

"Now, Mr. Lancer, I don't think you're being fair."

"It's my fault." No one had noticed Aunt Ellen reenter the kitchen. "I told him exactly where you were Thursday night."

"Told who?" Greer asked her.

"Mr. Seavers. He called Thursday afternoon to make sure you got the wire. I told him you were out on a date. I may have mentioned you were taking her to Zozobra." She paused as if trying to remember more of the conversation. "He had never heard about Fiestas. He had a lot of questions about all the celebrations, and he was excited to know you were out on a date." Ellen paused as if to judge whether she should say more, then she finished with, "I'm sorry. I thought he was your friend."

Greer was flaming mad. "Aunt Ellen, I'm not upset with you. Mr. Seavers *was* a friend But Mr. Seavers has taken advantage of our friendship. For the last time."

"Now, Greer, don't be hasty." Rick flashed his best and brightest smile.

"Don't worry, Rick. This has been a long time coming. You're fired."

"You can't fire me!"

"Wanna bet?"

"I have a contract and it's ironclad. Your lawyers, the ones I hired? Well, they'll rip their sharky teeth out trying to chew through our agreement."

Greer wanted to shout him down with the promise to pay whatever it took to wrangle free of his control, but she wasn't so naïve she didn't know her comments would come back to bite her. She'd deal with the logistics later. All she cared about right now was getting him out. She pointed to the door. "Get out!"

Rick appeared glued to the floor. He engaged her in an epic stare-down, but Greer wasn't about to waver. Her sense of betrayal won out, and finally he shook his head and made his way to the door. He paused before leaving, and Greer braced herself for the parting shot he fired in her direction. "Greer, honey?" His voice dripped sarcasm. "I hope you enjoy rehab. I already leaked it to the press, so you might as well make the most of it. Lord knows you don't do yourself any favors running wild in public."

❖

"The controller finally got all these revenue numbers ready to review." Paul set down the stack of binders and looked around the room. "Where's Drew?"

"I sent her home." At Paul's raised eyebrows, she continued, "For the day."

"I'll call her. We're overbooked and I need to talk to her to see if she has arrangements in place."

"She does. We have a walk rate with the Juniper down the street." Ainsley referred to the customary arrangements hotels had with one another to provide rooms for a small fee when the other was overbooked. "Drew called them before she left. I think she's more on top of things than I give her credit for." She paused. "Did you know her dad has cancer?" His sheepish expression told her he did. "I feel like such a heel. Why didn't you tell me?"

"You're not known to cut much slack."

"Seriously, Paul, cancer?" His silence sent her into a tailspin. She couldn't keep her voice from rising. "You think I don't have it in me to give her a break because her dad has freaking cancer?"

He ducked his head as he delivered his answer. "You have a tendency to demand a lot from people."

Ainsley could tell he was soft-pedaling and she was horrified to learn he thought she was incapable of simple human compassion. Had she given him or anyone else reason to believe otherwise? She worked hard, and she wasn't ashamed to admit she expected the same from everyone else. Was that so wrong? Especially when she didn't have anything else to focus her energy on? No partner to come home to, no close family ties, despite the sudden appearance of her sister Melanie.

Ainsley recognized she didn't have a life outside her work or even value outside of career ladder accomplishments. She realized she transferred her own ambitions to others, but she could still respect that others had different priorities. She knew this hotel was significant to Drew. After all, it had been in her family for years. Ainsley could comprehend how family could come before work, even if she couldn't personalize the priority for herself. But she had spent her life operating under the assumption if you gave someone an inch, they'd take a mile. Was it so wrong to expect the best from people?

Even as she formed the question, she knew it couldn't be answered by a simple yes or no. Of course it wasn't wrong to expect the best, but her expectations were demands, not goals. Was her demand for perfection always justified or were there occasions when a little slack on her part might make a huge difference to the recipient? If she faced reality, she would have to admit she had her own not-so-perfect moments. A nagging thought about the glaring imperfections of a certain fake redhead slithered its way into her consciousness. Ainsley slapped it down. *I may not be perfect, but I don't expect others to forgive my imperfections, and I don't have to forgive hers, I mean theirs.* She decided Paul's reaction was justified. She would attempt to project the image of compassion if she could figure out a way to do so without lowering her standards.

Ainsley spent the next few hours reviewing the books with Paul. Tim, the Steel controller, had spent the entire last week compiling the figures they needed to assess appropriate financial changes, a job complicated by the former Lancer controller's decision to vacate his position as soon as the rumors started about the takeover. His sudden departure had spared Ainsley the task of firing him, but it would have been nice to have some semblance of an orderly transition. Instead they had stack after stack of receipts and invoices and reports full of data holes. It was no accident Ainsley had sent Paul to collect the finished reports. The curses coming from the makeshift office Tim had set up in the cubby next to her office rivaled those of the most irate guests Ainsley had ever dealt with and, faced with a choice, she definitely preferred the latter. After all, the guests eventually checked out.

"If you say rev/par one more time, I swear I'll stick this pencil in your eye." Ainsley referred to the index of revenue to available rooms as she jabbed a pencil in Paul's general direction.

"Watch it, dragon lady. You might actually earn your reputation if I show up with a patch over one eye." Paul's teasing tone faded quickly when he looked at her. "Hey, I was only kidding."

"Knock it off, Paul. I'm not stupid. I hear what everyone calls me."

"It could be worse."

"I'm not sure how." Ainsley stood and closed the binder in front of her. "Command decision. Reserve a table in the dining room and catch the executive team before they leave. Dinner's on me. I want them all there." She caught herself and quickly revised. "I mean, if they don't already have other plans." She knew they would stay. Their jobs were still in the balance. Anything they could do to increase the remote possibility that they might be asked to re-interview for their positions meant any suggestion from her was viewed more like a direct order. For a brief moment she felt a tinge of regret that her power in the workplace didn't translate into the confidence to take another chance with Greer.

CHAPTER SEVENTEEN

I never liked him." Clayton practically growled the statement.

"How come you never said anything?" Greer felt like a fool. How could her uncle, who had met Rick probably twice, be a better judge of his character than she was? She had spent every day with the man. She couldn't blow her nose without him holding a Kleenex. She was instantly depressed when she realized the extent to which she relied on Rick. He'd hired her lawyers, her accountant, her travel agent, her property managers, and countless dozens of others who were charged with managing Greer Davis, Inc. If she couldn't put it on her Platinum AmEx, she didn't have a clue how to make a purchase. A week ago, she thought her life had spun completely out of control. She'd had no clue the bottom was a much longer drop.

"It wasn't up to me to tell you how to run your life."

"Well, then who was it up to, because I obviously know nothing about it myself." Greer knew she sounded petulant, but she wasn't ready to shoulder the blame for her current status. Hell, she didn't even know what her current status was. The only emotion she could summon was self-pity. "What am I going to do?"

"The first thing you're going to do is stop feeling sorry for yourself."

Greer's head snapped up. She recognized the growl in his voice, but it had never been directed at her. He didn't wait for her response before continuing. "Yes, you heard me. You're going to snap out of this downward spiral and pull yourself together. You can be mad at me later. Right now, I'm going to call my lawyer and ask him to come by. He'll help you get back control of your life. On one condition."

Greer waited with dread.

"You can stay here as long as you want and we'll protect your privacy, but while you do, you need to figure out a way to earn your keep. You choose, but I expect you to let me know by tomorrow. You may be richer than a Saudi prince, but you don't know diddley about what's really valuable in life. When you figure out what's really important, you'll be back in control." Clayton didn't wait for her response. He grabbed Ellen's hand and left the room.

Greer barely had time to digest his pronouncement before Drew slid into the seat beside her. "Finally, the golden girl gets a scolding, though it's much too late for you to learn any life lessons."

"Lay off, Drew. I've had a bad enough day without you adding to it."

"What's the matter? Not used to being dumped? Or I guess you're not used to being dumped once people find out you're rich and famous? Funny, I didn't think the dragon lady had any redeeming qualities until now."

"Don't call her that."

"Aww, how cute, sticking up for the lover who scorned you. Too bad she's not around to see you being so sweet, although I doubt she'd care. She saw you for who you really are."

Did she? Greer hadn't a clue who Ainsley thought she knew. The name Greer Davis, which usually translated into love potion, in this instance was love poison. But Ainsley had definitely liked whoever she thought she was with at first. A lot. Greer desperately wanted to be that person again.

"Are you going to be around?" Drew's sudden interest in anything having to do with her surprised Greer.

"Yeah." *Where would I go if I wasn't here?*

"I need to go back to the hotel. I can tell Dad's not feeling so hot and Mom's worn out from all the excitement. If they need anything, can I count on you to deal with it?"

"Sure. I'll handle whatever comes up."

"Just put a Band-Aid on it and call me. I'll do the heavy lifting."

She can't cut me a break. When did our relationship get so out of whack? "Drew?"

"What?"

"Seriously, I have it covered."

Drew grabbed her keys from the kitchen table. "Yeah, whatever." She started toward the door tossing the next words over her shoulder, "Seriously, though, call me if anything comes up. Later."

Greer knew Drew would eventually come around. They were family, after all. They'd had their share of sibling-like rivalry growing up, but their fights had eventually faded into friendship. Ainsley, on the other hand, was neither friend nor family. With only a week-long foundation to their relationship, Greer wasn't confident she could build what they had into something more substantial. But she wanted to. Oh, how she wanted to.

❖

"Why aren't you lounging in your Park Avenue apartment?" Ainsley pulled up a stool and joined her sister at the hotel bar. Dinner with the executive team had been the perfect idea. Paul assured her afterward they were finally convinced she was at least partly human. After two hours pretending to develop lasting relationships, all Ainsley could think about was having a drink in her room, but when she saw Melanie sitting by herself at the bar, she decided to use the opportunity to find out the motive behind her visit to the Southwest. She ordered a chilled Grey Goose and signaled the bartender to make another drink for Melanie.

"Our parentals were worried about you. I volunteered to provide a full report."

"Worried?"

"Darling, your picture was splashed across the front page of every paper in the country. Even our NPR-listening, *Wall Street Journal*–reading, career-driven parents couldn't help but hear you were the rebound sex kitten for the misbehaving Greer Davis. A bit out of character for Little Miss Workaholic. Do you blame them for being concerned?"

A plausible excuse, but Ainsley wasn't buying it. She knew from holidays and other special occasions that her parents knew how to use a phone. Melanie perceived some benefit from traveling across the country, ostensibly to rush to her side; otherwise, she wouldn't be caught dead in a hotel lacking the requisite five stars.

"So, how cozy are you with the famous Greer Davis?" The non sequitur told Ainsley half of what she needed to know. Melanie was curious, not concerned. The unanswered piece of the puzzle was why. "What's your sudden interest in my love life?" Ainsley was instantly sorry for her poor word choice.

"Love?" Melanie arched her eyebrows.

"Figure of speech," Ainsley answered. "Why are you really here?"

"I guess you haven't known her long enough to figure out if she's happy with her investment advisors."

"Damn it, Melanie. Don't tell me you flew your ass all the way out here because you want to handle Greer Davis's portfolio?"

Melanie's smile was catlike. "By my rough calculations, the price of the flight is nothing compared to the possible return. If you were handling everything else in your customary fashion, seems like I'd have an excellent chance."

"Sorry to be such a disappointment. Someday maybe you'll learn how to get business on your own without whoring out your little sister."

Melanie reached in her pocket and pulled out a slip of paper. "All may not be lost." She tossed the paper on the bar and Ainsley casually glanced at the unfamiliar scrawl. A phone number and one word. A name. Greer. Ainsley leapt from the bar stool and backed away from Melanie. Melanie stared at her with a perplexed expression. "Ain, what's wrong?"

"What's wrong?" Ainsley fought to keep her voice from rising. "I'll tell you what's wrong." But she couldn't. She couldn't find the words to voice her anger, choked as it was with wild jealousy. She had been made a fool of again. She remembered Greer standing in her office, looking contrite, asking for a chance. She must have given Melanie her phone number within moments of her declaration. Ainsley couldn't decide if this latest deception was worse than the first. It didn't matter. Any lingering thoughts she had about the emotional connection she had with Greer evaporated when she saw Greer's name on the paper Melanie had carried around all afternoon like a trophy. Ainsley knew Melanie's interest in Greer was nothing more than a financial one, but Greer obviously had her sight set on her next conquest. Melanie had been right. Ainsley was nothing more than a rebound girl, a brief stop in a parade of endless lovers.

"Ainsley, you look apoplectic. What's going on?"

Melanie actually looked concerned. Ainsley figured Melanie could afford to be magnanimous since she had what she wanted. She couldn't wait till Greer found out her sister preferred the other white meat and all Melanie was after was her millions. Ainsley almost laughed out loud, but she felt like crying instead. The roller coaster of emotions choked off all expression. "Don't worry about it. It's nothing." It wasn't nothing, but she wasn't about to give Melanie the satisfaction of seeing her spill tears over a woman who couldn't spare more than a few minutes to grieve what might have been.

Melanie looked relieved the subject was closed. She glanced at her watch, grabbed her purse off the bar, and slid off the bar stool. "Thanks for the drink, darling. I have to run. I'm headed out in the morning. I have a proposal to prepare. Lovely to see you again." Ainsley barely had time to process her abrupt departure when Tony the bartender interrupted her thoughts. He held the slip of paper Melanie had left on the bar. "This yours?"

Ainsley's answer was quick and short. "No." Yet, as she watched him ball it up and raise his hand to toss it into the nearby trash can, she heard herself call out, "Wait! Can I have it?" Tony handed the crumpled paper to Ainsley and she tucked it into her pocket. She had no idea what had gotten into her. *Oh well, I can throw it away myself. Maybe.*

"Your sister's kind of a bitch."

Ainsley looked up to find Drew perched on the stool next to her. "I think we've definitely found something we can agree on." She cocked her head. "I thought I sent you home."

"You did. And I appreciate it, but I checked in with my father and everything's fine. The hotel's packed and I figured I should be here in case you needed me. Besides, I understand you've been slacking off. Buying dinner for the management team instead of working." She delivered her comments with a smile and Ainsley grinned back. "Got me. Sorry you missed dinner. And as for my sister, she should be leaving in the morning."

"Any particular reason she traveled cross country to see you? Forgive me for saying so, but you don't seem to have a loving sibling relationship."

"You've got that right. She said she was concerned about my welfare, but the truth is she's stalking your cousin." At Drew's shocked expression, she added, "Call it financial stalking. She's a broker and she sees Greer as a gold mine."

"I doubt she'd be the first, but would she really try to take advantage of someone you're dating?"

Ainsley intentionally ignored the dating reference. "Your initial assessment—bitch? Well, that was spot on. Melanie would do anything to get what she wants. She's the picture in the dictionary under sibling rivalry."

Drew laughed. "Greer and I certainly have our differences, but I don't think she'd stoop so low."

"What's behind your differences, if you don't mind my asking?" Ainsley didn't care if Drew did mind. She wanted to know.

"I'm not sure I can put my finger on it. We were like sisters growing up, but we've grown apart. We live completely different types of lives. I feel like I don't know her anymore."

"Well, she's in for a surprise with Melanie. I'm sure Melanie has no clue Greer views her as her next conquest."

"What are you talking about?"

"Within moments of our rift, Greer gave her number to my sister. Rich, huh?"

"Are you sure?"

Ainsley held up the slip of paper in her hand. "Certain."

Drew shrugged. "Strange. Greer called me a few minutes ago. Asked me to get you to call her. If she's moved on, seems like she would've asked for Melanie."

Ainsley didn't know what to make of Drew's revelation. Greer wanted her to call? She knew the number to the hotel; why couldn't she call Ainsley directly? Well, she had been at dinner for the last couple of hours. What did Greer want to tell her? Why had she given her number to Melanie? Lots of questions. She glanced at the paper in her hand. Were all the answers merely a phone call away?

"Good morning, everyone!" Greer greeted Drew and her uncle and tried to ignore their surprised looks. She hadn't made early mornings a habit and doubtless they were curious about her seven a.m. appearance. The truth was she hadn't been able to sleep. After her uncle's gently delivered ultimatum the night before, she had spent the night wandering the ranch, considering her options. None of them seemed very appealing. She could dive back into the public fray, sans agent, and face her critics head-on, or she could hide out a while longer until she figured out a plan to take back control of her life. The last option definitely sounded more appealing except for the part where she was supposed to earn her keep and tolerate Drew's constant expressions of disapproval. Rick's idea about checking into rehab was almost tempting when faced with Drew's disdain. But Greer knew her real problem wasn't the drugs, it was what the drugs symbolized. She had lived her life with no responsibility, no accountability. Normal everyday concerns didn't apply to her and, as a natural extension, she was insulated from the consequences of her actions. Until now. Macy's death had set in motion a chain of events that toppled the structure of Greer's world. Faced with her choices, staying at the ranch was the most appealing alternative, and not only because it meant she was closer to Ainsley and a possible reconciliation.

But if she wanted to stay, she had to figure out a plan. She could afford to buy this ranch and all the surrounding property, but she was certain her uncle had a more personal investment in mind than money. Greer looked across the table and realized how tired Clayton looked. He held open a copy of the *Wall Street Journal*, but his eyes were squinting at the page as if he were on the verge of nodding off. She was curious about why her retired, ill uncle bothered to get up at this hour, but she was reluctant to engage in conversation until Drew left. It seemed every word Greer spoke was a lightning rod for Drew's derision. She didn't have to wait long before Drew pushed her seat back and mumbled something about how some people had to actually work for a living before she took her leave.

Greer waited till Drew was out the door. "Clayton, why are you up so early?"

He smiled indulgently at her. "Habit."

"You don't look so good."

"Treatment's wearing."

Greer realized she had been on the ranch for over a week, and she still didn't know jack about the status of her uncle's cancer or the treatment he was receiving. No small wonder Drew thought she was a beast. She decided to remedy the situation. "Tell me more about your diagnosis and treatment."

"I have lung cancer. What more do you need to know?" He shrugged and turned his attention back to the paper. Greer reached over and pulled down the edge of the paper and gave him an intense stare. "Humor me. I want to know more." She employed her best wheedling tone. "Please?"

Clayton folded the paper and methodically discussed his illness. Six months ago, at Drew's insistence, he'd gone to the doctor with a random array of symptoms. Shortness of breath, decreased appetite, fatigue. He figured the doctor was going to ride him about working too hard or put him on a fancy diet with fistfuls of vitamins. He was totally unprepared for the declaration "get rid of your damn cigars" and the extensive battery of tests that followed. Chest x-ray, CT scan, biopsy. His doctor had been direct and thorough and quickly confirmed his first impulse: cancer. Stage III lung cancer.

"What does Stage Three mean?" Greer asked.

"It means they still go full guns on treatment as if it will make a difference." Clayton's sarcastic tone was the first glimpse Greer had into the level of his optimism. She was surprised he let his despondency show.

"It's curable, right?"

"Sometimes. In a minority of cases. Most of the time the treatment results in partial remission. Recurrence rates are high. The reality is I probably have a few years."

"What's the treatment?"

"Radiation, like yesterday, and chemo. I'm on my second round. Finish up this week."

"And then what?"

"They do a scan to see if it did any good. Then they'll monitor me every few months to see if things are working."

Greer had a ton more questions, but Clayton looked tired and she decided she could find out a lot of what she wanted to know with a few clicks on the computer. She planned to take Betty to Pimentel and Sons for a tune-up, and she could pick up a laptop while she was in Albuquerque. She could think of several other things she needed to pick up in addition to a computer. Clothes topped the list. Normally, she would have directed Rick to get her whatever she needed, but she felt a rush of freedom at the prospect of doing for herself. Fear of being recognized didn't outweigh the anticipation of being her own person. As she plotted out her day she knew the thing—make that *person*—that ranked number one. She was concerned Ainsley hadn't called, but she wasn't ready to give up. Once she had a few other details well in hand, she was determined to take care of her top priority. "Uncle Clayton, what time is your lawyer coming over?"

"He's coming by after he leaves the office, around five thirty."

"Perfect. You don't mind if I run some errands today, do you? Do you need anything?"

"No. I'm drained, but no other nasty symptoms. The chemo makes me tired. It's the radiation that sucks the life out of me."

"You have chemo tomorrow, right?" When he nodded, she nodded back. "I'll see you tonight." She started from the table.

"Clayton?" When she had his attention again, she said, "I love you."

"I love you too."

CHAPTER EIGHTEEN

Ainsley was utterly unable to focus. She sat at the expansive desk in the management office with a half dozen open binders filled with spreadsheets crammed with figures. They needed to make some decisions, and Paul had scheduled a design team to come in the afternoon to give a presentation on their ideas for renovations. The Lancer hadn't undergone any significant design changes since its original opening years ago, and its dated look needed serious assistance. Usually this aspect of the transition was the most exciting. It was when Ainsley could feel the staff starting to rally together to make the "new" hotel everything it could be. Nothing like a new look to improve everyone's attitude.

But Ainsley's enthusiasm for this project was sapped by the energy she expended wondering about the women in her life. She was glad Melanie was well on her way back to New York. She couldn't take any more of her sister's not-so-subtle attempts to win access to Greer Davis. Melanie was convinced the tabloid stories were true, and she was as good as hitched to the client of her dreams. Nothing Ainsley said could dissuade her. Melanie had Greer's number in her BlackBerry and she couldn't wait to get back to New York to plot her next step. As mad as Ainsley was at Greer, she wouldn't wish her sister's relentless scheming on anyone.

Truth was she didn't wish any ill will on Greer. Her thoughts about Greer consisted of remembering Greer standing close, arms around her waist, pelvis nestled against her rear, gently kissing her neck. Ainsley shivered at the memory of the sparks skittering across her skin at even the lightest of Greer's touches. As angry as she was about Greer's deception, she couldn't help but admit those sparks had ignited a slow burn whose warmth she still felt.

Ainsley reached into her suit jacket pocket and pulled out the crumpled slip of paper she'd retrieved from the bar. She ran her finger over Greer's handwriting and relished the intimacy of tracing Greer's penstroke. Her signature was sharp and fierce. She had pushed the pen hard into the paper. Before she could shake a nagging feeling she was reading too much into the pseudo connection, Ainsley picked up the phone and started punching in the numbers to make the connection real. Greer's husky voice on the outgoing message evoked the wonderful, almost giddy feeling she felt while eating pie and making eyes at Tray just days ago. She listened as Greer told anyone who was listening that she was currently unavailable, but to be sure and leave a message and she would return the call. Ainsley's words were few. "It's Ainsley. Let's talk. Call me at the hotel." As Ainsley hung up the phone, she wished she could snatch back her words while at the same time she checked her watch to start counting the minutes till Greer called her back. Before she could give the matter more thought, the office door opened.

As Paul shut the door behind her, he asked, "Am I interrupting something?"

"No, not at all." Ainsley knew she probably looked flustered and the thought drove her to unnecessary explanation. She glanced at the phone near her hand. "I was making a call, but I'm done." She saw the odd look Paul cast her way and willed herself to shut up, biting her own lip to help her will along.

"Okay," Paul said slowly. "Sure you don't want me to come back later?"

Ainsley forced herself to smile instead of launching into more word vomit. "No, let's get started."

Drew joined them and they reviewed the information the design team had provided and prepared a final list of questions to be asked during the presentation. Ainsley caught her mind wandering more than once during the meeting. She searched her mind for all the reasons why making the call to Greer was a bad idea. She was angry with Greer for lying, but truthfully, the only deception had been a name. Greer had been careful not to spin a web of falsehoods, and Ainsley had chosen not to distinguish between outright lies and careful omissions. In her black-and-white world, both fell on the side of darkness. Only the intense pull of attraction prompted her to consider assigning shades of gray to the actions of Greer Davis. The draw was strong, but was she ready to give in?

❖

Greer was thankful her uncle was good friends with the Santa Fe County Sheriff. He'd instructed a few of his deputies to patrol the winding stretch of roadway near the ranch. Their vigilance meant Greer had a fighting chance of getting out of Tesuque before she was spotted. The media had taken to hanging out at the local Tesuque Market, lying in wait for cars to appear on the dusty road, hoping to catch a photo of Greer Davis worthy of a front-page spread. Greer loved the Vette but realized she would have been better off yesterday in Joey's beat-up Cavalier, especially with her uncle in the car. *I should borrow his car again for tomorrow.* She wasn't sure when she'd reached the conclusion, but she had obviously already decided she would be the one to take Clayton to the doctor for his chemo in the morning. While she was here, she might as well take him for his follow-ups too. Maybe she could get more information about his condition since he seemed reluctant to talk about it. She needed to see if Joey would agree to a longer term car-swapping arrangement. Clayton would be a lot more comfortable if he wasn't sitting on the ground, feeling the road on his trips to and from the doctor.

In the meantime, Greer was happy to have the Vette. She spotted the poorly disguised E! Entertainment TV media van as she whipped by the market and knew that even if they were poised and ready, their chances of catching her from a dead start when she was flying by at seventy-five was unlikely. She laughed as the van, followed by several others, disappeared in a cloud of her dust, unable to keep up with the powerful car as it twisted through the hairpin turns on the country road. She hoped the sheriff's deputies wouldn't be too hard on them when they were all pulled over for various traffic infractions from which she was luckily immune.

Greer wished she could take Ainsley for a ride in the Vette before she traded it in. She imagined Ainsley with her hair down, alternately laughing and screaming as they roared down the road. Ainsley would see a different Greer. Exciting and wild, and she would be so captivated by the risk, she would crave that Greer. Badly. Ainsley would reach across the gearshift and stroke Greer to a state of arousal. She would whip through the turns faster until the car seemed to lift off the ground, matching her hips lifting off the leather seat. Greer would max out the speed as she came, simultaneously in and out of control as she steered them both to safety.

Greer shrugged away the fantasy. Ainsley didn't want wild and risky Greer. She wanted safe and simple Tray with her scruffy clothes and scary hair. She wanted sweet love, not wild pleasure. Greer knew Ainsley had been a little freaked out after the first night they made love. Greer knew it was because she had allowed her public persona to show through. Hard and dark, rough and raw. But she desperately wanted Ainsley to know she was a whole person, capable of being both tough and tender. Greer decided her fantasies would be better spent figuring out how to get Ainsley to see all of her. She had the whole day to come up with a strategy.

Her first stop was Pimentel and Sons Guitar Makers. Betty deserved the best, and Greer was determined to remedy the years of neglect starting now. She was thankful Albuquerque was home to a premier luthier. Miraculously, Betty seemed to have suffered little during the time she spent locked away, but Greer wanted a second opinion from someone she trusted.

Mr. Pimentel Sr. himself greeted her as she walked in the shop. He and his sons handcrafted guitars for those who appreciated excellent work and could afford to pay top dollar. To them, her rock-star status meant nothing. Greer was just another musician who loved her instrument. Betty would get the same master care as any other highly prized instrument that crossed their threshold.

"How long since you've played her?"

"Years. Lots."

"She's been here in New Mexico the whole time?"

"Yes. In the case, in plastic." At least she'd remembered to provide some of the extra care a dry climate required.

His look told her he didn't understand why she would let such a beautiful guitar lay silent. She met his stare. "I'm going to start playing her again. Now."

He handed the guitar back to her. "You're lucky, then. She could still use humidification, but it's not necessary right now. You should also get a better case. One more resistant to the climate. I can make some recommendations. You may also want to have a new saddle made to adjust the action. I can match the ivory. Can you leave her with me for a few days?"

Greer nodded, but held Betty tight. Mr. Pimentel wrote out his notes while Greer worked herself up to leave Betty in his able hands. As she reluctantly handed the guitar to him, she kicked herself for all the years she'd wasted without her.

Greer's second stop was the Apple store in ABQ Uptown. Midmorning on a Tuesday seemed to be a good time to shop. She and one other customer had the store to themselves. Greer couldn't remember the last time she'd purchased a piece of electronic equipment for herself. She had her share of gadgets, but they all showed up magically unboxed and ready to use. She had a million questions for Walter, the attentive Apple employee. She wondered if his solicitousness was because he recognized her, but after listening to him drool over the "totally awesome" features of the tricked-out laptop she focused on, she decided he was more interested in gigabytes than superstars. He explained it would take about an hour to load all the programs she wanted, and he pointed out a nearby coffee shop where she could wait until he called her.

Greer decided instead to wait in the car. She'd nabbed a book from Drew's room and welcomed indulging herself in someone else's life story for a change. As she slid into the seat, she glanced at her reflection in the rearview mirror. Her dye job made her look like a beauty school reject and her eyes were constantly red from the contacts she wore. She decided she would have a better chance of regaining control of her life if she could at least recognize the person who looked back at her in the mirror. Besides, the scary-looking chick in the glass was as well-known by now as the real thing. She grabbed her phone and punched in a familiar number.

"Yeah?" Ethan's voice was crusty with sleep.

"Yeah to you too. Wake up, I have a question."

"Who is this?"

"It's me, Greer."

"Do you know what time it is?"

"Ethan, it's ten thirty."

"A.M.? This is not the Greer I know. She would know not to wake her friends so rudely in the middle of the night."

Greer laughed. She wasn't the Greer she knew either. Up early for breakfast, out running errands, all before noon. *I bet Ainsley has been at work for hours already.* Willing herself to focus, she said, "Just lie there and answer my questions."

"Okay," he mumbled.

"I want to go back to being a blonde. What do I need to do?"

"Greer, are you okay?" He sounded more awake and genuinely concerned.

"I'm ready to get my old self back." *Or at least the looks part.* "Seriously, Ethan, I need your help here."

He spoke slowly as if she had a learning disability. "Take. Off. The. Wig."

Oh, now she got it. No wonder he sounded like he was talking to the slow. "It's not a wig."

"Tell me you didn't!"

She could hear the edge of panic in his voice. She forced herself to sound nonchalant. "I couldn't keep wearing the wig. It kept slipping. I dyed it red to match. Used a color I picked up at the drugstore. I actually did a pretty good job, I don't think anyone could tell the difference—"

"You used color from a box? What the hell were you thinking?"

Greer felt tears well up, and she leaned her head against the steering wheel. She hadn't been thinking past the next moment for most of her life. She didn't need her best friend to point out her

DO NOT DISTURB

biggest shortcoming. Or maybe she did. "Look, I made a mistake. I've made a ton of mistakes lately. I don't need you to point out how stupid I am. Help me out here. What do I do?" Greer realized her question wasn't about her hair any longer.

"I'm sorry, sweetie. You know how I am when I don't get enough sleep." Ethan yawned as if to demonstrate the sincerity of his remark. "Okay, hair first, then we'll work on the rest of your life." He asked her some pointed questions about her home color job and then clicked off, promising to call her back within five minutes.

He did. "You're on Menual Boulevard? Great, you're around the corner from Salon Bello. Dan Padilla is waiting for you. He'll make you as blond as the day you were born, but it's going to take several hours. Get over there now. I had to promise unspeakable things to get you this appointment."

Greer didn't ask questions. She knew that after years on the *Phantom* tour, Ethan knew someone "special" in every city on the circuit. "Thanks, Ethan."

"Oh, you're not off the hook yet, dear. Tell me about this luscious babe you're smoochin' there in the Land of Enchantment."

"I don't want to talk about it."

"Not like you to kiss and not tell."

"She's special. Besides, it may be over. Too much exposure."

"Wow, you finally found one who doesn't crave the limelight? She sounds like a keeper. Does she know how special you are?"

"She doesn't know anything about me." Greer didn't try to hide the bitter tone.

"Her loss, babe."

Ethan was loyal to a fault. Greer didn't bother refuting his assessment, but she knew she was the one losing out. She had to figure out a way to cut her losses.

❖

Ainsley looked at her watch and sighed. Four o'clock was too early to start drinking. At least here at the hotel. She contemplated sneaking out and running down the block to a nearby bar, but she

• 191 •

knew she wasn't safe out there. Reporters and news vans still lurked outside waiting for a glimpse of the woman who had captivated Greer Davis and taken her mind off the death of her lover Macy Rivers. Ainsley had given them no satisfaction, steadfastly refusing to leave the hotel since she had been smuggled in. She couldn't help but follow the stories—tidbits about Greer Davis were everywhere in the hotel from magazine covers scattered throughout the lobby to televised reports blaring from all the flat-screen TVs Paul had insisted be installed in the bar. Someone who didn't know would think Greer herself had died, the way the entertainment news droned on and on about her path to stardom.

"Has rock and roll's favorite leather girl decided to quit the music biz? Our reporter in the field, Delia Gadsby, has been investigating. Don't go away if you want to hear the rest of the story."

"And if you don't want to hear the rest of the story?" Ainsley answered her own question by clicking the remote till she found a local news channel to replace the insipid entertainment drivel on *TMZ*. She became thoroughly engrossed in a story about a local adoption agency when she heard a light knock on the door.

Greer Davis stood in her doorway, and she was smoking hot. Denim, leather, and spiked blond hair. She leaned against the door frame with her arms crossed. Everything about her appearance shouted confidence, and Ainsley felt her own drain quickly away. She met Greer's cool blue eyes for the very first time and gasped at the icy wave of want coursing through her. Greer answered with a hint of a smile before she entered the office and locked the door behind her.

"What are you doing here? Shouldn't you be hiding out from the press?" Ainsley made no effort to conceal her anger, but she suspected the source of her passionate tone couldn't be exclusively linked to fury. She felt magnetized by the brilliant color of Greer's eyes. *I should've known I was falling for my usual type, blue-eyed blonde.* Ainsley brushed away resistance to the conclusion she'd fallen at all and tried to reconcile Greer Davis, rock star, with the brown-eyed redhead who lurked in her thoughts.

Greer slid into the chair across from her desk and crossed her legs, acting like she owned the place. Well, Ainsley thought, up until a few weeks ago her family did. And, she recalled, Greer had worked here while she was in high school. She found herself wondering if Greer had enjoyed this business, if it was in her blood the way it was in Ainsley's and Drew's. Obviously not or she wouldn't have left. *She left to become a rock star, silly. She was supposed to stick around and deal with the day-to-day grind of running a hotel when she could travel the world with hordes of screaming fans in her wake?*

Ainsley realized she didn't think what Greer did for a living was real work. She didn't have regular hours. If an emergency happened, she called or made her agent call one of her many minions to handle it. Greer never worked overtime because someone else didn't show up. She had no responsibilities. Not even her own. Nope, rock star did not equal real job. Ainsley felt the acid burn of resentment wind its way down her throat and she snapped, "What are you doing here?"

"I got your message, but when I called they said you were in a meeting. I came to apologize."

"Not necessary," Ainsley lied. She did want an apology. Remorse was a sign Greer wasn't callous. Yet she found herself unable to ask for what she really wanted because she knew it wasn't possible. She wanted a do-over. She wanted to go back to meeting Greer on the plane and figure out if the feelings she felt for her were real, not colored by shades of gray.

Greer wasn't easily dissuaded. "I get that you don't like Greer Davis, but you don't really know her. You liked her when you thought she was someone else. Didn't you?"

Ainsley tried to follow, but Greer talking about herself in the third person merely added to the confusion already fueled by her proximity. Would it feel as good to run her hands through those blond spikes as it had to caress the red ones? And those warm lapis eyes? Was it her imagination or did they seem to see right through her? She hoped not because if so, Greer was witnessing a powerful struggle between heart and mind.

"I'm not sure the person I met exists."

"Come on, Ainsley, you did more than meet her." Greer was up now, coming around the desk. Words rushed from her brain to protest the affront, but they dissolved on Ainsley's tongue. Greer was behind her now, spinning her chair around, leaving no barriers between them. She slid a hand along Ainsley's face, cupping her chin, stroking her lips with her thumb. "I never meant to hurt you, to lie to you. Take all the time you want to tell me how angry you are with me, but don't throw me out. Let me have equal time to tell you how I feel. I promise, I can explain why I did the things I did."

Ainsley felt her lips betray her resolve and part against the gentle pressure of Greer's touch. Her mind no longer controlled her physical actions. She could only watch as Greer leaned forward and traced the path of her fingers with soft lips. She opened to the touch and her tongue invited Greer inside. Greer didn't vary the intensity of their touch, but added slow and steady strokes of her tongue to the intimate dance. Ainsley's arms joined her unfaithful lips and circled Greer's waist to pull her in. The kiss wasn't enough. She yearned to be closer. Greer balanced on the arms of her chair and Ainsley took advantage of the forward movement to hold each of her breasts. The groan she elicited from Greer made Ainsley come up out of her seat.

"We had our very own Greer Davis sighting this afternoon. Coronado Mall was overrun with news vans as Ms. Davis made her way through the shops, outfitting herself with a new wardrobe. But it was our very own Linda Thomas who got an exclusive from the rock star herself. Linda?"

"Good reporters look for stories wherever they happen to be. Well, today I was sitting in a chair at the Salon Bello, when who should walk in and sit down next to me but the recently elusive Greer Davis herself."

"Did you get to talk to her?"

"I certainly did, Tom. She asked me to pass her a copy of People *magazine. Can you imagine that? I struck up a conversation, and we whiled away the afternoon under the heat lamps."*

"Did she have any insight to the recent events in Chicago or anything to say about Macy Rivers?"

"She did, Tom. She said—"

Ainsley's abrupt exit from her chair nearly toppled them both to the ground. She ignored Greer's surprised look and moved out of her reach, grabbing the remote and killing the power to the television. *Shopping? Greer spent the afternoon shopping? Oh, wait, she hadn't shopped the whole time; she had also found time to visit a salon and chat with reporters.* Any residual sympathy she felt for all the supposedly unwanted attention heaped on Greer was apparently unwarranted. Greer was whoring herself out for the reporters. She deserved whatever she got in return. She started to tell Greer what she could do with herself, but the look on her face paralyzed her. She looked at the now-silent TV and her expression was wistful, shy almost. Ainsley realized she was catching a glimpse of the woman she'd met on the plane. A sweet, shy woman whose uncle had cancer, whose parents had abandoned her, and whose cousin was prickly at best. A piece of her wanted to pull Greer into her arms, stroke her head, and murmur endearments.

For God's sake, Ainsley, she's not a puppy. You can't let her flash those hangdog eyes at you and melt your heart. Everything she's ever told you is a lie. Have a spine, for crying out loud!

Her thoughts swept her feelings aside, and Ainsley pulled back. She didn't meet Greer's eyes as she spoke. "I'd like it if you left." It wasn't what she would like, but she didn't trust what pleased her to be a proper guide.

"Baby, are you sure? I think we have a real connection. I know I owe you an explanation—" Greer moved closer and the proximity was dangerous.

"You spent the day shopping?"

Greer was confused. Why was the mention of her shopping trip a catalyst for Ainsley to dismiss her? It had to be something else. "I had to get a few things. Oh, and have my hair restored to its natural color." She smiled, hoping to lighten the tension swirling in the room. "Do you like it?"

Ainsley did. She liked everything she saw, but she wasn't sure she could trust her eyes. She wanted to curl back up in Greer's arms, but she wasn't sure she could trust her instincts either. "Let me get something straight. Why did you adopt an alternate identity in the first place?"

Greer was relieved for the opening. "You know what happened in Chicago, right?" Ainsley nodded. "Well, you can't imagine what a scene it was. My hotel was covered in protestors. People toting signs accusing me of killing Macy. A guy tried to kidnap me to rescue me from my wayward life. Reporters were everywhere. I had to get out of there and the only way to do it was to totally change how I looked, who I was."

"I see. And today you suddenly decided talking to reporters was a good idea." Ainsley hoped her sarcasm was a clear message. Greer obviously craved the attention she had missed while hiding out.

"I didn't plan on giving an interview. I was at the hair salon and one of the other customers turned out to be Linda Thomas. She's an anchor on one of the local stations. You wouldn't know her, but back when she was a field reporter, she interviewed me for my very first TV appearance." Greer heard her own voice. She was babbling, but with purpose. As long as they were talking, she was still here, inches from Ainsley and her warm embrace.

"And you couldn't resist the chance to be back in the spotlight?"

"I wish you'd listened to the whole interview."

"I can't think of a reason I'd want to do that."

"Because I told Linda that the woman I'd met here in the Land of Enchantment was truly enchanting. I told her I wasn't going to divulge anything else about you, or about us, for fear of blowing any chance I might have at having a relationship with you."

Ainsley sighed. The words were perfect, but she didn't know if she was ready to trust them. The call she'd made that morning was as much risk as she was willing to take for now. If she took any more steps outside her comfortable black-and-white existence, she was scared where they might lead. "We got off on the wrong foot and you're not my type. We have absolutely nothing in common." Greer didn't look the least bit dissuaded by her proclamation, so Ainsley roughed it up. "I think I made it clear I don't care for Greer Davis, and if I'd known you were her, we never would have even had a conversation, let alone…"

She didn't have a description for what they had shared. She didn't have a framework by which to judge their encounter, and she didn't have the words to give it a proper name. But it didn't matter. Ainsley could tell by the combined expression of sadness and anger that crossed Greer's face that her remark had done the trick.

Greer closed the distance to the door as if the room were about to explode. She paused briefly in the doorway, her back to Ainsley, her words barely audible. "I'm sorry."

Her departure sucked the life out of the room and Ainsley was at once relieved and disappointed. *Might be time for that drink now. The hotel bar is going to have to do.* She waited to allow enough time for Greer to make her exit from the hotel and then walked to the hotel bar.

"Ms. Faraday, do you have a minute?" The young lady at the front desk looked genuinely distressed and Ainsley detoured in her direction. "I have a problem with the…"

Ainsley didn't hear the rest of her words. She was focused on the site of Greer climbing into the oldest, ugliest car ever to grace the valet entrance of a Steel hotel. *I thought the news said she was driving a shiny new Vette.* Cursing herself for having internalized any part of the constant stream of gossip about Greer, she decided to do some fact checking of her own. Ainsley strode over to the bell stand and tried to appear casual. She maneuvered so she could read the young man's name badge: Joey. "Can you believe that clunker?"

Joey blushed a deep red and his tone was defensive. "It may not look great on the outside, but my car is tougher than it looks. I've driven it since high school. I had planned to drive it until it fell apart on the road."

Ainsley started to remark that it looked as if that could happen any moment, but she stopped herself and replayed the words Joey had spoken. "I thought I saw Greer at the wheel?"

"I thought she just wanted to borrow it, but she said she would need it longer. Her uncle isn't comfortable in her car because it's too low to the ground. She's going to be taking care of him. I told her to keep it as long as she needed, but she insisted we make a permanent deal." He held up a shiny new key and stared at it as if it would evaporate. "She traded me for the Vette."

Ainsley was as confused as he was flustered. Trading her sleek and shiny car for a jalopy? Sure didn't seem like the Greer Davis she knew. She chastised herself. *All you know about Greer Davis is what you read in the paper or see on TV.* She hadn't shared more than a dozen words with the bell captain since she arrived at the hotel, but she felt compelled to ask, "She's taking care of her uncle?"

"Clayton Lancer. He used to own the hotel before your company bought the place." He offered a sheepish grin Ainsley found strangely engaging. "I guess you know that already." Ainsley smiled back and nodded in encouragement. "Anyway, he was, is, a great guy. The Lancer Hotel was his pride and joy. It's a shame he got sick."

"How is he doing?"

"Not so well. Drew says the doctors aren't very optimistic. The treatment is supposed to prolong his life, but it won't save it. Guess it's good he sold the place so he can relax a little in retirement. If he was working, he wouldn't be able to spend time visiting with Greer."

It was the longest string of conversation she had shared with any of the employees who weren't on the management team. Everyone else clammed up whenever she walked in the room. Apparently, Joey hadn't signed on to the "don't talk to the big bad corporate villains" petition, and Ainsley decided to take advantage by pressing him for more information.

"Are they close?"

"Super close. Mr. Lancer is like a dad to Greer. She lived with them all through high school and spent most summers during college staying at the ranch and working here at the hotel."

None of these bits of information fit neatly into the mental image Ainsley carried around of Greer Davis. She shoved them into her head and quickly shut the door before they could all come tumbling out. She'd sort out the mess later when her head wasn't fuzzy from the combination of sizzling kisses and mixed-up messages. *Why do I even care?* Despite her rattled condition, the answer was clear. Ainsley wasn't done with Greer Davis. Nor did she want to be.

Chapter Nineteen

G reer jumped at the sound of the alarm. It was the first time she had used one since…well, she couldn't remember the last time she had used an alarm clock. She had staff trained to deal with most situations, which kept her from having to wake before her body decided it was ready to greet the day, but this morning she had a promise to keep.

As she dressed in her hastily purchased new clothes, she was relieved to see her old self looking back in the mirror. Being a natural blonde was indeed everything it was cracked up to be, except when it came to winning over a certain hotel executive. Greer wondered what her relationship with Ainsley would be like if they had been seated on the plane and Ainsley had actually known who she was. Would the same sparks have flown between them? Would she have had the courage to kiss her? Would Ainsley have slapped her instead of returning the kiss? Greer shrugged at her reflection and decided her idle mental reflections would get her nowhere. She desperately wanted to win over Ainsley, but after yesterday's encounter, she knew she had to start by being the kind of person Ainsley obviously preferred. Responsible.

"Greer, honey, are you up?" Aunt Ellen poked her head in the door and Greer laughed at the incredulous expression on her face. "Didn't expect to see me up, let alone dressed, did you?"

Ellen smiled indulgently at her. "Not really." She pointed at Greer's head. "I'm glad to see you back to your old self."

"I'm not so sure my old self is what I want to be right now."

"We all have baggage, dear. It's how you carry it that counts."

Greer drew her into a bear hug. "Why are you always so damn nice?"

Ellen squeezed hard. "Don't get me wrong, you are a chore sometimes, but we love you. All we really want is for you to be happy." Ellen pulled back and looked her square in the eyes. "You have reached the pinnacle of success, but I don't know if you've been happy in a long time. Am I right?"

She could only nod. Ellen pulled her back into the hug and whispered in her ear, "It's not too late. It's never too late."

Greer relaxed into her motherly embrace and felt some of her stress fade in the face of the love flowing between them. As if she could tell when Greer was finally feeling better, Aunt Ellen released her and stepped back. "Are you sure you don't want to stay home and relax today? I'm going anyway. I don't mind driving."

"Actually, I'm looking forward to having something useful to do. And I have a more comfortable car for Uncle Clayton to ride in." Greer imagined the surprised look her aunt would have when she ushered them into Joey's jalopy. Truth was even though the old sedan didn't look so hot, it was still in great shape and was a very comfortable ride. Greer had announced at dinner that she planned to contribute to the household by serving as the house's chief chauffeur and errand runner. She wanted to be more involved in her uncle's medical treatment. She figured by taking care of whatever needs they had in town, she would free them up to relax at home and Uncle Clayton could concentrate on getting well.

They seemed surprised at her announcement she planned to stick around until her tour started. She shared with them the gist of her meeting with Clayton's lawyer, and her decision to employ a temporary agent to help her manage her affairs until she had a more permanent solution. What she didn't share was the primary reason for her decision to stay. She had a very important mission: win the love of Ainsley Faraday.

❖

"Why don't you two come on back?" the nice, pretty nurse called out to Ellen and Greer. As they passed through the door leading into the inner sanctum of the doctor's office, Greer paused by the familiar pit bull seated at the receptionist desk. When the receptionist glanced up, she could feel a growl coming her way. Greer offered a tentative smile. "Hi, I'd like to reintroduce myself. I'm Clayton Lancer's niece. I appreciate how well all of you have been taking care of him. Thank you." Her prepared speech delivered, Greer didn't wait for a response, instead following her aunt into the doctor's office.

"We'll wait a few weeks to run another scan, but I'm hopeful. The PET scan performed midcycle was promising. I believe we'll have even better results with additional treatment." Dr. Prescott leaned back in his chair. "Questions?"

"I have a couple," Greer heard herself say. She glanced at Clayton as if to ask permission. At his nod, she continued. "Can you define 'promising' and 'better results'? I'd like to have a point of reference."

Dr. Prescott looked at his patient, and Clayton answered, "You can speak freely to my niece."

"Your uncle has small cell lung cancer, Stage Three. We're treating him to prolong his life, but I can't guarantee, nor do I think it's likely, we'll cure the cancer. The best we can hope for is to keep it at bay and allow him to have some quality of life for longer than he would without the treatment. We'll scan him every so often and make determinations as we go about whether additional treatment would be helpful."

Greer quickly realized she hadn't braced herself adequately for the heavy dose of realism the doctor had just delivered. She wanted to shout questions about the point of all the gut-wrenching treatment her uncle was having to endure if all he could expect was a vague prognosis of a "longer" life. She held her tongue. Clayton was a grown man and a wise one too. The questions she needed to ask were how she could best take care of him.

"I'm sure you've explained this to the rest of the family in the past, but I want to know what else we should be watching out for?"

As if he knew she needed the encouragement, Dr. Prescott said, "Good question. Clayton here has a tendency to minimize his symptoms. Watch for anything out of the ordinary." He shook his finger at both Greer and Ellen. "But don't hover." They nodded their understanding. "If something doesn't seem right between now and the next scan, bring him in, and we'll check it out. I'll have my nurse give you a pamphlet on your way out with tips about what you should watch out for."

He walked them out of his office and shook hands with Greer before leaving them at the receptionist's desk to wait for the nurse. Greer had her back to the desk and didn't notice her trying to get her attention until her aunt pointed out she was waving a copy of *People* magazine in her direction. Greer remembered her tirade from earlier in the week and dreaded the payback she was about to receive. She leaned in, an apology on her lips, but before she could say a word, the receptionist spoke first.

"My fifteen-year-old niece would like your autograph. Do you mind?" She didn't wait for an answer, but began spelling "E-U-N-I-C-E."

Greer smiled, took the offered pen and autographed her photo on the cover of the magazine. She wanted to write words of condolence for the rock 'n' roll–loving teenager with the old-fashioned name, but she scrawled a more general dedication and returned the magazine to Ms. Grouchy-pants.

❖

Ainsley was instantly annoyed at the sight of Paul consuming a monstrous plate of what looked like a rapidly sinking submarine. She jerked a chair back and plopped into the seat at his table. "What the hell are you eating?"

"The most amazing meal ever."

"I can't believe we serve something so hideous." She couldn't bring herself to try the food, but from the menu it was apparent piles of tortillas, cheese, and random other goopy substance qualified as haute cuisine here in the outpost of the Southwest. Tourists and locals alike flocked to eat the stuff. She picked up a fork and poked at the green and red mess on Paul's plate. "I ask again, what is it?"

"Breakfast burrito," Paul mumbled between bites. "Christmas."

Ainsley decided Paul had been body snatched. The trim and dapper man she knew lived for five-star cuisine. The mess on his plate was anything but. He was so far gone, he thought it was a holiday. "Christmas?" she asked, thinking she was probably starting a pointless conversation.

He paused between bites to explain with great deliberation, as if Ainsley were the slowest person on earth. "Red chile. Green chile. Together, it's Christmas." Ainsley shook her head. Paul picked up a fork from the other place setting, heaped it high with a glob of the mixture on his plate, and shoved it Ainsley's way. Ainsley pursed her lips in protest, but Paul kept coming at her, and to save her suit from flying food debris, Ainsley finally opened her mouth and let the mess enter.

Soft, buttery flavors from the egg, cheese, and tortilla danced with the tang and heat of the chile sauce to form a taste nirvana. She chewed slowly to savor every last sensation. As the last bit dissolved in her mouth, she closed her eyes and sighed with regret. Charlie Trotter's, watch out!

Paul laughed out loud. "See, isn't it wonderful? Now do you get why I don't want to mess with the menus?"

"Shut up and give me another bite."

Drew joined them at the table. "I see how it is. Current management does all the work, while you two sit around eating." She placed a box next to Ainsley. "This was just delivered for you."

"Weird. I'm not expecting anything."

"Well, it's from Señor Murphy, so if you don't want it, I get first dibs."

"Who is Señor Murphy?"

Drew gave her a disdainful look, but her tone was teasing. "Do you not get out at all? Señor Murphy Candymaker is a premier Southwestern chocolatier, right here in the City Different. If you haven't had Señor Murphy's candy, you haven't lived."

"Then I suppose I should see what's in the box." Ainsley unwrapped the box and glanced inside. "Peanut brittle? It looks different."

Drew pulled the box out of her hands. She rifled through the wrapping and handed Ainsley a card. "This isn't peanut brittle. This is chile piñon brittle. Completely different thing. Much, much better."

Paul reached over and snagged a piece of the reddish brown candy while Ainsley read the card. *I hope you enjoy this even though it's not what you're used to. Here's hoping you like a bit of spice with your sweets. Yours, Greer.*

Ainsley read the card half a dozen times before she noticed Paul waving a piece of the brittle in her direction. "Who's the amazing person who sent this? I want to write them a thank-you note. I'll write you one too since I'm about to eat this entire box myself."

Ainsley slapped his hand away. "None of your business, and that's your last piece, by the way. This is mine." Ainsley placed the lid on the box and left the table, ignoring the questioning looks on Drew and Paul's faces. She was surprised and touched by the gift. She hadn't expected to hear from Greer again, let alone in such a thoughtful way. Ainsley took the box to her room, where she could experience the dual sensations of hot and sweet in private.

❖

Greer carried in the last bag of groceries from the car and plunked it on the table. She felt good doing normal things like buying groceries. Except for her trip to the drugstore when she'd first arrived, she couldn't remember the last time she'd actually purchased everyday things like toothpaste and bread. People at the market had recognized her as she pushed a cart through the aisles and consulted with her aunt about the list, but the locals left her alone. A few tourists ventured closer, and Greer had braced herself for an onslaught of displeasure. Instead, the few who talked to her told her they had seen her TV interview and they hoped her life would return to normal soon. She signed a few autographs on random grocery lists and then helped her aunt load the car. Pretty normal.

"Greer," Ellen called out, "there's a Mr. Berkley on the phone for you." The name sounded familiar. Oh yeah, the agent her uncle's lawyer had lined up to assist until she found someone permanent to replace Rick. Berkley would be working on a trial basis for now, and Greer had a task ready to test his skills.

"Thanks, I'll take it in the den." Greer spent the next twenty minutes outlining her request. She wanted to kick off her world tour early with a concert at Paolo Soleri Amphitheater in Santa Fe—a benefit for the Lung Cancer Society. The Paolo Soleri was a rustic outdoor amphitheater on the grounds of the Santa Fe Indian School with terrific acoustics and a breathtaking view of the Sangre de Cristo mountain range. Young Greer Davis, playing all the smoky bars in town, had once equated success with taking the stage at the Paolo Soleri. The storm of success blew her by that dream, ultimately landing her at venues like Madison Square Garden, Wembley Stadium, and Red Rocks Amphitheater. Two weeks ago, she would have said she had experienced all the success she had ever dreamed of having. Now, all she wanted was to make her teenage wish come true.

She outlined her general take on the event. She wouldn't take any of the proceeds, and she would cover the cost of her band. All she wanted him to do was make the arrangements on a tight time frame.

She was pleasantly surprised at his response. After a few pointed questions, he simply said "I'll make the arrangements" and ended the call, presumably to do just that. Rick would have spent more time and energy listing the reasons she couldn't and shouldn't do a freebie concert than it would have taken to put the concert together in the first place.

Greer hung up the phone feeling happy but unsatisfied. She needed to make calls to her band members, who were enjoying a well-deserved vacation, but all she wanted to do was pick up the phone and call Ainsley to tell her what she had planned. She knew it was a selfish need. *See, I'm not such a bad person after all.* Was Ainsley past the point of caring? Greer thought she might be except when they were in the middle of their last kiss. Ainsley's hungry lips and tongue told Greer she cared very much.

Greer picked up the phone, but refrained from dialing the number for the Lancer. Bragging about one step in the right direction wasn't likely to win her any points with Ainsley. Ainsley had her number, and if she wanted to talk to her, she could do so anytime. Instead Greer dialed the number for Harry Lowe, the band's drummer. Harry and the rest of the band had traveled to a tropical island to enjoy some time off before the kick-off of their world tour. Greer knew her phone call asking them to come back a few days early to do a charity event was not going to be well received, but she and the guys had been together for so long she knew they would do anything for her. As she dialed, her mind buzzed with all the details she would need to handle. She wasn't accustomed to buying her own groceries, let alone planning the details of her events, but instead of feeling like a chore, the prospect of doing more than merely showing up was invigorating.

❖

Paul cleared his throat and Ainsley shot him a dirty look. She knew he'd caught her daydreaming, but paying attention to business was distracting her from flashes of Greer and a box full of chile piñon brittle. She realized she hadn't been at the top of her game ever since she'd run into Tray, make that Greer, in the square two weeks ago. Since then she had engaged in a downward spiral of crazy antics, all revolving around an inexplicable attraction to Greer Davis. All her actions were completely out of character for someone looking to move up to a cushy corner office at corporate headquarters. If she had never seen Tray after the flight, she would have remained focused on her work, but at the rate she was going, she was more likely to wind up working the front desk.

All day her moods swung between anticipation and frustration. The candy delivery from Señor Murphy's sparked both. She wanted to call Greer and thank her for the thoughtful gesture while at the same time she wished Greer hadn't muddied the waters by reaching out. Ainsley clenched her fists in her pockets and flinched when she came into contact with the well-worn slip of paper with Greer's number. She didn't have to pull it out to see the big flowing cursive in her mind's eye. Did Greer use the same script when she signed autographs for her fans? Did she include her phone number to many of those? Ainsley cursed her jealous thoughts and wadded the paper up in her fist as if she could squeeze away its meaning. Finally she allowed herself to breathe and unclenched the tangible tie to Greer. She had to let go, or she would never get all the things she really wanted.

Chapter Twenty

The last two days had flown by. Greer was starting to feel the stress. No wonder she paid Rick so much. Preparation for the benefit concert gave her a small taste of what it took to manage Greer Davis, Inc. She definitely had a new appreciation for his seamless management style, but she would never again give up the freedom she now experienced at being in control of her own affairs. Her uncle's lawyer had hired a firm in New York to begin the process of terminating Rick's contract and locating a new management firm. Berkley was good, but she needed a comprehensive team in place. Greer was done letting one person call the shots, unless that person was her.

She was taking control on the relationship front as well. Ainsley had thanked her for the candy from Señor Murphy's, with a short and guarded voice message. Instead of returning the call, Greer sent another gift, this time a bright red chile ristra. The note she included said: *Locals hang these beauties as a sign of welcome. I'd welcome a sign you'd like to see me again. P.S. Doesn't this blazing red look better on these peppers than on my head?*

Ainsley hadn't responded to the overture, but Greer still held out hope. In the meantime, she was determined to closely oversee the details of the upcoming concert. She and Berkley had selected a promoter who had secured the venue and purchased ad spots on all the local radio and TV outlets. Since Greer was underwriting the entire event herself, there were no sponsors to appease, so decisions about what to do and when were efficiently made. Tickets would go on sale in the morning, and Greer planned to spend the rest of the weekend sorting out the playlist. Harry and the rest of the band would arrive in town the evening before the concert. One of the major benefits of the band's long tenure together was they could pick up and play together, seamlessly, even after a long absence. Because the venue was comparatively small and outdoors to boot, they would offer their fans a stripped-down, raw version of their rock 'n' roll standards. Greer planned to pack the lineup with tunes from her early days with Betty to help her along. Right now, though, she was starving. Greer stowed her guitar and headed downstairs.

"Something smells terrific." She opened the lid of a large pot and breathed in the smoky aroma of her aunt's homemade green chile stew. She grabbed a nearby spoon and started to fish around for a perfect bite only to promptly drop the utensil when her aunt poked her in the side.

"Get out of there. It's not ready." Her smile belied her scolding tone. Ellen handed Greer a tortilla. "Here, munch on this. Lunch will be ready in about forty-five minutes. Go find something to do so I can finish getting it ready."

"Where's Uncle Clayton?"

"I think he's out back."

Greer wandered out to the back yard of the house, but she didn't see him anywhere in sight. Their property stretched out as far as she could see into a break lined with tall pine trees. She decided to while away the time till lunch by wandering around. When she reached the break, she could hear the light ripple of running water. She recognized the old acequia that served as the irrigation system on the ranch. She leaned down along the earthen wall and reached her hand into the cool water and wondered idly about its source. These ancient ditch systems had been developed to combat the usually dry desert conditions by catching water from the river and spring flows from the mountain range and diverting it to the local farms. Each acequia system had a commission led by a majordomo who regulated water rights. Greer learned about the intricacies of these systems and their effect on the state's development in high school. She couldn't help but marvel at the need for such a complex system of managing a resource she always assumed would be present at the turn of a handle.

Greer's thoughts were interrupted by the sound of a voice calling out. She looked around, but couldn't immediately detect the source. She stood and started walking along the edge of the ditch, past a clump of sagebrush and gasped when she saw her uncle lying in the dirt. Greer dropped to her knees and leaned in close to his face.

"Oh my God, are you okay?"

Clayton sat up and offered a crinkled smile. "I'm okay. Just got a cramp in my leg and I've been trying to stretch it out."

"Geez, you scared me to death." Greer frowned at her insensitive choice of words and barreled on. "Let me help you back to the house." Clayton looked as if he might protest, but then shook his head and took the hand Greer offered to him. As Clayton leaned against her, she was again dismayed at Clayton's appearance. His breathing was labored and he had lost a significant amount of weight. Greer decided to talk in order to distract herself from focusing on the toll the disease was taking on her uncle.

"I have a surprise."

Clayton smiled. "You do, huh?"

"Do you want to know what it is?"

"If you tell me it won't be a surprise anymore, will it?"

"You're going to find out soon anyway."

"You haven't changed one bit. You never have been able to keep a secret when it carries good news for someone else." His words were affectionate. Greer wondered if they were accurate. She did have hazy childhood memories of revealing enough information about already wrapped presents to give the recipient the ability to guess the contents. She loved surprises, but she hated waiting. As an adult, she didn't wait. She reveled in her ability to experience instant gratification in all aspects of her life. Whatever she wanted was within her quick grasp. *Except the love of Ainsley Faraday.*

The mere possibility Ainsley might someday return her feelings made Greer want to speed into town and beat on Ainsley's door, declaring her desires, until Ainsley relented. This new method of patiently waiting, desperately seeking the right moment to try again rather than forcing a choice was so foreign to her usual style, Greer felt she had to physically restrain herself from assuming her usual ways. For the first time in her life, she wanted something different, but she was going to have to go about getting what she wanted differently in order to get it. Somehow matching a new method to a new desire made sense.

"Are you going to tell me your surprise, or were you only teasing?"

"Sorry, I was lost in thought." Greer decided it wouldn't hurt to get a little instant gratification now as a tiny reward for behaving about her bigger goal. "Yes, I'll tell you. The band is flying in next week. We're doing a concert at Paolo Solari."

Clayton raised his eyebrows. "Wow, what's the occasion?"

"It's a benefit. For the local chapter of the Lung Cancer Society."

Clayton stared into her eyes, and the love she felt reflected in his look was overwhelming.

"It's no big deal, really. I've always wanted to perform there. I figured this would be a good opportunity."

Her words were squeezed off as he wrapped her in a tight embrace and whispered in her ear, "I love you, Greer. You are an amazing person. I am proud to be your uncle."

Greer didn't meet his eyes again for fear she would start bawling, but she held him close and whispered back, "I love you too." They were standing in the middle of a field, about halfway back to the house. The mountain range rose up in the distance and the sun shone down, bright and full. Their breathing was the only sound. Greer lost herself in the comfortable embrace of unconditional love and marveled at how good it felt to revel in the simplest of things. She was so comfortable it took her a few moments to realize her uncle's breath had become jagged. His slight frame slumped against her. She remembered his leg had been hurting. She needed to get him back to the house.

Drawing back from the embrace, she felt him stagger. Greer looked closely at his face. It was ashen and his breathing was ragged.

His eyes were mere slits. "Clayton, Clayton? Are you okay?" His lack of response answered her question. Greer desperately fought to channel her panic into a plan of action. She needed to get him back to the house, but she couldn't carry him. She didn't want to leave him in the yard, but there didn't seem to be a choice. She conjured up the image of the brochure she had gotten from the doctor's office. Maybe he was experiencing side effects from his treatment earlier in the week, but she wasn't convinced. She needed to get help, and she needed to get it now.

Greer eased him onto the ground and made a pillow with her hooded sweatshirt. She kissed him on the forehead and made two promises: she would be right back, and he would be okay. As soon as he was settled, she took off running toward the house knowing for sure she could keep one of the promises she had made.

❖

Ainsley reached a hand up to rip down the poster someone had slapped onto the brand new glass doors of the hotel. Some bellman was about to get his head ripped off for letting what amounted to graffiti mark the entrance of the pristine hotel. If she hadn't accomplished anything else, at least she had managed to bring the sleek style of a Steel property to this Mom-and-Pop operation. The renovations were not yet complete, but the new signage and polished entryway signaled the start of a new era for the formerly frumpy hotel.

"Ms. Faraday, please don't take that down."

Ainsley saw the hulking bell captain, Joey Vega, who had so helpfully answered her questions about Greer the other day. Awkwardly stuffed into his stiff new uniform, he didn't project the image she would have preferred the hotel's front door personnel to have, but she couldn't help it, she liked him. He was always ready with an easy smile and sparkling eyes. She decided to scale back the scolding she was poised to deliver. After all, he was the only employee who didn't act like he should dive into a foxhole every time she walked by.

"Joey, would you like to explain why you thought it was okay to mar the front doors of this fine hotel with advertisements?"

"This isn't an advertisement, Ms. Faraday." He looked at her as if cautiously deciding whether or not to proceed. "Did you read it?" His tone conveyed an innocent question and eager anticipation regarding her response. She hadn't read it. Since the poster shouldn't be there in the first place, it didn't really matter what it said, but she found she couldn't ignore the enthusiasm in his voice. She looked up at the playbill. The headline screamed, but it was the picture that riveted her attention. Greer Davis, her hands cradling an acoustic guitar, looked down at her. The look on her face mirrored the wild abandon Ainsley had seen the very first night they had made love. The force of it made Ainsley want to rip the guitar from Greer's hands and make those talented hands stroke her instead.

"So, is it okay to leave it?" Joey's voice startled her. She didn't have a clue what the poster said, she only knew the woman featured there called out to her. No matter how she rationalized it, she had made love with Greer Davis, wild and crazy superstar, not Tray Cardon, meek and lost traveler. If that was true, was it also true that Greer was capable of the easy, sweet affection Tray possessed? *Dammit, Ainsley, Tray doesn't exist.* She had repeated the thought over and over since she learned Tray's true identity, but it wasn't till now she realized the knowledge held possibility as opposed to self-incrimination. She flashed on the unique and thoughtful gifts of local flavor Greer had sent. What if the only real difference between Greer and Tray had been a name? Didn't she owe it to herself to find out?

Decision made, Ainsley started toward the office but she only made it a few steps before she felt a touch on her arm. She looked over her shoulder into the face of a bewildered Joey. He must think she was crazy, but she didn't have time to explain. If she altered her focus now, she might lose her nerve.

"By all means, leave the poster up." She returned his grin and practically ran across the lobby. Once in the office, she shut the door and scrambled to locate the slip of paper with Greer's number. She didn't allow herself an instant to second-guess, instead punching the numbers into the phone as if she was opening the combination to a safe full of riches. When she heard the other line ringing, she finally settled into her chair and allowed herself to breathe. *Three, four, five, six...* Finally, she heard the click of a receiver and she braced herself for the expected sound of sultry tones.

Hi, you've reached Greer Davis. Well, my cell phone anyway. I can't get to the phone right now, but leave a message and I'll be in touch.

Ainsley let out a pent-up breath as she listened to Greer's recorded voice. She had no intention of saying what she wanted to say to a recorded message. She gently replaced the receiver. *Damn.* She leaned back in her chair and folded the small piece of paper into a variety of shapes while she contemplated her next move.

A quick knock on the door preceded Paul sticking his head in. "Have you seen Drew?" Ainsley shook her head. Paul gave her a funny look. "Are you okay? You look like you lost your best friend."

She shrugged in response, and he left as quickly as he'd entered. Greer wasn't her best friend, but she was important. She must be or Ainsley would've been able to put her out of her mind like the countless others she had shared a bed with over the years. A slow thought, chased by feeling, crept into her mind. Greer was different from those others. And she might not be her best friend, but Ainsley wanted her to be. She wanted her to be her best friend, her partner, her lover. She wanted those things fiercely. She wasn't going to wait a moment longer to have what she wanted. If she couldn't reach Greer on the phone, she knew someone who might know how to find her.

Ainsley raced through the office door. Paul was at the front desk. She grabbed his arm. "Did you find Drew?"

"Someone said she's in the restaurant. I sent Joey to get her. She has an urgent phone call." Paul's expression signaled he was dying to know why she was so intense in her request. She waited in silence for Drew to appear. Finally, Drew jogged up to the desk.

She gave Paul and Ainsley a questioning look, probably wondering why the senior members of the transition team were standing by the phone waiting for her. Paul spoke first.

"Drew, there's an important call holding for you."

Drew took the phone, but before she punched the line to connect it, she shot a look at Ainsley. "Did you need something?" Her tone was cool and dismissive. Ainsley felt her resolve falter slightly. She bought herself a moment by pointing at the phone. She could talk to Drew after she'd taken her call. As Drew began to speak into the phone, Ainsley began an internal dialogue to rebuild her courage. Drew's call didn't last nearly long enough, but Ainsley decided to plunge ahead once she saw her put the phone down.

"Drew, I wonder if I could talk to you for a minute?" The minute the words left her mouth she registered Drew's pale, anguished expression, and Paul shaking his head and mouthing "no." Before she could say anything else, Paul circled an arm around Drew's waist and ushered her to the front door, waving Joey over. Ainsley followed close behind and heard Paul tell Joey to get Drew's car, pronto. The pieces started to form a picture. *Drew gets an urgent call and has to rush out. Paul is protective of her.* Suddenly, Ainsley realized something was wrong, terribly wrong. She wondered if it had to do with Greer. Whatever it was, she needed to find out, in person. She called out to Joey's disappearing back, "Get my car instead."

Moments later, Ainsley found herself driving like a madwoman through the streets of Santa Fe. If she thought being in the car with Drew would give her more information about either what was going on or about Greer's whereabouts, she was wrong. The only words Drew could seem to form were the directions to St. Vincent's Hospital. Ainsley didn't push her. She was too scared of what Drew might say.

CHAPTER TWENTY-ONE

B eing Greer Davis meant never having to wait. Until now. The emergency room was the great equalizer. Rich, poor, famous, or unknown, it didn't matter. Who she was didn't factor into the process.

Greer's fame might not have moved Clayton up in the line, but his arrival by ambulance was one of the variables that worked in his favor. Greer's first instinct had been to drive him to St. Vincent's herself. The drive wasn't long, but most of it was along undeveloped stretches of land, and she worried about a possible breakdown in Joey's old jalopy. Ultimately, Ellen made the decision to call 911 and they waited together for what seemed like hours for the ambulance to arrive. Their patience at the front end of the trip had the benefit of getting Clayton through those double doors faster than the poor folks who had been sitting for who knew how long in the busy waiting room. Ellen was with Clayton and a team of professionals in his curtained-off "room." Nobody had any idea what was going on, so Greer left to give them room to figure it out. She entered the waiting room and slid into a hard plastic chair and pretended to read a magazine while she waited for Drew to arrive.

She didn't have to wait long. They had trouble getting through to Drew at the hotel, but she must have run every light and stop sign to get to the hospital in record time. From her chair in the waiting room, Greer could see her dash through the double doors and head directly to the frazzled nurse working the intake desk. Greer moved quickly to intercept her before she encountered the same frustrating lack of information she had faced when asking for an update.

"Drew, over here." Greer waved at a chair beside her. Drew looked from Greer to the receptionist and back again before walking over and settling in the chair next to her.

"What happened?"

"I don't know. We were walking around the ranch. He got a cramp in his leg and he looked like he was about to pass out. I called nine-one-one."

Drew puffed up. Her voice was a low growl. "What in the world were you thinking? He's in no condition to be walking all over creation."

Greer's first inclination was to growl back a protest. Her uncle was the kind of person who did what he wanted to do. If he wanted to traipse up the side of a mountain, he wasn't likely to heed warnings to the contrary. As she started to form the words, she realized Drew already knew these simple truths about Clayton. Her accusations were rooted in fear, not blame. Greer wanted to tell her she understood, that she knew it was easier to lash out than feel the pain of loss and fear, but tender words weren't part of her repertoire. She acted instead and swept Drew up in a tight hug.

"Hey, get off me." Drew didn't back her words up with action, so Greer held tight. She imagined Drew might even be hugging her back. After a few minutes, Drew relaxed in her embrace.

"Where's Mom?"

"She's back there." Greer pointed to the "Only Authorized Personnel Allowed" doors next to the intake desk. "The nurse said only one person could be back there with him at a time."

"And the mighty Greer Davis acquiesced?"

"Knock it off. I was waiting for you. I figured the two of us could take her if we work together." Greer nodded in the direction of the scowling nurse manning the admission desk. She stood and held out a hand. "Come on."

Instead of taking her hand, Drew looked anxiously at the double doors. Greer followed the direction of her gaze. "Expecting someone?"

Drew looked as if trying to decide whether to answer. "I got a ride here." She paused. "From Ainsley."

"Faraday?" The inane question was all Greer could manage.

"You know some other Ainsley?"

"Don't be a smart-ass."

"Don't let a crush make you stupid."

Greer started to protest, but she didn't know which part of Drew's admonishment to challenge. She was stupid. Stupid for letting Ainsley get away, but she was at least smart enough to realize her mistake. On the other hand, what she felt could in no way be characterized as a crush. A crush was a sharp, quick press of feeling. What she felt for Ainsley was deep and abiding passion. Suddenly, she knew what to say.

"I'm in love with her."

Drew frowned and placed her palm on Greer's forehead. Greer knocked her hand away. "Cut it out."

"You cut it out."

Greer smiled. "You realize we sound like a couple of kids."

"I guess we never outgrew sibling rivalry. I always thought of you like a sister, you know."

"Yeah, I know. Me too, you. Go on ahead, I'll wait for her."

"Okay." Drew started toward the entrance to the emergency room. She was a couple of steps away when she glanced back. "You should tell her." Then she dashed through the double doors on the heels of a medicine cart before Greer could respond.

❖

Ainsley envied the casual physical play between the two cousins. They looked like teenagers sparring, but the warmth behind their teasing looks belied any true conflict. Obviously the affection in their relationship ran deeper than the hostility she had witnessed between them at the hotel. She pressed her face against the glass and wished. Wished she had a relationship with her sister like the one she witnessed between Drew and Greer. Wished she knew the loving, affectionate Greer others knew. She could see her now in the concern of her furrowed brow, the love in her easy smile, but she didn't know if she was ready to trust what she saw as real.

Ainsley looked through the glass smeared with handprints from dozens of visitors who had entered seeking healing. Suddenly, she realized Greer Davis was a regular person, sitting in a waiting room like all the other regular people suspended in time while waiting for news about their loved ones. Greer could probably use a friend, and Ainsley could think of no good reason not to fill the slot. She shrugged off her apprehension and pushed open the door.

As Ainsley made her way to the chairs, she heard a commotion from her left and she looked up in time to see Drew barreling toward Greer, ignoring the nurse who shouted for her to stop running. She grabbed Greer's hand and hauled her back the way she had come. Ainsley couldn't be certain, but she was fairly sure neither Drew nor Greer had noticed she was even in the room. She closed the distance to the nurse.

"What's going on?"

"I'm sorry. I'm not at liberty to say."

Ainsley knew she wasn't going to get information from hospital staff. She wasn't family. She wasn't anything. As she sank into one of the nearby chairs, she resolved to become someone special in the life of Greer Davis.

❖

"I thought he was having complications." Greer huffed the words between pants as she followed Drew through the maze of curtained off cubicles.

"He is, but the complications are more severe than they thought." She pulled to a stop outside a curtain and her next words were short and clipped. "He has a blood clot. It's large. They don't think treating it with blood thinners will be effective. They want to do surgery. They want to do it right now."

"So, what are they waiting for?"

"It's risky."

Greer braced herself. "And?"

"Clayton wants this to be a family decision."

Greer swallowed back tears as she realized the meaning behind Drew's words. She was being included in the decision. Whatever they decided, this might be her last chance to talk to her uncle. Whatever she was feeling now, Drew must be feeling full force. "What do you think?"

"I think we should get in there and do some talking."

Greer moved through the curtain and joined Drew and her aunt at Clayton's bedside. He was conscious, but the rest of the news was bleak. Any sign of a climb back to good health had been struck down, and his pale and weakened body didn't appear to have the strength to hold him up for what could be the most important conversation of his life. As if their lifelines were connected to his, Drew and Ellen seemed deflated, unable to speak. Greer decided she had to step in, or they would all merely sit and watch any sign of his life slip out of the room.

"I understand we need to sort this out." She looked at her uncle. "Clayton, would you like to say anything?"

"I've lived a good life. I wonder if I'm being greedy, asking for more." His comment elicited sobs from Ellen. Drew watched with watery eyes and quivering lips. Greer considered his question. She thought about all the years of her life she had burned away, living fast and loose, with no depth or feeling. In contrast, her uncle had built a business, a home, a loving family. He had character in spades. Everyone who came in contact with him walked away a better person for having known him. No, it was she who was the greedy one, who had squandered all she had. Taking life's gifts for granted. Her uncle deserved a long future.

She pulled the wolf fetish from her pocket. *Healing.* Greer squeezed the tiny talisman in her fist and leaned over his bed. "Do you want more?" He nodded, and she kissed him on the forehead. "Even if it means risking everything?" Another nod. "Then let's do this." She looked at Ellen and Drew. "You okay with this?" They both nodded, relief that Greer had taken control apparent in their expressions. She felt good knowing she had somehow won back their trust, but more important was the message she read from her uncle's decision. Even when things seemed bleakest, giving up only meant certain failure. If Clayton didn't have the surgery, he would die. The risk of surgery meant he had a chance.

Greer realized she could pine away for Ainsley, letting the "what if" of uncertainty be her only reward, or she could take the chance of declaring her feelings. Gifts and notes weren't doing the trick. Greer braced herself for baring her soul without accessories she could hide behind. If Ainsley turned her down, Greer knew her heart would heal. If she never took the risk, she might never recover from the pain of playing it safe.

CHAPTER TWENTY-TWO

Ainsley stared at the poster in her hand. Joey had left a small stack of the bills advertising Greer's benefit concert on the desk. In the photo on the picture, she was animated and vibrant, jamming on her guitar while rocking across the stage. Ainsley hadn't seen Greer since Friday, but she knew from Joey's reports that Greer and Drew had spent every moment of the weekend waiting at the hospital.

"You look beat," Paul said. "Why don't you run up to my room and take a nap? It's quieter there. Let me take over for a while."

Ainsley was beyond beat. She had spent the last three days substituting for Drew at the hotel in addition to her transition duties. With her room connected to the office, she had no peace at all. She didn't mind. It was the least she could do for the Lancer family. Paul only made halfhearted efforts now to try to get her to stop, but she was reaching a breaking point and was about to give in. An hour of sleep sounded like paradise. If she could shut her mind down, it might be heaven. Before she could take Paul up his offer, she had to know. "Have you heard anything today?"

He shook his head. "No. Do you want me to call?"

"No, no. They have enough to worry about without keeping us updated." The last thing Ainsley had heard was Clayton had come through surgery, but his condition was rocky and he was in ICU. Every ounce of her wanted to be there, to wrap Greer in her arms and be a strong, supportive lover, but she knew her desire was more about fulfilling her own needs than those of Greer and Drew. She was doing more for them by giving Drew the freedom to be where she needed to be. She realized she might be even more effective if she got a little rest. "Paul, I think I will take you up on your offer. But I want you to get me up in two hours. Deal?"

"Deal." He handed her his key and ushered her out of the office. Ainsley made her way toward the elevator in a haze. She noticed a huddle of hotel employees near the front desk, but she didn't even have the energy to urge them back to work. *Let Paul handle it.*

Finally, the elevator doors opened and she almost fell in. She pressed the button for her floor and willed the doors to close quickly. After what seemed like infinity, the doors started to slide slowly into place. Through the closing gap, Ainsley noted the crowd breaking up. She figured Paul had dispersed the employees, but when she saw who had been standing at the center of the crowd, she gasped.

❖

Greer knew even if she wasn't running on empty, she would never make it to the elevator before the doors closed, but at the sight of Ainsley staring at her through the closing metal doors, she broke away from Joey and the rest of the gang. This wasn't how she wanted this scene to go—her running like a bat out of hell toward Ainsley, ready to blurt out her declaration of love. She hadn't slept in days. She had huge black bags under her eyes, and the pieces of her hair jutting out around her head could no longer be mistaken for a fashion statement.

The fear behind her hesitation flashed, then fizzled out. If she had learned nothing else from her uncle's brush with death, she had discovered even small victories were worth big risks. If all she got out of a face-to-face was the chance to apologize and tell Ainsley in no uncertain terms how she felt about her, no matter what response she got, then no risk was too big. The thin slice of Ainsley she could see through those closing doors was all she needed to confirm her desire to declare her intentions. What if the elevator Ainsley was in crashed to the ground? What if a meteor struck the hotel lobby, sizzling all the occupants to a fiery crisp? What if this moment was all she had, all she would ever have? Messy hair, messy clothes, baggy eyes. None of that mattered. Greer rubbed the fetish in her pocket. *Pathfinder. Safe journey.* The right path was mere steps away. Greer launched herself across the lobby.

She was mere inches away when the doors shut and Ainsley had not met her gaze as the steel stole the space between them. Damn. Greer sagged against the frame of the elevator and shook her head. Her sprint across the lobby had been fueled by adrenaline. She could feel it leaving as fast as it had come.

"Greer?"

She looked up at Joey. She hadn't even heard him approach. He shuffled his feet and glanced back at the rest of the group who had witnessed her failed maneuver. "Yes?"

"Are you okay?"

Greer grimaced. Apparently, her mad dash had not gone unnoticed. Should she pursue this quest for unrequited love by standing outside another closed door? Greer decided she had nothing to lose except her pride. Determined to track Ainsley through the halls of the hotel, she reached behind her back and pushed against the doors to right herself, but instead of moving forward, she fell back through the doors as they opened behind her. Joey reached out to grab her arm, but they didn't connect. She hit the floor of the elevator with a thud. Greer winced and opened her eyes.

"Not exactly a rock-star entrance." Ainsley grinned down at her. "Are you okay?"

Greer rubbed her head and grinned back. "Pretty sure my pride is hurt worse than my head. I wanted to see you so badly, but this wasn't exactly what I had in mind."

Ainsley extended her arm and helped Greer to her feet. Greer fell into Ainsely's arms, hating that lack of coordination was the only reason she was there. Ainsley's next action wiped away any thoughts of regret. Greer melted into soft lips that delivered the perfect balm for her bruised ego. Time was suspended as their kiss deepened. She held Ainsley close and enjoyed the déjà vu of their touch. No one else had ever felt like this. No one else ever would. If this kiss, this hug was all she could have, she was determined to imprint herself with the memory so she could return to these feelings when she was alone.

As if Greer had conjured up their separation, her thoughts were accompanied by the empty feeling of Ainsley pulling back. The look in her eyes was impossible to decipher. A mixture of desire and frustration, which Greer read as the prelude to a good-bye, though a much gentler one than Ainsley had offered before. She opened her mouth to blunt the emotion, but Ainsley beat her to words.

"I think we have an audience."

Greer glanced at the doors and realized for the first time they were standing open. Joey and the rest of the Lancer crew were standing in the lobby, staring at them kissing in the elevator. Could their public display be the source of frustration she saw on Ainsley's face? She inclined her head toward the open doors. "Does that bother you?"

"Surprisingly, no." Ainsley offered a slow smile. "As out of character as it seems, I kind of want to give them a reason for staring."

Greer returned the smile and pushed away her insecurities once and for all. Ainsley wanted to kiss her. In public. Right now. "I can help you with that."

"Well, Greer, what are you waiting for?"

Greer stopped midway to Ainsley's waiting lips and glanced away so Ainsley wouldn't see the tears forming in her eyes. She felt arms encircle her and pull her close. Ainsley whispered in her ear, "Baby, what's wrong?"

She felt silly for crying, but it couldn't be helped. Ainsley's words were fresh and new, and they unearthed cravings Greer didn't know she had: comfort, acceptance, love. She had to answer soon if she wanted Ainsley to stay. She could already feel her failure to respond being met with the tentative pull back of potential rejection. She cupped Ainsley's chin in her hand and met her eyes. "My name. I've never heard you say my name…" She wanted to say more, to explain the irrational emotion behind her teary response, but she couldn't manage the words and the emotion at the same time.

Ainsley saved her the trouble. She pulled Greer back into her embrace. "How about I promise to say it so much you become desensitized to it? I'll say your name every day until you beg me to stop. Do you think that would work?"

Greer heard the tacit offer beneath the words. She wanted to accept, but she was looking for something less vague. Would her bid for more be viewed as an unwanted push or a gentle nudge? *You've come this far, why stop now?* It was her uncle's voice she heard, blending with her own, and she knew she wouldn't be happy with anything less than the prize that risking it all might bring. She fought to hide the fear from her tone and gave her answer, which was really more of a question. "If you said my name every day for the rest of our lives, I would never beg you to stop."

Ainsley didn't hesitate. "Let's see about that." She planted a kiss. "Greer."

CHAPTER TWENTY-THREE

G reer ushered Ainsley into her room at the ranch and closed the door behind them. She had a couple of hours before she was supposed to meet the band for a sound check at the amphitheater, and she planned to spend every minute of it alone with Ainsley. Although they talked on the phone several times a day, Greer had barely seen her over the past week between keeping vigil at the hospital and preparing for the concert.

"I can't remember the last time I had a girl in this room."

Ainsley took her time looking around the room. Greer shuffled her feet in embarrassment as she saw Ainsley inspect the walls covered in posters. Her high school favorites were well represented: Def Leppard, Mary J. Blige, Guns N' Roses, U2, Paula Abdul, Queen. Ainsley finally spoke. "You certainly had eclectic taste as a teenager."

"Still do."

"I guess I do too."

Greer noted the undercurrent of Ainsley's omission. "You a Greer Davis fan?"

"I'm a recent convert. I have a backstage pass for her concert tonight."

"Do you now?"

"I hear once you get backstage, you can get really close to the artist. It's a girl's best chance of getting a date."

"Well, in my case, a date with the artist is available to only one particular ticket holder." Greer pulled Ainsley into her arms. "I can't tell you how much it means to have you there with me tonight."

Ainsley kissed her cheek. "There's nowhere else I'd rather be."

"I'm sorry for not being honest with you from the start."

Ainsley shrugged. "You didn't know me."

"I wanted to."

"We barely know each other even now." Ainsley's tone signaled hesitation, and Greer heard her need.

"I promise I'll never lie to you again, either directly or by omission. I'm sorry I ever did. I was only thinking about myself and, if I've learned nothing else in the past few weeks, I've learned the best way to look out for myself is to nurture the relationships I have with the people that matter the most."

Ainsley heard the force behind Greer's words, but years of guarding herself from intimacy made it difficult to recognize, let alone embrace. She needed something to quiet the last trace of lingering doubt. "Am I one of those people?"

"You are absolutely one of those people." Greer was emphatic.

The assurance was enough. For now. Ainsley, ever businesslike, wanted to know the next steps. How often would they see each other? Where would they meet? What did it mean to "matter most"? As much as she craved answers, she decided to be content with Greer's first step and hope the rest would follow soon.

As if she could hear her thoughts, Greer asked, "How long will you be in Santa Fe?"

"A couple more weeks."

"And then?"

"I've been offered a different job. Still with Steel, but at the corporate office. No more moving from place to place."

"I envy that. I have five houses, but I spend most of my time living out of a suitcase. Where's the new position?"

"New York."

"We'll be playing Madison Square Garden a couple of months into the tour."

"Great. We'll make a date of it." Ainsley faked her enthusiasm.

She'd wanted answers. Well, now she had them. Greer would be off on her tour and she would be living and working in Manhattan. They would hook up for an occasional date when Greer's tour blew into town. She might be one of the people that mattered most, but Greer, like herself, put business before pleasure. They were more alike than she had thought.

Greer sat on the edge of her bed and patted the covers. "We still have a little time before I have to meet the band." Ainsley resigned herself to making the most of the little time they had. She raised her eyebrows. "Here? With all your heroes watching?"

"I like to think they'd approve of the choices I'm making now." She leaned back, pulling Ainsley with her. They were both startled when Ainsley smacked her head on a hard surface.

"Ouch!"

Greer lightly rubbed the back of Ainsley's head, then set her brand-new guitar case on the ground. She opened the case and lifted Betty out. "Ainsley Faraday, I'd like you to meet Betty Martin. My first love." Greer spoke directly to the guitar, "Betty, I'd like you to meet Ainsley Faraday," she paused, "my lover." Her playful introduction fell short of what she wanted to say, but the words "my last love" seemed premature. Well, not to her, but she had no idea if Ainsley felt the same way. She'd taken enough risks lately. "Lover" was enough for now.

Greer realized her internal musings left an awkward silence in the air. She decided to remedy the awkwardness by taking action. Even if she wasn't ready to speak the words, she could show Ainsley the depth of her feeling. Her kiss sang the most touching ballad she had ever penned and her hands strummed Ainsley's body with more passion than she had ever experienced onstage.

❖

Ainsley was amazed at all the activity taking place backstage. Greer told her the small venue at Paolo Soleri made for a modified experience compared to her usual appearances, but she was still amazed by the flurry of activity. Watching Greer in action, Ainsley was embarrassed she'd ever thought Greer's life as a rock star was an easy ride. Since they'd arrived at the venue, Greer had been consumed with every detail of the upcoming performance. Ainsley had offered to lend a hand, but Greer had only given her one task, insisting she could handle the rest herself.

Ainsley busied herself with her assignment as if it were the most important job of her life. She stood to the side of the stage and arranged the video camera so it would capture the perfect angle of Greer and the band when they took the stage. The cable from the camera was connected to Greer's new MacBook, and once the concert started, Clayton would see the whole event streaming live into his hospital room. He had finally been moved out of ICU, but was expected to remain in the hospital for at least another week. The news of an extended stay didn't sit well with him, and he had made his displeasure known. Ainsley was the one who had come up with virtual attendance at the concert to serve as a short-term pacifier, and Greer placed her in charge of the logistics. With Drew back at work and Paul filling in, Ainsley was glad to pitch in.

She was happier at that moment, doing the simple work of setting up a camera to film Greer's performance, than she had ever been as the manager of some of the top hotels in the country. Frank had called the night before to discuss the status of the transition and details about her future. Everything she had spent her life working hard to achieve suddenly seemed to have dropped out of her focus. All she could see was herself with Greer. The logistics were a hazy perimeter.

"When did you become a computer whiz?" Paul's voice startled her from her thoughts. Ainsley acted on impulse and hugged him.

"I have all kinds of special talents."

"Besides hotel management? Well, do tell. Planning on using any of those other talents on the road?"

"What are you talking about?"

"Just wondering what's in the cards for you and the rock diva?"

"Leave it to you to plunge right in. I didn't get you a backstage pass so you could quiz me."

Paul held up a hand. "Easy there. I came back here to congratulate you. I heard Frank offered you the job at corporate."

"Thanks. A few weeks ago, I would have been ecstatic. Now, I…I'm not sure how I feel."

"I guess if you want to be with her, one of you is going to have to make a choice."

Paul's declaration made the issue sound so simple. It was anything but. "I suppose that's true, but I haven't a clue how everything will play out."

Greer walked up and interrupted their conversation, but as happy as Ainsley was to see her, she was distracted by the replay of her discussion with Paul in her head. Greer was scheduled to leave on her world tour next week. Now that Frank had finally offered Ainsley the coveted corner office she had worked her whole life to achieve, a choice was in the offing, but no choice would fulfill both of their needs.

Ainsley shook off the creeping edge of despair and focused on the present. She stood silent as Paul thanked Greer for the backstage pass and wandered off to mingle with the local celebs who were gathered backstage for the VIP reception.

Ainsley realized she hadn't said a word since Greer joined her, and she searched for an innocuous topic of conversation. "I have the camera all set up."

"Great. Join me at the reception?" Greer offered her arm. Ainsley started forward, then abruptly stopped. Greer cocked her head. "Everything okay? I know it's kinda crazy back here."

"It's crazy, but crazy in a good way." Ainsley took a deep breath and plunged on. "This life—you love it, right?" Greer nodded. "And you should. I mean, you've worked your whole life to achieve this kind of success and you deserve it. I know how much you deserve it. I've worked hard too. For different things."

Greer placed a finger on her lips. "I love you. Do you love me?" She moved her finger slightly to allow Ainsley to answer.

"Yes. Greer, I love you." Her use of Greer's name elicited the desired smile. She loved Greer's smile, and she couldn't bear the thought of compromises that might rob her of experiencing her future smiles. She tried to imagine how they could both have what they wanted, what they needed, and still have each other with all the closeness and passion they deserved. On the heels of her wish, came the answer. Greer's finger was back in place, but she blurted out the solution anyway.

"Christmas."

"Christmas?"

"You know, Christmas!" Ainsley desperately needed Greer to interpret the code. "Like the chile. Red and green. So we don't have to choose between the things we love, the things we need. We can figure out a way to have it all, right?"

Greer's grin was huge. She enveloped Ainsley in a sweeping hug and kissed her soundly. "Ah, Christmas! I've always been a big fan."

About the Author

Carsen Taite works by day (and sometimes night) as a criminal defense attorney in Dallas, Texas. Though her day job is often stranger than fiction, she can't seem to get enough and spends much of her free time plotting stories. Her goal as an author is to spin tales with plot lines as interesting as the true, but often unbelievable, stories she encounters in her law practice. Her first stab at fiction, *truelesbianlove.com*, was a pure romance, released as one of the debut novels in Bold Strokes' Aeros e-book line. Carsen's second novel, *It Should Be a Crime*, for which Carsen received a 2010 Lavender Certificate from the Alice B. Readers, draws heavily on her experience in the courtroom and was selected as a 2010 Lambda Literary Award finalist. She is hard at work on novel number four, *Nothing but the Truth*, scheduled for release in January 2011.

Carsen is married (Canadian-style), and she and her spouse live near White Rock Lake in Dallas where they enjoy cycling and walking the trails with their four-legged children.

Books Available From Bold Strokes Books

Witch Wolf by Winter Pennington. In a world where vampires have charmed their way into modern society, where werewolves walk the streets with their beasts disguised by human skin, Investigator Kassandra Lyall has a secret of her own to protect: She's one of them. (978-1-60282-177-4)

Do Not Disturb by Carsen Taite. Ainsley Faraday, a high-powered executive, and rock music celebrity Greer Davis couldn't be less well suited for one another, and yet they soon discover passion has a way of designing its own future. (978-1-60282-153-8)

From This Moment On by PJ Trebelhorn. Devon Conway and Katherine Hunter both lost love and neither believes they will ever find it again—until the moment they meet and everything changes. (978-1-60282-154-5)

Vapor by Larkin Rose. When erotic romance writer Ashley Vaughn decides to take her research into the bedroom for a night of passion with Victoria Hadley, she discovers that fact is hotter than fiction. (978-1-60282-155-2)

Wind and Bones by Kristin Marra. Jill O'Hara, award-winning journalist, just wants to settle her deceased father's affairs and leave Prairie View, Montana, far, far behind—but an old girlfriend, a sexy sheriff, and a dangerous secret keep her down on the ranch. (978-1-60282-150-7)

Nightshade by Shea Godfrey. The story of a princess, betrothed as a political pawn, who falls for her intended husband's soldier sister, is a modern-day fairy tale to capture the heart. (978-1-60282-151-4)

Vieux Carré Voodoo by Greg Herren. Popular New Orleans detective Scotty Bradley just can't stay out of trouble—especially when an old flame turns up asking for help. (978-1-60282-152-1)

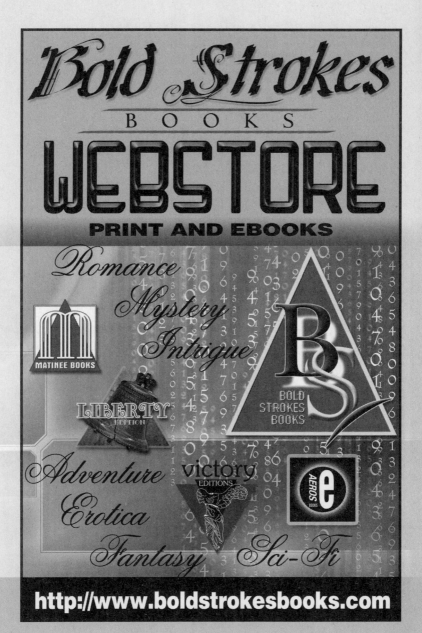